May 26, 2004

HELLBOY

THE BONES *of* GIANTS

HELLBOY

THE BONES *of* GIANTS

by

Christopher Golden

Illustrated by

Mike Mignola

POCKET BOOKS

NEW YORK LONDON TORONTO SYDNEY

This book is a work of fiction. Names, characters, places and incidents are products of the author's imagination or are used fictitiously. Any resemblance to actual events or locales or persons, living or dead, is entirely coincidental.

POCKET BOOKS, a division of Simon & Schuster, Inc.
1230 Avenue of the Americas, New York, NY 10020

Published by arrangement with Dark Horse Comics, Inc.

ISBN: 0-7434-6283-1

First Pocket Books printing February 2004

10 9 8 7 6 5 4 3 2 1

Cover Art by Mike Mignola

Manufactured in the United States of America

Original Book Design by Cary Grazzini

FOREWORD

I created Hellboy back in 1993. Since then I've come up with hundreds of Hellboy ideas. Some are complete stories, but most are just fragments, bits and pieces that rattle around in my head banging into each other. Some of those bits eventually cobble themselves into stories. Others settle into that dark corner of my brain where even really bad ideas never quite die.

In 1997, Chris Golden wrote *The Lost Army*, the first *Hellboy* novel. It was well received, and right away we started talking about doing a second one. We thought it might be interesting to collaborate on a story, so I went into that dark corner and pulled out what I thought was one of the better ideas. Chris liked it, ran with it, added more characters than I would have thought possible, and really created something wonderful.

I think *The Lost Army* is great, and I don't mean to take anything away from it, but *Bones of Giants* is better. A lot better. Chris is a better writer than he was four years ago (just look at his recent novels *Strangewood* and *Straight on 'til Morning*), and hopefully I'm a better artist. And we both benefited greatly from having all of Norse mythology to draw upon. Was there ever a group of people that believed in better monsters?

My thanks (as usual) to Chris and to Scott Allie. And also to designer Cary Grazzini, who has been making *Hellboy* (and me) look good since the very beginning. I would be lost without him.

And to you, whoever you are—enjoy.

Mike Mignola
New York City

DEDICATION

It's customary, right here at the front of the book, to dedicate it to someone . . . to say who it's "for." My wife and children have received the lion's share of my dedications, along with a handful of my close friends, like Tom Sniegoski, Bob Tomko, and Jose Nieto. Last time out (with *The Lost Army*), the dedication was for Mike Mignola, who of course created Hellboy. He deserves even more thanks this time around because the way this novel opens, the situation and the images that set it all up, came from Mike. And editor Scott Allie deserves thanks and kudos as well. But you know what? I'm about to do something I've never done in my career as a novelist. *Bones of Giants* was born for me decades ago, when I read a book called *Thunder of the Gods* by Dorothy Hosford over and over and over again in elementary school. So here's my dedication. This one isn't for my wife or my kids, it's not for Mike.

This one's for me. Just for me.

Christopher Golden

For my pet rat, Admiral Dot, who, tragically, ended up in the freezer.

Mike Mignola

PROLOGUE

Like the death cry of an antique god, thunder tore the night sky asunder and the northland trembled at its fury. It was loud enough that Jan-Olaf Kjell felt its rumble in the hollow of his chest. He turned, boots crunching the snow, his fishing gear and his catch for the day banging against his back and legs.

A quarter of a mile back, the river raged; ice floes swept along with the current as it twisted and turned through the frozen hills of Lapland. Twelve miles south, the river flowed through Skellesvall, and some hundred miles beyond that, into the Gulf of Bothnia. Jan-Olaf lived by himself outside of Skellesvall and had never been south of the Arctic Circle. This was what he knew of the world, but this he *did* know. This land, this river, these hills. Forty-seven years he had fished the banks of the river at a secret spot his father had found decades before that. His father was dead now, but Jan-Olaf still believed what his father had told him.

The gods had blessed the river. As long as it was approached with the proper respect, it would never fail to provide all the fish he could hope to carry home. Forty-seven years, Jan-Olaf had seen the proof of it, and his father and grandfather, and who knew how many Kjell men before them? Always a secret, though, because the men of Skellesvall would surely taint the blessing of the gods and ruin it all.

Jan-Olaf smiled. *The gods.* He was a Christian, but his father had always said that the old gods were forgotten but not gone, that it was best to give them the respect they were due, just in case. Just in case . . .

With a brilliance that made him flinch and shield his eyes, lightning tore a wound in the sky, fire from the heavens reached an accusing finger toward the ground. Three seconds later the thunder came again, a crack so loud it was as though the earth itself had split in two. Jan-Olaf swore

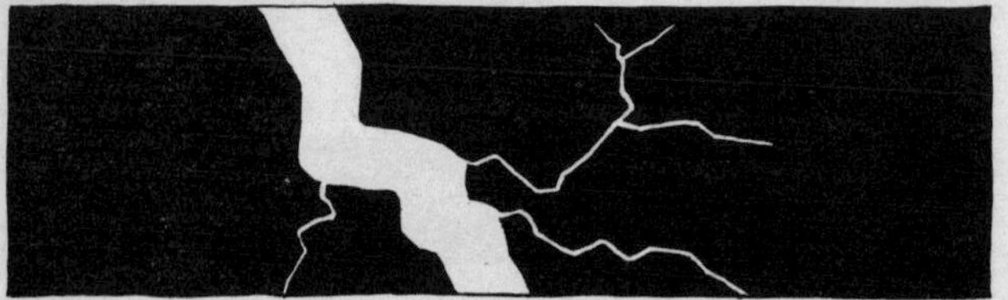

aloud and nearly covered his ears, though of course it would have been too late to protect them from the roar.

A deep frown creased his forehead. He knew this land. This was his world, and he understood all there was to understand about it. But now, this early evening, lightning split the night from a perfectly clear, star-filled sky. Thunder roared without storm or heat or even much wind.

Impossible.

Again the sky brightened as a fresh tendril of lightning sliced the dark from earth to stars. It was followed immediately by yet another, this slashing down at an angle, cutting diagonally across the horizon. Thunder rolled across the land, echoing in the hollows and thumping upon the snow.

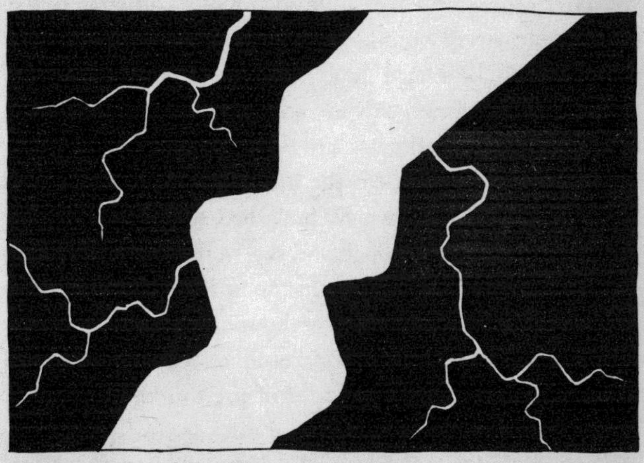

Jan-Olaf stared, eyes narrowed, at a spot to the northeast where the first bolt of lightning had touched ground. The first, yes, but also the second, and the third . . . and again the lightning split the night. The roar of thunder now had enough power to rattle his remaining teeth, and Jan-Olaf was certain that the snow *moved* under his feet.

An absurd thought went through his mind, then, but he could no more prevent it than he could touch the sky.

The gods, Jan-Olaf thought, and a shiver passed through him that had nothing to do with the temperature.

It angered him, this thought. He glanced around to mark his place—he was perhaps half a mile from his truck, just below a cleft in the hill where he and his father had camped once, long, long ago. Then Jan-Olaf dropped his equipment and his catch and set off on a direct course to the northeast. With the snow giving way beneath his boots, it took him more than half an hour to make the trek up the steep hill and then down the other side. Large stone outcroppings jutted from the ground and served both as landmarks and resting areas that would prevent him from tumbling the rest of the way down.

The sky remained pristine and clear, only the stars to mar the perfect darkness. Or that was how it ought to have been, were it not for the unnatural lightning, which only increased in frequency. It flashed so bright in those moments, it was as though the sky were on fire, and the thunder bellowed so loudly that soon his hearing seemed muffled, eardrums numbed by the sound. Jan-Olaf pulled his hat down and pulled his jacket up to cover his ears, but it did not assuage the onslaught of the thunder. The roar of the heavens was inside his head now, in his heart.

At last, sliding and grabbing hold of rocks, he came down a steep incline that he recognized. Just ahead it ended in a rock ledge five feet above a wide stretch of riverbank where the snow was thin and patches of earth showed through. He usually fished downriver, but had come this far north many times. Now, even as he reached that overlook, lightning scorched the air perhaps thirty feet away and Jan-Olaf froze, covering his eyes to protect them from the blinding light. The thunder was deafening, but he no longer cared.

He knew this land, thought he had understood it, but this was like nothing he had ever seen or experienced in his life. Thoughts of ancient warriors and chariots across the sky clashed in his head against the rational logic of the modern world.

When he opened his eyes he had to blink several times as his vision adjusted to the darkness again. At last he was able to peer down over the edge. The wide swath of riverbank was dappled with snow and ice save for a scorched and blackened patch of ravaged earth. At its center lay a withered corpse larger than any man Jan-Olaf had ever seen. Part of the hillside seemed to have given way, for there was rubble strewn about down there as well. Whether the desiccated thing had been thrown ashore by the river or torn out of the breast of the earth, he did not know, nor did his mind have space to consider such things just then.

His eyes were wide and he had ceased breathing in that moment, simply forgotten how to draw breath. Jan-Olaf knelt in the snow on that ledge and stared at an ancient truth that numbed him more deeply than the frozen land ever could. Everything he knew was wrong.

He stared at the wasted thing, there on the riverbank, at the iron weapon it clutched in its dead fingers.

The lightning came again, and this time when Jan-Olaf closed his eyes, he wept frightened tears, for he was lost now. Lost in a world that was suddenly new to him, and yet also so incredibly old.

CHAPTER ONE

When he set eyes on the figure that emerged from the limousine into the moonlit night, Officer Aaron Bruckner nearly wet himself. It was taller than any man, its flesh a dark crimson like drying blood. Though there were things about it that suggested humanity—the thick sideburns on its cheeks, the jacket and pants it wore—the thing was far from human. How else to explain the long tail that thrust up from beneath the duster jacket, the hooves that clicked on the pavement, the broad flat spaces on its forehead that could only have been the stumps of horns.

"Sweet Jesus," Officer Bruckner whispered as he unholstered his weapon.

He ignored the limousine, ignored the rest of the cops around him. Half the Hollis, Virginia police department were there in a cordon around the Playtown USA amusement park. Calls had been coming in all day from parents whose children had been terrified—pants-wetting, catatonic, scarred-for-life terrified—by some freak hiding in Playtown. *Ugly. Scary. Big. Red.* That was about the best description the kids had been able to give of the thing that had frightened them . . . chased them . . . even choked a couple of them, though thankfully none were seriously hurt.

Freak, Bruckner thought, and he laughed at the word. This thing was no molester or lunatic. There was only one word for the monstrous, inhuman thing that stalked across the lot now. *Demon.*

Despite the heat of that August night, a chill ran through Bruckner as the thing came toward him. Beyond that limousine was nothing but darkened, empty parking lot, and past that, the trees that lined Route 82. The press had been kept away, save for the helicopter that even now buzzed above. Behind Bruckner were dozens of cops and park officials, but in that moment it was just him and the creature. Him and the demon.

Aaron Bruckner stood his ground. His throat was dry and he felt tears beginning to form at the corners of his eyes, the sting of salt and fear. His fingers felt numb and his limbs moved as if of their own accord, some distant cosmic puppeteer pulling his strings. Holding his breath, he stared at the blood-red beast, its features angular and hard as though hewn from stone. Its right hand was enormous, huge beyond all sense of proportion, and he thought for a moment that it might well *be* stone.

Something was frozen inside Aaron Bruckner, but it kept him steady as he raised his service weapon in both hands and took aim at the monster's chest.

Movement at his side. Aaron flinched, glanced to the left, and found Sergeant Wilkie staring at him. The heavy-set sergeant had wide, dark eyes, a missing upper incisor, and a nose that looked to have been broken at least twice. A thick vein throbbed in his temple whenever he was stressed, which was just about always.

"Bruckner," Sergeant Wilkie snapped in a low voice.

"What the hell are you doing? Put that weapon down!"

The gun wavered in his hand. Bruckner stared wide-eyed at the demon, then back at Wilkie. "But Sarge . . ." Didn't he see it, for God's sake? "The thing . . . in the park . . ."

Wilkie stepped right in front of him, blocking his view of the demon, this fiend that would haunt his dreams for years thereafter with a throaty laugh and eyes of fire, its long tail swaying behind it. The sergeant pushed Bruckner's hands down, his numb hands, and Bruckner let him, too stunned to fight it.

"Damn it, kid, don't you ever read the papers?" Wilkie muttered. "It's that *guy* . . . that Hellboy. This is just the sort of thing he gets involved with."

Even as Wilkie's words sunk in, the demon strode up behind him, towering over him. It paused a moment there, as Wilkie turned and the two cops stared up into the grizzled, granite features of the creature.

"Hey," Hellboy said. "Anybody seen a monster around here?"

Playtown after dark was a surreal, nightmarish landscape. Under normal circumstances the power would have been shut down at the end of the day, but the park had been evacuated several hours before dusk. There were no floodlights—no need, since the place was supposed to close at dusk—only the multi-colored bulbs and glowing neon on the rides themselves. They were just enough to twist the golden light of the moon into a sickly, hallucinatory sort of illumination.

From the Ferris wheel came a tinny calliope music, clashing with the melody coming from the distant carousel. Other than that, Playtown was silent.

Creepy little place, Hellboy thought, though Playtown wasn't exactly little. It was a small but modern amusement park whose roller coaster, Whiplash Mountain, had some local notoriety. Of course, Hellboy would not have ridden the thing even if he had a gun to his head. He was not fond of roller coasters. Too rickety. Not that he had had a great deal of experience with them. Save for a couple of trips Professor Bruttenholm had specially arranged for him when he was small, his only visits to amusement parks had been like this one: go in, figure out what the hell was haunting or stalking the grounds, get the heck out.

What sort of unnerved him, though, was that the few times he had done this in the past, the amusement parks had fit the mold better. Ancient relics of good times past, barely able to stay open, but apparently attractive to spirits, demons, and, in one case, a woman with the head of a boar. He didn't like to think about that last one. It had been a while since he had been asked to look into one of these places. Once a decade, it seemed. And Playtown was next.

But it was too new, too nice, too well kept, or at least that was how he figured it. Playtown did not follow the pattern. It had none of the things that usually seemed to attract the supernatural.

Freaky.

Hellboy walked the paved path that wound in and out of the rides, past gift shops and take-out windows, past picnic tables and abandoned ice-cream and pretzel and cotton-candy vending wagons. The smell of fried dough was strong on the breeze, but he couldn't see a wagon for that anywhere. Paper drink cups with straws jutting from them sat atop an overflowing trash can, precariously balanced, waiting to fall. No one was going to empty the trash until Hellboy handled the pest control.

Pest control. He hated thinking of it that way, but sometimes he could not help it. The really intriguing stuff, the stuff that made his employers at the Bureau for Paranormal Research and Defense wet their pants, did not come along as often as this kind of mundane ghostbusting crap.

Of course, whatever was lurking around here at Playtown, he didn't think it was a ghost. The reports that had come in had referred to a tall creature, skeletally thin, with leathery red skin and long, shaggy hair. It was supposed to move in a kind of dance, arms windmilling around. And it scared the crap out of a bunch of kids. Hellboy wasn't particularly fond of the research part of the BPRD's name, but the Bureau had a guess as to the monster's ID within an hour.

The night was hot and dry, but, as he passed the log flume, Hellboy could feel the air grow heavier with the moisture of evaporated water. There was a Tilt-a-Whirl and the Octopus and the Roundup, all of which were designed to make riders scream and vomit, and a hydraulic tower that would lift riders hundreds of feet above the ground and then plummet them toward the ground before slowing at the last moment. The lights were brightest in that area, turning the pavement an odd mélange of color, like the inside of a nightclub.

Further on he passed a clutch of rides for small children: kiddie canoes and Red Baron planes and slowly spinning teacups. The Red Baron ride had been split in half by a thick oak tree that grew up through the metal works and shattered it from the inside.

Hellboy grunted as he looked at it. That was new. He had heard reports of the trees that had suddenly burst up through the ground—that was what had finally forced the park authorities to evacuate—but seeing it was another story. No wonder the little kids had run screaming. By now their parents were probably talking lawsuit.

Other than a couple of dropped ice-cream cones—long ago melted to almost nothing—and a child's backpack with colorful clowns painted all over it, there was no sign of trouble here save for that intrusive tree. A couple of the Red Baron planes had actually broken off and smashed to the ground. How this all had happened without any children being badly hurt was beyond him.

Unless whatever was responsible had not wanted to hurt the children at all? He frowned and rolled that one over in his mind. Hellboy glanced at the backpack again and shuddered. Clowns creeped him out. No one was that happy. It was unnatural.

From the kiddie corner, he went past a garishly painted funhouse and an entire alley filled with those ring-toss and basketball-throw-type games that no one ever really won except by sheer luck. Then, on the other side of a small building that housed vending machines and restrooms, he came in sight of the bumper cars and the carousel. The music from the Ferris wheel had receded behind him now, and as he walked toward the merry-go-round, its sweet carnival melody grew louder. It made him think of the ice-cream man—of watching the ice-cream man out the window and being forbidden to chase him . . . after that first time, the BPRD had decided it would be better for all concerned. The late Professor Bruttenholm, who had raised Hellboy within the confines of the BPRD's facilities, had always been more than willing to go and get something for him from the white truck, but it wasn't the same.

The carousel was still spinning. The horses and other animals in the painted menagerie upon its platform went up and down on their poles, some in time with the music and others to their own mechanical rhythm. A second tree, much larger than the first, grew up out of the ground only a few feet from the edge of the turning carousel. It was dark and gnarled, twisted limbs thrust out at all angles. Some of the branches extended into the carousel itself and scraped against the poles and the wood and plastic animals as they went around. The ends of those branches had been stripped of leaves, a few of which were on the ground. Hellboy figured the others had blown away.

He stared a long moment at the carousel, wondering if he should climb aboard to search it. But after a minute, it was clear to him that here, as well, there was nothing out of the ordinary save for that tree.

Then something moved.

On the other side of the carousel, in the shadows beside another row of those rip-off carnival games, a tall figure slipped forward. The moonlight glinted off its skin, red as reported, though much brighter than Hellboy's own. Like a candy apple, and just as sticky looking. It spun as it moved, hands swirling above it, hopping from one leg to another in a kind of mad, capering dance. Shaggy hair hung halfway down its back, but otherwise the thing was naked. It leaped upon the carousel and swung 'round the pole that jutted up from the back of a dolphin.

The carousel came quickly around, happy music filling the air, and the thing stared at Hellboy as it swung past him. Its face was skeletal, yes, and thin, its chin pointed, cheekbones high and jutting from beneath leathery skin.

Hellboy shivered. The thing was pretty damn ugly.

It rode the carousel around twice more and then leaped off in an acrobatic tumble that sent it twisting through the air. Its clawed feet hit the pavement in utter silence and it continued its wild capering, dancing around him with flailing limbs. Hellboy rolled his eyes as the thing circled him, staring, studying. Dr. Manning at the BPRD said the thing was supposed to be able to become invisible when it wanted to be. But Hellboy often saw things other people didn't.

When it danced past in front of him again, Hellboy glared at the thing impatiently. "I can see you, moron."

The thing faltered, its expression almost comical. It had a mouth full of jagged teeth that were crusted with a green moss, scraped clean in spots, and now that it had stopped

moving, Hellboy could see that its skin had a texture closer to bark than leather.

It spoke to him in quick flurries of words in a language Hellboy quickly realized was an old dialect of Portuguese. He figured that pretty much confirmed the monster's identity.

"You're Caypór, I guess."

Again, the thing rambled on quickly in that fluid language, but now Caypór began to move again. It danced around Hellboy, yellow eyes staring in fascination, trying to figure him out, to understand why Hellboy could see him. Hellboy couldn't speak the language, but he understood enough to get the gist of what the demon was saying. And, according to the file he'd been given on the creature, Caypór was a demon. A Brazilian forest demon, to be exact. It was a sort of bogeyman there who frightened children away from the forests.

If what the ugly bastard was saying was true, though, it had always been a servant of the parents of those children. It kept the children safe, scaring them away from the forests. Now it had been summoned here by a group of Brazilian mothers whose families had settled in the United States. If Hellboy understood Caypór correctly, the mothers

had grown concerned that American popular culture had somehow worked an insidious dark magic on their children's minds, and would obliterate any interest in their own culture and heritage.

A breeze kicked up and Hellboy's duster flapped behind him. He scratched at the bristle on his chin and stared at the demon. "Let me get this straight. These women raised a demon to scare their kids away from an amusement park, probably giving 'em years' worth of nightmares, hoping it would make them more interested in their homeland? So you wrecked some kiddie rides and terrified the crap out of a whole bunch of *other* kids who aren't Brazilian and did *not* ask you to come here?"

Slowly, Caypór did a pirouette, limbs fluttering. Then it bowed, as though proud of what it had done.

"Jeez," Hellboy said, sighing. "That's the stupidest thing I ever heard."

Caypór froze, narrowed its feral yellow eyes, and shook back its long, matted hair. Hellboy realized he probably should have been more diplomatic, but he'd never been able to master diplomacy, believing it most frequently the province of liars and idiots.

"All right," Hellboy said, offering a small shrug. "I guess you were just doing the job. They called you, right? But you oughtta go now. Grab a brew and some Peking ravioli or something."

A flurry of angry words rolled off Caypór's tongue and it pointed a long, bony finger at Hellboy.

Hellboy crossed his arms and glared sternly at the demon. "I'm not kidding, schmoe. Cut this crap out. Get gone."

Caypór threw his hands up and the ground rumbled as a thick tree trunk shattered the pavement beneath Hellboy's hooves and shot up from the earth beneath him. It knocked him backward, but already its branches spread, and it grew up around him, lifting him off his feet. The carousel's lights blinked and the music sounded suddenly warped. A branch twisted around Hellboy's torso.

He raised his enormous right hand, and brought the stone appendage down in a blow that splintered wood and snapped branches all around. He tumbled to the ground, landed on the pavement on his stomach, and struck his chin. His teeth clacked together and he bit his tongue, tasting his own blood.

"Always gotta choose the hard way," he mumbled as he rose. His gun was heavy in its holster at his hip, but he didn't bother taking the time to retrieve it.

Caypór pranced around like a court jester, but there was nothing merry about the way it moved. It swung fluidly through the air, danced in near Hellboy and planted its hands on the ground, then whipped its legs around. Taloned feet slashed at Hellboy's chest. His hide was tough, durable, and so the attack did not draw blood. But it stung.

"Hey!" Hellboy shouted. He swung a left hook at the demon, but it cartwheeled away from him. "Hold still!"

With a gesture, the demon called forth another gnarled,

haunted tree from the trembling ground. It burst through the sundered pavement and shot at Hellboy. But he was ready this time. The upper limbs of the tree stretched toward him, sap-scented tentacles whose bark rippled in the light of the moon and the colorful glow of the flickering carousel bulbs. They tried to wrap themselves around him, but Hellboy dodged, snapping off smaller branches, and brought his heavy right hand down in a splintering blow that sheared off the top ten feet of the tree.

The demonic bogeyman did a little crab-like scuttling, arms flying around him as it moved behind Hellboy. Caypór flew at Hellboy again, lashing out with its feet. With a grunt, moving faster than most would think him capable of, considering his size, Hellboy bent and lifted the shattered trunk of the tree. He spun, swung the tree trunk, and struck Caypór with such force that the demon screamed—the sound like wood shrieking, about to break. The blow sent Caypór tumbling to the ground between the carousel and the gazebo that housed the bumper-cars.

The demon tried to rise and Hellboy struck him again. Caypór slammed into one of the posts that held up the roof of the bumper-car gazebo, and the post snapped in half. The corner of the roof sagged there but did not collapse.

"I told you to cut it out," Hellboy reminded him.

There were cracks in the demon's bark-like flesh, and a dark brown substance that might have been its blood had begun to ooze out. Caypór's shaggy hair fell across its eyes as it struggled to stand. Yellow, bestial eyes blossomed with rage and then plant-like shoots of new growth appeared in its wounds. Like flower petals, they spread over the injuries and began to heal that red bark skin. In his archaic Portuguese, Caypór snarled a quick ballet of words that Hellboy only half-understood. The meaning was clear, though. Caypór wasn't going to leave, and it could heal itself fast enough that Hellboy wasn't going to be able to destroy it by hand.

Then Caypór spit on him.

"All right," Hellboy said, jaw clenched. "Now I'm ticked." They had restored the lost spider scene to *King Kong*, and it was showing that night on cable. Hellboy could have been watching it with Abe back in their hotel room if not for Caypór.

The demon lunged at him, a flurry of limbs and wicked claws. Hellboy ignored them, felt the scraping at his skin and just waded right into it. He brought down his right hand again and it shattered the demon's left arm. Caypór shrieked. Hellboy slugged it with a quick left to the jaw, breaking some of those mossy teeth and shutting the demon up.

Then he lifted Caypór with both hands and tossed it into the bumper-car gazebo. The demon landed, sprawling, on the sheet-metal floor. Hellboy strode grimly to the operator's platform, still buzzing with electricity, and ripped the control box off its moorings. It trailed a thick tangle of high-voltage cable. Hellboy crushed the metal and plastic box in his hand and it sparked, exposed wiring crackling. He hauled on the cables, ripped them loose, then dropped them over the side of the gazebo and onto the sheet-metal floor.

Caypór was just getting up again when the electrical

current surged through the floor. The demon froze, then began to jitter in an obscene pantomime of the prancing it had done moments before. Hellboy could hear the sizzle and pop as electricity coursed through it, and the lights in the park were slightly dimmed by the power drain. The smell of a woodstove or chimney smoke filled the air, and reminded Hellboy of autumn. Then Caypór's eyes popped, one after the other, and fire began to lick from the empty sockets. The demon's chest began to glow orange, and gray flakes formed at the edge of that burning ember. Its skin split, and fire spat from the wounds and began to consume it. There would be no new growth now, no sprouts of life.

The breeze that had blown steadily suddenly ceased, as if pausing for breath, and the fire that consumed the demon hesitated as well. The sizzle of electricity filled the air. Then the wind kicked up again and the fire engulfed the demon completely, shooting toward the ceiling, catching there, and beginning to spread.

At length, Hellboy shook his head in disgust and turned to go. "Always gotta be the hard way."

The cops kept their distance as he walked out. *Jeez, what, do I smell?* Hellboy thought in annoyance. Virginia was so close to D.C. that between the politicians and the FBI headquarters over in Langley he figured people down here would be used to weird crap happening all the time. But Hollis was just a little podunk town like a million other places in America. The people there probably wouldn't have known what to say to Julia Roberts either. Not that she was ever going to kill a demon in Hollis, but still . . .

One of the policemen stepped out to meet him as he walked toward the limousine.

"Hellboy," the portly cop said, as if tasting the word. "I'm Sergeant Bob Wilkie. Did you find anything in there?"

"Yep." Hellboy scratched at the back of his neck, where what little hair he had was tied in a tight knot.

Wilkie's eyes widened. "What is it?"

"It's on fire. Probably wanna call someone to put it out."

With that, Hellboy strode to the limousine, opened the door, and carefully climbed into the back. The car tilted low as he slid onto the seat. When he glanced up, just before closing the door, he saw Sergeant Wilkie barking orders at a few of the other cops. That was good. Hopefully they'd get the fire out before it could spread.

He pulled the door shut and settled in beside Dr. Tom Manning, the director of the Bureau, who was on the cell phone. Dr. Manning held up a finger to indicate that he'd be just a moment longer on his call, so Hellboy just stared out the window as the limousine started to roll. The director had brought Hellboy and several other operatives for the BPRD to Washington to testify in front of the committee that would decide how much money the U.S. government would contribute to the Bureau's budget. Hellboy hadn't testified yet, and he had no clue what he was supposed to say.

"Sorry about that," Dr. Manning said as he slid the phone back inside his suit jacket. He regarded Hellboy intently, eyes narrowed. "So, how did it go?"

"Research boys were right. It was Caypór."

"Really?" Dr. Manning asked, fascinated. "What was he like?"

"Stubborn. Look, how long before we get back to the hotel? I'm gonna have a heck of a time falling asleep as it is with this testimony thing tomorrow."

"Ah, that," the director said. The expression on his face was all professional then. "Well, you'll be pleased to know you won't be testifying tomorrow. You're leaving first thing in the morning for Sweden."

"Sweden?" Hellboy turned as best he could in the cramped confines of the limousine and stared at Dr. Manning. "What the hell's in Sweden?"

Manning's features were grave, but there was a kind of awe in his voice. "Even with all you've seen, even with what you are, I don't think you'd believe me if I told you."

CHAPTER TWO

In a suite in the Fitzgerald Grand Hotel just outside of Washington, D.C., Abe Sapien did his best to relax and avoid thinking about the testimony he was meant to give in the morning. The air conditioning hummed soothingly and the room was a cool sixty-six degrees, but he wore only pants and a white cotton undershirt.

When he shifted, his rough skin slid across the sheets and made a sort of rasping noise, but he did not hear it. Abe wore headphones connected to a portable CD player and he tried his best to focus on the book in his hands while Sting's *Ten Summoner's Tales* played.

The book was called *Streets of Laredo*, a western by Larry McMurtry that concerned the last days of an aging Texas lawman. It was just about the saddest, most mournful thing Abe had ever read, and Sting wasn't helping. The music and the book combined to nurture a sort of melancholy in him, but at least they were a distraction from fretting about the morning. Yet they had another effect as well. Though it was not quite ten o'clock, Abe was quite drowsy. The book kept sagging in his hands, his chin bobbing onto his chest every few minutes or so. He had read the same paragraph several times.

When the book actually fell out of his hands, Abe

snapped awake, startled, and removed his headphones while rising from bed. He sighed and flipped a few pages until he found where he had left off and then folded down the page. There were people, he knew, who thought it nothing short of blasphemy to fold the page instead of using a bookmark. Bookmark zealots. Paperback fascists. Abe ignored them.

Restless now, he wandered the suite. He did not feel confined in that small space—with his amphibious appearance he was used to retreating from public view—but he felt unsettled. The mirror over the bureau drew his attention and Abe stared at his own reflection for several seconds. He had no idea why Dr. Manning had brought him. No way the Congressional committee was going to pay attention to what he had to tell them when even in their internal correspondence they had referred to him as "that fish guy."

Idiots, Abe thought. *Fish guy. Don't they even read their own files*?

He felt thirsty suddenly and wandered to the mini-bar. Still preoccupied, he opened it and glanced within. Three-dollar bottled water. Four-dollar Sprite and Coke. Two-dollar candy bars. Macadamia nuts, cookies, and trail mix. Even though Abe would not have to foot the bill himself, he still thought the prices outrageous. But he missed his room, missed his things, and worst of all, he had missed the Red Sox game on television that afternoon. Living at Bureau headquarters in Connecticut, Abe had grown to be a devoted Red Sox fan, intrigued by the legendary curse that popular wisdom said had haunted the team for nearly a century.

After a few more seconds' hesitation, Abe took the Macadamia nuts and a Sprite out of the mini-bar and closed the door with a rattle of tiny liquor bottles.

A beep sounded in the suite. As Abe glanced toward the door, it swung inward. Hellboy blocked out nearly all the light from the corridor and he was momentarily silhouetted as he entered. Then Abe saw the tears in his jacket and the already healing scratches on his chest.

"Guess you found what you were looking for," the amphibian said.

Hellboy shrugged out of his jacket and threw it on the couch in the outer room of the suite. "Ruined another coat," he said as he unsnapped the holster from his waist and slipped it off. Then he paused and gazed at Abe, narrowing his eyes. "What's with the Macadamia nuts?"

Abe stood with the soda in one hand and the nuts in the other. A bit sheepish, he smiled and held the can out to Hellboy. "Want some?"

"Nah. Macadamias don't have any flavor. They're like those stupid white things they put in Chinese food. Whaddaya call 'em? Water chestnuts. Might as well eat tofu."

For a second, Abe considered putting the nuts back. Instead, he sat on the edge of his bed, set his soda on the night table, and defiantly popped the top of the can of nuts with a hiss of the freshness seal. Idly, he scooped out a few nuts and tossed them into his mouth. They were sort of chewy, maybe a little stale, and truth be told they didn't have very much flavor. But he wasn't going to tell Hellboy that.

"So?" he prodded.

Hellboy snatched up the cable television guide the hotel had provided and then went to sit on his own bed, tail curled up behind him. The bed sagged deeply under his bulk, but he did not seem to notice.

"Wanna watch a movie?"

Something in his tone alerted Abe, who studied his best friend more closely. Hellboy was tired and annoyed by both his scratches and ruined coat, but there was more to it than that.

"What?" Abe pressed him.

"I asked if you wanted to watch a movie," Hellboy replied. With his hard, angular features and dark red skin, most people did not notice when he smiled. When he smirked, though, as he did now, only a few people in the world would have recognized the facial expression for what it was.

Abe glared at him, the gills on his neck fluttering.

"What?" Hellboy asked innocently.

"You tell me. Did the bogeyman turn out to be an attractive Hellgirl or something?"

Hellboy scowled. "With that attitude, I'll just go by myself."

"Go where?" Abe demanded.

Hellboy lay back on the bed, arms under his head, and gazed at the ceiling. "Sweden."

"Sweden? What's in Sweden? I don't want to go to Sweden. It's cold there. I interrupted my chess game with Kate to come here, and I'm still rearranging my books. They're all over the place."

When Hellboy sat up again, the bed springs squealed in protest. He stared at Abe, disappointment plain. "Kate doesn't even like chess. She only plays because you won't leave her alone about it. And your books will still be there when you get back."

Abe took another handful of Macadamia nuts and popped the top on his soda. He took a sip, then picked up *Streets of Laredo* again and lay back while Hellboy stared at him.

"Kate loves chess."

"Not what she said," Hellboy replied calmly.

"Only because she doesn't like to lose."

"Abe."

The amphibian glanced up from his book with a sigh. "I don't want to go to Sweden. Remember our last trip to Scandinavia?"

Hellboy nodded. "Of course. But there aren't gonna be any lunatic shapeshifting seals this trip."

"How do you know?"

"You don't want to go? Be that way," Hellboy said with some finality. "I just figured you'd be glad you didn't have to testify in front of that committee tomorrow."

"They weren't seals."

"Whatever."

"I don't like the cold."

But Hellboy must have heard the wavering in Abe's voice, for he sat forward a bit further, his enormous stone hand hanging nearly to the floor.

"Y'know, I heard Swedish chicks dig fish guys. It's a well-known fact."

Abe rolled his eyes, closed his book and stared at Hellboy. "Pick a movie."

Stiff, nervous Swedish government types met Hellboy and Abe at the airport in Stockholm. The mouthpiece—the only one among them who was either capable or willing to speak English—was a man named Fredrik Klar. He wore thick, rimless eyeglasses and had his blond hair cut short and swept back in a style that struck Hellboy as just a little too Aryan for comfort.

Stockholm was a picturesque city, combining the elegance of the Old World with the sophistication of a new century. Though cool, the weather was beautiful this time of year, the sky a crystal blue that seemed to hang lower than it did elsewhere in the world. As though the heavens were closer there, somehow.

In all the years the late Trevor Bruttenholm had been his mentor, not to mention his adoptive father, Hellboy knew he had disappointed the man time after time with his lack of enthusiasm for study. But he remembered a little of what he had learned of Norse mythology. When he gazed up at the sky, it seemed to him no wonder that the Scandinavian peoples imagined their gods so much a part of the world. Far away in Asgard, yes, but also so very close.

Klar wasn't going to give them time to explore Stockholm, however. The agents from the Swedish government escorted Hellboy and Abe to the Swedish naval vessel

Kiruna for the long journey north through the Gulf of Bothnia to the coastal city of Lulea. Abe retreated to their cabin almost immediately, but Hellboy spent some time on the deck. The crew gave him a wide berth, which was just fine, seeing that he did not speak Swedish. Klar passed him once or twice in a hurry and greeted him with a nod. Hellboy wondered exactly what the rush was. It wasn't as though he had anywhere to go.

Eventually, as the hours passed and they forged further north, the sky turned gray, and now its nearness seemed ominous rather than comforting. With the change in the weather, Hellboy at last went below. He found Abe reading in their stateroom, still wearing the thick wool sweater he had donned as soon as they got off the plane back in Stockholm. His skin had a pallid cast that concerned Hellboy.

"You all right?"

Abe nodded. "I just wish it was a little warmer in here."

They moored off Lulea and slept the night on shipboard. Klar roused them at five in the morning. The sky was already light this far north and Hellboy was heartened to see that the sun was out once more, but Abe buried himself beneath a thick parka with a hood, a fringe of fur framing his face. A number of wisecracks occurred to Hellboy, but one look from Abe and he thought better of it and kept silent. He only hoped that whatever Dr. Manning had sent them to investigate was truly as astonishing as the Bureau director had claimed, or Hellboy would never hear the end of it.

Two large trucks awaited them in port, vehicles with thick tires wrapped in chains and laden with supplies as though they were heading out on a true Arctic expedition rather than merely visiting a northern village. Abe glared balefully at the gear in the back of their truck, then he sighed and climbed into the backseat. Hellboy lifted himself up into the passenger seat and the truck rocked under his weight.

Klar sat patiently behind the wheel as he strapped himself in.

Hellboy glanced at him. "Okay. Let's go. Mush."

A sort of scowl flickered across Klar's face. "Mush?" he asked.

"The faster we go, the sooner we come back," Hellboy replied. He glanced into the backseat, but Abe had already closed his eyes and was breathing deeply, either asleep or on the way.

Great, Hellboy thought with a sidelong glance at Klar. It looked like the ride was going to be packed with scintillating conversation.

On the hilltop overlooking the Dalbard River, Karl Aronsson held up a hand to shield his face. It was not snowing, but the wind swept over the ground and pulled it up, driving old snow into the air in enough quantity that visibility was negligible. The gale was strong enough that, despite his bulk, Karl had to lean into it to keep from being knocked off balance.

He wiped his goggles and looked down at the riverbank below. Despite the wind, from his vantage point he could see his team spread out, planting stakes around the remains the old fisherman had found. Rope would be used to delineate the area and then once the corpse had been carefully removed, the dig would begin. Thus far, the weather had prevented them from photographing the discovery in its surrounding environs, or from taking samples of it on site. The wind would not last forever, but the lightning was an issue as well.

As if summoned by his own thoughts, the sky lit up with a vein of electric light that cut through the driven snow. The thundercrack was deafening, even with the earmuffs Karl wore. His team, down there on the bank of the river, had earplugs in, and already they had begun to complain that it was not enough. The lightning made them all scurry away from the remains, and they gazed at the sky warily, as though they might be the next targets. Which was absurd. Though the frequency of the lightning strikes had slowed dramatically, even in the time since Karl and his team had arrived, its target was a constant. He was certain there was a scientific explanation, some sort of circuit that had been formed between the electrical activity in the atmosphere and the weapon clutched in the fingers of that corpse, but that was not his field.

Whatever the explanation, they could not very well remove it until they knew that the circuit could be broken. None of them relished trying to move what was essentially the most consistently effective lightning rod in the world. And, if it came to that, they had not yet received government clearance to remove it anyway. Not that Karl cared very much for the role the government had decided to play in all this. It was an archaeological discovery, after all, not some spy satellite.

And what a discovery it was. In all his life, he had never encountered such a significant find. If it was not a hoax, of course. He did not think it was, but until they had been able to test the remains there would be no way to truly know.

The wind gusted even harder and Karl took a step back, taken off guard a moment. He turned his back to it and found himself looking down the other side of the hill toward where they had left their vehicles. Somewhere down there, the old fisherman, Kjell, sat in a truck awaiting the arrival of government representatives whom he hoped were going to reward him for reporting this find. Karl thought the only reward they might give him was a little publicity, which was almost certainly not what the old man had in mind.

Again he wiped off his goggles, but as he turned back toward the riverbank he saw dark shapes moving in the valley below. The gale lashed all around him and the snow blotted out his vision a moment, but there came a sudden lull, and he could see that there were more vehicles in the valley. The dark shapes he had seen were people swathed in parkas and wearing goggles much like his own. Karl counted six of them, but there were two out in front, one of whom towered over all the others.

Another sudden gust cast a shroud of white across the land again, wind whistling all around him, buffeting his entire body. The party below became nothing but dark shapes in the snow once more, and it was several minutes before they drew close enough that Karl could make them out. They seemed like ghosts, as they loomed up from below, rising up the hillside as though drifting on the wind.

He shielded his goggles again, trying to get a better look at them. When he spoke, he had to raise his voice to try to be heard over the storm.

"Are you the American scientists?"

The wind lessened and the two in front were perhaps ten feet away. Karl stared at them, eyes wide behind the lenses of his goggles. The huge one had skin the color of drying blood, and a long red tail thrust out behind him, swaying in the air. His enormous right hand seemed carved from stone. The other had green, reptilian flesh, and thin, inhuman lips, and he shivered with the cold.

"Not exactly," said the red man. "But we're the closest you're gonna get."

His hooves slid on the snow-covered hill and Hellboy planted them more firmly. From what he had learned on the ride up, this Karl Aronsson was a professor from Stockholm University and, despite what Klar's arrogance implied, it was really the university that was in charge of this site. Professor Aronsson seemed odd at first, staring at Hellboy and Abe like he'd forgotten for a moment what he was doing there in the first place. Then he smiled, the grin barely noticeable above the rim of the thick scarf around his neck.

"You're Hellboy," the rotund man said. "I've heard of you."

"He's a celebrity," Abe said dryly.

Hellboy held out his left hand and Aronsson shook it.

"A pleasure," the professor said.

"Likewise. This is Abe Sapien. He's also with the BPRD. It's been a long trip, Professor. Maybe you could show us exactly what it is that the Bureau sent us up here for."

"Of course, of course." Aronsson glanced at Klar and hesitated a moment, a look of distaste on his features. Then he turned and started down the hill. Hellboy and Abe followed, with the government monkeys in tow.

The hill sloped down toward a river nobody had bothered to tell Hellboy the name of, and they picked their path carefully. Stones thrust up from the ground at intervals, and several of the government men paused at each of these spots to reassure themselves of their footing. Hellboy paid them little notice. His attention was instead upon the people who milled about on the riverbank, busying themselves with measurements and hammering stakes and digging soil samples or some such. He could not really tell what they were digging for because of the windstorm and the snow that blew all around, whipping against him.

Then they were on a ledge five feet above the riverbank and Hellboy squinted, not sure he was really seeing what he thought he was seeing. In the midst of this buzz of activity, like the queen in the hive, was the withered corpse of a man who would have been at least as tall and broad as Hellboy had he still lived.

"Long lost brother, you think?" Abe asked beside him.

Hellboy frowned and shot him a dark look, then dropped off the ledge to land with a crunch of snow and earth on the riverbank. A woman chipping at the rocky wall of the ledge jumped, startled by his sudden arrival. She let out a little cry and backed against the wall, eyes wide.

"Sorry," Hellboy said, a bit sheepish.

The woman glanced up quickly to see Professor Aronsson climbing down a tall metal ladder that had been set against the ledge. The others were gathered at the top awaiting their turn. When she saw him, the woman seemed to calm down a bit, and even spoke a few words in Swedish to Hellboy. He smiled dumbly, the universal expression used by those who did not want to admit that they had no clue what somebody else was saying. When Abe and the professor had made it down the ladder, Hellboy was relieved.

Klar and his lackeys were next. Hellboy pulled his goggles off and gave the man a long look. "Give us some space, all right?"

He was surprised when Klar only nodded.

"So, am I to understand that no one explained to you what we have found?" Professor Aronsson asked as the snow whipped around them.

"Great job, huh?" Hellboy asked. "Actually, the Bureau usually provides its field operatives with boatloads of research. In this case, the boss decided we would have a more 'objective' investigation if we went in blind."

Together they walked toward the corpse. It was not perfectly preserved like some of the ancient specimens that had been found in the previous century. This thing looked mummified, like a dried husk of skin had been draped over the massive skeleton beneath.

"Objective," Hellboy repeated. "Who the hell could see this thing and be objective?"

"If it is real, I would agree with you," the professor replied.

"You doubt its authenticity?" Abe asked, moving closer to them.

Professor Aronsson froze, there on the riverbank. He turned to regard them both, looking first at Abe, then at Hellboy. "How could it be what it appears to be? Do you realize what that would mean?"

Hellboy shrugged. "I've seen a lot of weird stuff. That's life."

He glanced over at Abe, who no longer looked bored, irked, or even cold. They stood perhaps half a dozen feet from the corpse and now Hellboy moved closer. His tail traced a line in the thin layer of snow. Wispy remnants of the dead thing's hair and beard moved with the wind. Around its neck was an enormous bronze pendant fashioned in the shape of a cruel-looking serpent. The size of the cadaver, its obvious age, that bronze pendant; none of it would have stirred within Hellboy a fraction of the fascination he felt at the moment were it not for that weapon in its right hand. Gnarled, dead fingers had clutched at its haft for forgotten millennia.

Hellboy crouched to get a better look at it. Though the handle was short, the head was many times the size of a sledgehammer. It had been forged of a dark metal and etched with some sort of symbolic engraving, twin lines that turned outward and curled in upon themselves. The hammer was not squared, but came to a sort of peak on the top, and had protrusions on either end that would likely have made it more deadly. For this was no workman's tool, but a war hammer.

"Has anyone tried to lift it?" Abe asked, shouting to be heard over the wind.

"You mean have we attempted to remove it?" Aronsson replied. "The weather has prevented us from taking the proper precautions in transporting the remains, but yes, we did try to . . . remove the hammer."

Remove, Hellboy thought. *That wasn't the question.* But he could tell from the man's tone that the professor knew exactly what Abe was really asking.

"You couldn't lift it," he said. It was not a question. Even as he spoke, Hellboy reached out with his left hand. He paused, however, and stared at his own thin red fingers in hesitation. Then he flexed the huge fingers of his right hand, so much stronger and more massive than the other. Withdrawing his left he reached out with that huge right hand and brushed at the fingers clutching the war hammer. He expected them to snap and fall to dust, but they opened like the petals of a flower. Hellboy grasped the handle of the hammer, marveled that the leather wrapped around its length was still intact, did not seem to have rotted at all.

"You couldn't lift it?" Hellboy asked, his back to Abe and the professor, blocking their view of what he was doing.

"Actually, we only tried to lever it out of position to see if . . . well, to see if it *could* be moved. It could not. It

might as well be rooted to the ground. Of course, no one tried to lift it by hand because of the lightning."

Hellboy stood up, the hammer clutched in his hand, huge even in his massive grip. He tested its weight, the feel of it. The hammer was heavy, but not so much that he would have been unable to wield it in battle if he wanted to. He stared at the thing in his hand and a kind of awe swept through him as he wondered if this could really be what they were all thinking it might be. His gaze went past the hammer to the cadaver on the ground, its sunken eyes, its dry, papery skin. If the hammer was for real, then the dead guy would be too. And that was just too wild to even think about, no matter what Hellboy had said to Professor Aronsson.

Professor Aronsson, he thought. He had just said something about—

"Lightning?" Hellboy asked, turning to face them. "What about lightning?"

Abe started to move closer, clearly fascinated that Hellboy had lifted the hammer. But Professor Aronsson had the opposite reaction. Eyes wide behind his goggles, he raised his hands and backed away in horror.

"No, no," the stout man said in a panicked voice. "You must put it—"

A blaze of lightning arced from the sky, its brightness searing his eyes. The air was filled with the acrid burning stench of an electrical fire. It struck the hammer and the charge passed through Hellboy, paralyzed him, sizzled through his body. He felt the hair at the nape of his neck stand up, and his teeth clamped painfully together.

Through those clenched teeth, he roared in anguish as the handle of the war hammer fused to his hand.

CHAPTER THREE

Shattered spires. Smoke from fires. Funeral pyres. That was all that remained of the city now. The master of Himinbjorg had blown a warning on his great horn, Gjall, and the Aesir had awoken to find that the prophesied day had come at last. The ramparts of Bifrost had shattered and the darkling beasts had gathered on the plains of Vigrid just outside the city walls. The hosts of Valhalla marched out to meet them, nearly half a million strong.

Bodies burning. Waters churning. The river Iving ran red with blood and the soil was saturated with it. The battle had been sown with death, and now the reaper had come. The harvest of both armies lay pale and ravaged, scattered across the plains. Aesir and Einherjar, Nidavellim and Svartalves . . . and the giants. The largest of their corpses stretched a league, too far to see head from foot. The war had lasted so long that trees grew up through their guts, leaves blossoming blood-red cast shade over mountains of rotting flesh.

Now it was near the end of things. The end of all things. Vigrid had been taken, the wolf and the serpent driving the last of the Aesir back to the city walls and then through. They crumbled, great halls fell, and the children of the gods screamed. This final clash of sword and bone was bereft of the honor that had imbued millions of previous conflicts. It would not end with tankards raised high in the halls of Valhalla, but in the venom of Jormungand, in the gnashing jaws of Fenrir, and at last in a cleansing fire that would raze the nine worlds of all traces of what had come before.

The glory of an age was passing.

Hammer clutched in his hand, he stood his ground before the palace of his father and would not be driven back again. His coat of mail had been torn away, and he had lost his helmet as well. With torn and bloodied cloth his only armor, he roared in fury that tore his throat ragged.

"Come, then, nephew!" he shouted in the language of his father's ancestors. "The world will suffer your presence no longer."

Before him was the head of the serpent, as high as the tallest spire, jaws as wide as the fallen rainbow bridge. Its body disappeared into the distance, in some places visible and in others buried beneath the mounds of the dead. Its tongue lashed out and its jaws snapped and the earth trembled as it slid slowly toward him, but its eyes were dead and still, as though it, too, realized that the end was near for all of them.

He brought the hammer down on the ground and the earth split open, a fissure cracking wide and running out be-

neath the serpent's head. Storm clouds spun in on themselves above and seemed to spill into a river of sky that swept away from the city as though chasing the serpent's tail. And below, under the serpent's belly, the earth raced the storm, tearing itself open and swallowing Jormungand in what was now a canyon miles long. The ruins of Asgard and the dead on the fields of Vigrid began spilling into that canyon after it.

The hammer rang and trembled in his hand. Jormungand hissed and surged, slowly, inexorably, pushing its maw up toward the edge of the canyon. He raised the hammer again, blood raging with the lust for battle. For all those he had seen slain during this everlasting war, his children and siblings, his friends and comrades, he desired nothing more than to destroy the serpent. Somewhere nearby he heard the screaming howl of a monstrous wolf, and he knew his father and Fenrir were locked in bloody combat. He tasted the copper of his own blood upon his lips, his hair and beard matted with it.

The ground shook again as the serpent rammed its head above the edge of that pit. He leaped at it, and the hammer came down and crushed the socket of its right eye. The eye exploded in viscous fluid, and he grabbed hold of the serpent's scales and hung on as it thrashed. Lightning tore from the sky and struck it along the length of its body. The world trembled beneath them and the serpent tried to shake him off.

Again the hammer came down, splitting the serpent's skull.

His heart rejoiced. It could die. Jormungand could die and there would be vengeance. He was bathed in the gore of its wounds, and yet still he clutched at the sharp edge of a scale and kept his grip. Raised Mjollnir again. The skies opened with a torrent of rain that fell with such sheer ferocity that the storm nearly tore him loose from his perch atop the serpent's jaw. The hammer was stripped clean of gore in seconds and he hesitated.

Upon his chest swung the pendant crafted for him centuries before by the Nidavellim. It was a representation of the serpent itself, of Jormungand. It banged against him, reminded him that victory was already hollow, all was already lost. The end had been determined long ago, and he could only play his part in that.

But he would not retreat, would not allow the serpent one more inch of ground. He would not take a single step backward toward his father's palace. Again he raised the hammer. Again the serpent bucked its head. And then he fell, tumbling to the ravaged ground in the rain. It rose up again and then lunged for him, tongue flicking out, fangs like swords glistening with venom.

He climbed to his feet, but the serpent was too fast. As he lifted Mjollnir again, Jormungand snapped its jaws closed over him, rows of teeth slicing through his chest, snapping bones. His upper body inside the serpent's mouth, face coated with venom, fangs grinding up inside his body against his ribs, he swung the hammer and cracked its lower jaw. It hung loose and the serpent roared its fury as he forcibly pulled himself up off those lancing teeth that had impaled him.

It recoiled, pulling back and away from the palace, the one untainted hall in all the city. Painfully, clutching at his wounds, he rose. His skin grew tight across his face as though it might split, and his eyes were scorched by poison, his vision fading as blindness came on. The venom of the serpent was inside him, burning through his veins.

He waited until it tried to come for him again, hissing through its shattered jaw, unable to snap any longer, hoping perhaps merely to crush him. Jormungand shot forward once more, and he leaped atop the serpent's head again. The hammer came down and the thunder roared and the lightning split the sky, searing the serpent's flesh over and over. With Mjollnir tight in his grip, he battered Jormungand's skull again and again, pendant swaying around his neck.

It shuddered, and then it fell with such force that the great hall of the Allfather cracked and collapsed in upon itself. The city was destroyed in total now. Asgard was no more.

He slipped off the serpent and faced it one last time, this thing that his own brother had spawned. And then, blinded by poison, venom withering his flesh, he staggered backward, nine steps, giving up the ground he had sworn to defend.

And then he died.

When Hellboy opened his eyes, he was underwater. Only then did he realize he was drowning. His chest hurt and he gagged and sucked even more of the river into his lungs. He felt hands on his arms and shoulders, pulling at him, dragging him. Violence filled his head like a melody, and he drove his hooves into the river bed and thrust up out of the water. With a single sweep of his arms he knocked away the men who had been touching him, drowning him.

Choking, gasping, he staggered to the riverbank with the wind-driven snow buffeting his face, but he did not fall. Several of the men rose and backed away. Only one dared come forward, hands raised in a calming gesture.

"Hellboy, it's all right. You're all right."

"Touch me again and I'll feed your innards to my goats!" Hellboy raged, taking two shaky but imposing steps forward.

The man—not a man at all, though, was he—pulled off the goggles that shielded his eyes and stared at Hellboy dubiously. Not a man, not with that skin and those markings, the gills that fluttered at his neck.

Abe, Hellboy thought. *This is Abe.* It frightened him that he had not known that.

"What language is that he's speaking?" Abe asked, glancing around at the other men. "Does anyone know it?"

Another man, portly and tentative, moved toward the river's edge now. A kind of odd smile was on his face. *Professor Aronsson.* Faces and names were coming back to him now, but they were crowded in his mind with so many other images, of monsters and bloodshed and winged women and flashing swords and battles that lasted centuries.

"Some of the words sound familiar. It's an ancient tongue, certainly," Professor Aronsson said. "I think he said something about goats."

Abe shook his head and stared at Hellboy again. "That can't be right." He stepped forward, offering his hand. "Can you understand me? Are you all right? I thought you were drowning."

Suddenly very tired, Hellboy swayed a moment and thought he might throw up. "Abe?" He felt as though he had been drugged and his thoughts were only now beginning to clear. The images that crowded his mind were fleeting, beginning to fade, and he was left with the immediate sensory memory of having struck out at people who had been trying to . . . drown him. *No, not that. Trying to help.*

Hellboy looked around, still unsteady. Fredrik Klar and his trio of silent, somewhat sinister associates stood just behind Professor Aronsson. Klar had his hand inside his jacket, and Hellboy realized there must be a gun in there. He almost laughed at the intense expression on Klar's face, as though the man thought he could actually do Hellboy some damage that way. But now was not the time for levity. Abe was all right, and several members of the archaeology team had backed away up the riverbank, no worse for the wear save that they were wet and would now have to return to their accommodations. A man with thinning reddish-blond hair and a mustache sat nearby cradling his wrist and staring at Hellboy. Yet another lay on the

ground, panting, as the woman who had screamed when she first saw Hellboy went to his side.

"Did I hurt anybody?"

Professor Aronsson spoke in quick, rhythmic Swedish to the woman who knelt by the fallen man. She looked up, an expression of relief upon her face, and replied even as she helped the man to sit. From the look of things he had only had the wind knocked out of him. The man who cradled his right hand said something in Swedish as well and began to stand, wincing in pain.

"Anders believes he has broken his wrist, but other than that, it appears we are all well."

"Jeez, I'm sorry," Hellboy said, hoping Anders understood. "Don't know what got into me."

Boots sliding on the snow near the river's edge, Abe moved to his side. "I can't believe you aren't hurt worse. But that lightning scrambled your eggs, I think. What language was that you were speaking?"

Hellboy frowned. *Lightning*?

He remembered then, the pain that surged through him, the burning in his veins as the venom . . . no, no, the lightning . . . tore into him. Agony had torn through him, and he had staggered backward into the river.

Nine steps backward, he thought, although it seemed odd for him to remember exactly how many steps.

Yes, the lightning. It had struck him just after he had picked up . . .

"The hammer?" Hellboy rasped tiredly. Slowly, anxiously, he glanced down at his right hand and saw the huge war hammer with its engravings still clutched in his grasp. And he knew it.

Mjollnir, he thought, and his head filled with images again, horrible images of giants and journeys across the evening sky with thunder rolling along beneath him.

"Gahhhh!" he shouted, and he tried to throw the hammer down.

It would not come free of his hand. He could not open his fingers. The hammer was fused there as though it had been welded in place. He swung it, stared at it again.

"Oh, crap."

"No kidding, huh?" Abe replied.

The amphibian glanced around at the others, most of whom had already begun to go back to work buzzing around the huge dead husk just a short way up the riverbank. Professor Aronsson approached slowly, gaze ticking from the hammer in Hellboy's hand to the gray sky and then back down again. It took a moment for Hellboy to realize what he was waiting for. More lightning. Hellboy flinched and followed the professor's upward gaze, but there seemed to be no more lightning forthcoming.

"Guess you're stuck with it until we can figure out how to get it off," Abe observed. "You all right otherwise?"

Hellboy considered before he answered. "No. I don't think so."

But before Abe could respond, Klar approached cautiously. The officious little man with the sculpted blond hair stood before Hellboy as if at attention.

"That . . . artifact is the property of the Swedish government. You will release it," Klar insisted.

Abe sniffed. "Maybe you haven't been paying attention."

"Or maybe he's just stupid?" Hellboy suggested reasonably. "Look, Mr. Klar, I don't want this thing attached to me, but it's not exactly in my control, is it?"

"You were brought here to investigate," Klar went on stiffly, gazing up at Hellboy and not backing off in spite of the other's imposing presence. "It is upon you, then, the responsibility to find a way to separate yourself from that artifact. Until you are able to do so, you will not be permitted to leave Sweden."

The distress on Abe's face was pitiful to see. "Now wait just a minute. We came here on a consultation. You can't just—"

But Hellboy was barely listening. Klar's tone had woken something in him. *Thunder and lightning. The roar of warring giants. The clash of sword against shield.* He sneered, baring his teeth, and bent down over Klar to glare at the man.

"Hold your tongue, little man, if you wish to keep it in your head."

Hellboy's eyes went wide and he clapped his left hand over his mouth. "Did I just say that?"

"No idea," Abe replied. "Whatever you said, it wasn't in any language I've heard before. Maybe we should talk, huh? Better yet, let's call home. Dr. Manning may have an opinion about this, and you can bet Kate will."

Hellboy felt the weight of the hammer in his grip, and yet in some ways it had no weight at all. He studied the markings on the side, the two lines that swirled up and curled under, and suddenly he understood what the symbol represented. *Yggdrasil.* It was the world tree, the foundation of all life upon the nine worlds. And he had not gotten that from studying.

"Good idea," he muttered without looking up.

When he did, Klar was still standing in his way, though the man looked both unnerved and slightly miffed to have been so thoroughly ignored. Professor Aronsson was behind him, still obviously fascinated. The scholar gazed up at Hellboy in wonder.

"Can it truly be?" Professor Aronsson asked, though the question seemed to be directed to no one in particular.

"Yeah," Hellboy said slowly. "Yeah, I think it can." He stretched, his muscles aching. His teeth stung like he had been chewing aluminum foil, and there was a metallic taste in his mouth. From the lightning, he figured. *You got hit by lightning,* he reminded himself, still amazed by that. Somehow it was easier to confront that than to spend any more time considering the hammer. Mjollnir. He knew it was, because whatever lingered inside the weapon itself, like the sound of metal striking metal echoing down through the ages, had once been aware. It had its own identity, he reasoned.

"Its own memory," Hellboy muttered, staring at the hammer.

"Come on," Abe urged. "We've got a lot to figure out and I want to do it somewhere warm. If there's any warm to be found in the Arctic."

Hellboy allowed himself to be propelled along by his friend. Klar hesitated only a moment before at last moving aside. The thin man grumbled and pursued them as Professor Aronsson led them back up the ladder and over the hill to the valley where the trucks awaited.

Once in the passenger seat again, Hellboy tried to rest. His eyes closed as the engine roared to life, but instantly he was barraged with images again, and not merely that, but sounds and scents. He saw stumpy, gnarled beings in black armor and thin, exotic creatures with copper skin who moved like wraiths. The urge to crush them beneath the hammer was powerful.

Somehow, with the rumble of the truck over the frozen land, he began to drift off. In sleep, though, another image superceded the others—*an enormous beast clad in fur, ice hanging in ridges from the folds of his garments. In the midst of a blizzard, he saw it staring down at him, easily ten times his height. Face a blue-white, hair and beard white with a covering of snow, eyes like orbs of clear ice, gleaming from within with an insidious blue glow. The axe over its shoulder covered with frost.*

It laughed at him.

The truck bumped over a rut in the road, and the stumps of Hellboy's horns clacked against the passenger window. His eyes snapped open and he stared out at the harsh terrain. The sky was still gray but the wind had died now and the day was clear.

"What the hell?" he muttered.

Then he turned to look at Abe, who huddled inside his parka, eyes closed, also resting. Klar was behind the wheel again, but now they had another passenger. Professor Aronsson looked at Hellboy with great concern.

"What is it, my friend?" the professor asked. "Something is haunting you."

"That's one way to put it," Hellboy grunted, sitting up. He rested the hammer on his lap and it was starting to annoy him, having to carry the damn thing around all the time. He cast a hard look at Klar. "Turn this thing around, Mr. Klar. We're going the wrong way."

Klar only spared him a sharp, angry look before returning his focus to the road ahead. "We are driving to Skellesval so that you may contact your superiors. This was at your request, I remind you."

"Hellboy?" Abe asked quietly from the backseat.

"Turn it around," Hellboy told Klar again. "We're going north. There's something up there that's . . . not right."

The trucks rolled north approximately seven miles before Hellboy instructed Klar to stop. He had to open the door with his left hand and then he climbed out onto the hard-packed snow. The truck's shock absorbers squeaked loudly and it rocked as he took his weight off it. The windstorm that had raged at the ocation of the body's discovery was nonexistent here. More than that, the ominous gray clouds above had given way to a clear sky that was almost pure white, as if it too was solid and covered with snow.

"At least tell us what we are likely to find here," Klar said, walking up beside him. The man had an almost permanent frown now and his lips were pursed as though he had a great deal more to say but did not dare.

"I don't know," Hellboy replied honestly. "But it's

connected. I can feel it. All of this feels . . . familiar to me somehow."

"Or maybe to that?" Abe noted, pointing at the hammer.

Hellboy raised it up as though saluting his friend. "Maybe."

Professor Aronsson was staring at the hammer again, but then he met Hellboy's eyes. "This feeling you have. You cannot offer more detail. But are there other feelings?"

Taken slightly aback by the question, Hellboy did not respond immediately. After a moment, he laid the war hammer across his shoulder casually and looked out over the snow-covered hills and the mountains in the distance. He shrugged.

"Yeah. Like pictures flashing in my head. Fighting. Monsters. That kind of thing."

"You've done plenty of monster fighting," Abe reminded him, his lips thinner and grayer than usual thanks to the cold. They shivered.

Hellboy nodded. "Plenty. But these aren't my memories."

They were all silent for nearly a full minute as the other government agents came up from the second truck. The men were armed with automatic weapons. Hellboy frowned at the sight of the guns. He didn't like guns at all and was disturbed that Klar's men had been transporting these things without his knowledge. Not that it was any of his business, but still, he would have liked to know.

"Well?" Abe asked.

"That way," Hellboy replied, pointing west. "You up to it?"

Abe did a courtly little half-bow. "Lead on, god of thunder."

Hellboy shot him a hard look. "That's not funny."

"Who's laughing?"

They trudged across the snow, over hills that gradually increased in size, for more than a mile. Though Hellboy felt drawn more and more strongly toward that spot, he also worried about Abe. His friend's face had taken on the same greenish-gray hue as his lips, and the amphibian had been mostly silent for the trek. He had no idea why the cold should bother Abe so much—he was cold-blooded, after all—but in the end decided, that while it was obviously uncomfortable for him, the weather would probably not be too detrimental. As long as they did not spend too much more time out there on the frozen landscape.

He might have turned around then anyway for Abe's sake, as well as for Professor Aronsson's. The portly man had begun breathing heavily after the first hill and many times they had to pause and wait for him. Klar's lackeys seemed in fine health, but if they had not been, Hellboy would have happily left them and their automatic weapons behind.

The hammer seemed to hum in his grasp, a buzzing murmur as though it were resonating like a tuning fork. And the closer they came to their destination, the more certain Hellboy became that something insidious was going on here. Though the day gradually became more and more pleasant, the sky blue and clear, the sun warmer upon them, the air grew closer and more oppresive. Hellboy felt the weight of dark expectation settle over his heart, and a sense of menace that exuded from the very land about them.

Soon enough they came into the shadow of a small mountain that rose up before them, contorting the horizon. Its stone and earth face was bare in some places and covered with snow and ice in others, and yet in his mind he saw an image of trees thrusting from the mountainside. Trees with crimson leaves. Yet there was no vegetation to speak of, even in the foothills around it.

He frowned, his eyes drawn to a ridge not far above the base of the mountain. They had been traveling almost due west. A little to the north, up on that ridge, he saw a black hollow that stared out at him like the eye socket of a skull.

"Don't tell me it's up there," Abe said sullenly.

Hellboy glanced at him, saw that his friend was not merely tired but unnerved. "You feel it too, don't you?"

"Evil," Abe replied. "I guess maybe you don't need a hammer to get the vibe off this place."

"I guess."

But when he had led them to that northern ridge, patiently awaiting his companions, both those welcome and those unwelcome, Hellboy felt the murmur of the hammer diminish. A slide of rock and ice was on the ridge below the cave entrance, and evidence of a campsite was nearby.

"This slide wasn't natural," Klar declared only seconds after arriving at the mouth of the cave.

"What gave it away?" Abe asked. "The whole someone-blew-up-the-mountainside décor?"

For that, indeed, was how it appeared. Someone had set explosives around the ridge and blasted a portion of the rock away. The cave was natural, but it had to have been hidden for some time, perhaps by some previous landslide. Or perhaps on purpose.

"It's not here anymore," Hellboy said, so quietly that only Abe and Professor Aronsson could hear.

"What isn't?" the professor asked, even as he moved further into the cave, examining the runes that were engraved on the walls.

They did not have proper equipment to investigate further, but Hellboy searched the many pouches and pockets on the belt around his waist and came up with a small but powerful flashlight. He led the way, and they took a closer look at the runes. Some were indeed etched in the wall and others painted with ochre dyes, and possibly blood.

A short way inside the cave there was an iron door set into the stone wall, its face engraved with the same sorts of runes. The lock on the door had been shattered and it hung open just slightly.

"Whatever was here was very well hidden," Professor Aronsson observed. "Someone did not want it to be found."

"Makes you wonder *how* it got found," Hellboy replied.

He swung open the iron door, but, as he suspected, the small vault within was empty.

"I guess I don't even have to ask if you think this has something to do with the . . . the body down by the river," Abe said. "But do you have any idea exactly what the hell's going on here? How the body got there? Or what was in this cave that was so important?"

Hellboy stared at the runes on the iron door for a long moment. Then he turned to Klar. "Send someone back to the trucks. Get a photographer up here to take pictures of this."

Klar bristled. "I don't see what this has to do with—"

"Something started here," Hellboy said abruptly. "Can't tell you what it is yet, but trust me on this part. You *will* want to stop it. I'm guessing you're going to want help with that. So get me a photographer."

Klar hesitated, then exchanged words with Aronsson, who replied with a name. Probably a photographer from the university, Hellboy thought, or someone back at the other site. Then Klar glanced at one of his associates, and the other man turned and left the cave to start the long trek back across the snow alone.

Hellboy looked at one of the others. *Gustaf,* he thought the guy's name was. "Go with him," he said. "I don't have a clue what might be out there."

The first flicker of fear crossed the men's faces, and then Gustaf took off after the first man without even glancing at Klar for approval. Hellboy tried not to smile. Then he looked at Abe and Professor Aronsson.

"Now we go to Stockholm."

"Stockholm?" Abe asked. "The hammer tell you that?"

Hellboy only looked at him. "We're going to see a guy I used to know."

"An old friend of yours?" the professor asked.

Hellboy frowned. "No."

CHAPTER FOUR

The brassy, celebratory lilt of jazz horns sounded through the neighborhood surrounding the Storkyrkan. The song ended with a riff of drums and cymbals and then applause echoed from the open doors of the cathedral. Upon the steps of the squat building where she and her elderly father lived, Pernilla Aickman sat and pulled her sweater a bit tighter around her. Though summer, it was chilly this late in the evening. Still, she would not have wanted to miss the concert at the cathedral.

Pernilla did not like the crowd, so she would not actually attend the performance, but if she sat on the steps of their home on Trångsund—little more than a stone's throw from the royal palace—she could hear every note. Sometimes her father, Edmund, joined her there, but he had been overdoing it of late and was too tired tonight.

The music started again, a sweet, high trilling of horn accompanied by a slow piano melody. In a moment the drums would come in . . . and there they were. A thin smile blossomed on her lips and she hung her head, dark hair tumbling in waves across her face, and just listened. The music was so sweet it spread a warmth through her that the chill of the night should not have allowed. It spoke to her of ballrooms and chandeliers, dapper men and ladies in beautiful dresses, of a world far, far away from the dusty libraries and remote excavation sites where she spent her life.

Pernilla laughed softly to herself. *What else is there? I'm my father's daughter.* And yet there were times when the mysteries of the past seemed dull and dreary to her, and she wondered how to go about investigating the secrets of the present, of modern rather than ancient society.

Perhaps the music does not transport me so far as I would like it to, she thought.

A deep bass guitar reverberated out of the cathedral and the tempo of the music picked up. From where she sat, Pernilla could see just the corner of the cathedral far off up the street. That angle offered no view of the open front doors, but she saw the light that spilled out of them and splashed onto the stairs that led down to the street. She could barely make out the figures of a small crowd standing on the stairs to listen and try to get a peek within. The cathedral was full tonight, the concert attended by locals and tourists alike.

The song ended and another wave of staccato applause rippled through the air. As it subsided, and in the seconds before the piano began to play once more, a new sound insinuated itself into Pernilla's mind. From off to her left there came a kind of *trip-trop* sound that made her think of horses. Yet something was off about that sound. It was like hooves on the cobblestones, yes, but the rhythm was wrong.

She turned away from the cathedral to peer along the street in the other direction, trying to find the source of that sound. The music began again in earnest, drowning it out, but Pernilla's curiosity was piqued. The music danced across the wooden shutters and fat drainpipes on the sides of the buildings. Black metal streetlamps glowed with a golden light that shone down upon the street, creating islands of illumination upon the cobblestones. But the islands were too far apart and traveling from one to the other required passing through long seas of darkness that might hide almost anything.

Even as she stared along that street, a pair of figures came into view as they approached the nearest streetlamp, half a block away. One was small and thin, dressed in shades of gray. He wore a fedora, its brim pulled low enough that the light from the streetlamp could not reach it. The other man was enormous, his long coat swaying around him. For a moment, in the wash of light from above, Pernilla was convinced his skin was actually red, but a moment later the streetlamp was behind them, and she realized that could not be. Of course it couldn't. It was the cast of the light. He was probably merely possessed of a dark or ruddy complexion.

But she could not tear her eyes from those two figures. Over the music, she could not hear the *trip-trop* sound of hooves, if it was still there to be heard.

The pair passed from that island of illumination into a sea of darkness, coming nearer to her all the time. But as Pernilla watched, they reached the edge of the light's influence and were silhouetted by it, backlit as though their bodies were rimmed with a divine aura.

Her breath caught in her throat. Suddenly she could not hear the music anymore. There were ridges on the big man's head that she had at first taken to be some kind of hat or perhaps large glasses he had pushed up atop his pate. But now a new possibility had occurred to her. And even as it went through her mind, she saw his tail swing out from behind him.

Oh, Lord, no, she thought. All the warmth went out of her. Her hands felt clammy suddenly and her chest hurt as though her heart had swollen and was pressing against it from within.

Pernilla leaped to her feet, stared for one more long moment at the two figures as they became nothing more than wraiths in the dark, approaching her building. From the cathedral came a long, twisting saxophone solo that she felt was almost propelling her now. A foreign taste filled her mouth, metallic and antiseptic, as though she had just come from the dentist. She ran up the few steps to the front door and flung it open.

Once inside, she slammed the door and double locked it, then stood leaning against the thick wood, her breath coming quickly, palms spread out upon its surface. Pernilla opened her mouth and tried to call for her father, but all she managed was the thinnest croaking voice. And then she froze. *No, no, don't call for him. Don't bring him downstairs. Just stay quiet and maybe they'll walk on, maybe they'll go away.*

The knock on the door made her yelp and jump back. With a hand over her mouth, she stared in horror as the knock came again, the door shuddering with the power of it.

"Go away!" she cried in Swedish. Then, remembering what her father had told her, she shouted again in English. "Go away, demon! Stay away from here! I'm not going to let you kill my father."

Hellboy paused with his left hand only inches from the door, a puzzled expression on his face. Abe could not blame him. It had taken them a while to locate Edmund Aickman's address. Though Hellboy had not bothered to tell Abe exactly how he knew the old folklorist, the way the young woman on the front steps had fled in terror at the sight of him did not seem a promising start.

"Exactly what did you do to these people?" Abe asked.

"What did I . . . not a damn thing, Abe. And thanks for that vote of confidence." Hellboy scratched thoughtfully at the small patch of hair on his chin and stared at the door. His right hand was thrust into a trash bag that was tied around his wrist to hide the war hammer that was fused to him. He opened his mouth several times as though he had thought of some response, but long seconds went by and he said nothing.

It was silent within as well, and Abe had a mental picture of the raven-haired woman waiting in breathless terror within. It would have been funny if it wasn't so sad. Once more he glanced at Hellboy, who shrugged.

"I got nothing. Short of breaking the door down."

Abe sighed and rapped lightly on the door. There came a tiny yelp from within but no more verbal abuse.

"Ma'am, can you hear me?"

Nothing. Not a whimper.

"Hi. Good evening. Your English is pretty good, by the way. I'm . . . my name is Abe and I represent the Bureau for Paranormal Research and Defense. My friend and I were hoping to speak to Professor Edmund Aickman on a consultation for the Bureau? I gather that's your father."

"I'll die before I'll let you hurt him!" came the desperate voice from within.

Abe was stumped. "Nobody wants to hurt him, Miss Aickman. We found something that—"

"I *saw* Hellboy out there!"

Hellboy cleared his throat. "Yeah. I'm here. What's your point?"

"Oh, that tone's helpful," Abe chided him softly. The two of them looked tiredly at one another.

"Miss Aickman, here's the deal. I don't like your father, but we need his help. I'm not here to hurt anybody. Just tell him I'm here, would you? Tell him we found Mjollnir. He'll know what I'm—"

There was a clicking as the door was unlocked, and then it was yanked open. Abe took a quick, ragged breath, startled by the woman within. Her dark hair hung across her face, and her wide copper eyes stared at them from beneath that ebony curtain. There was something almost wild about her, and she burned with an intensity that stunned him. It wasn't necessarily a physical response or even attraction, but a simple awareness that this was a unique individual.

She was not alone. To her left, holding open the door, was a thin, nearly bald man who must have been in his late seventies at least, possibly older. He wore square spectacles that for some reason made Abe think about that old story about the cobbler and the shoemaking elves.

The woman said something in Swedish to Professor Aickman, but the old man just brushed at the air in dismissal. She flinched as though the gesture had hurt her.

"I saw you briefly at Trevor's funeral," Aickman said.

Hellboy stood on the stoop and stared at him. "I saw you too."

"I have wondered many times how much of a grudge you held after our shared . . . experience with King Vold."

Aickman's daughter stepped closer to her father, staring at Hellboy as though she expected him to attack at any moment.

"You almost got me killed," Hellboy acknowledged. "I'm over it. From what I remember, you got the worst of it."

A smile twitched at the edges of Aickman's lips. "Eloquent as always."

"Screw that. You want to see the hammer or not?"

For the first time, the professor's daughter seemed to relax. Her gaze ticked toward Abe and he smiled. Given the restrictions of his facial musculature, most people found it difficult to tell his emotional state based upon expression, but a small smile flickered across her own features as well before she looked back at Hellboy.

"Have you really found Mjollnir?" she asked, the last word hesitant.

Hellboy raised his right hand, brandishing the trash bag

in their direction. "Pretty sure, yeah. But that isn't all. Something's brewing and your father's the expert in this part of the world."

All eyes were on that bag.

"By all means, then, do come in," Professor Aickman said. He stepped back from the door, took his right hand off the knob for the first time, and executed a stiff little bow.

Abe stared at Aickman's right hand. The skin was pale and dry and spotted with age, but in the middle of it there was a hole the size of a half dollar. When the old man let his hand hang at his side, Abe could see the thick gray twill fabric of his pants right through the hole.

"Gentlemen, please allow me to introduce my daughter, Pernilla. She is also an accomplished folklorist and archaeologist in her own right. I fear I have infected her with the loneliness of a life of academia. One day, perhaps, the world will forgive me the crime of stealing her away from whatever other destiny awaited her."

"Father," Pernilla chided him, embarrassed. She was roughly mid-thirties, and the professor probably eighty, and yet he obviously had the capacity to embarrass her the way all parents seemed to. Abe was fascinated by this phenomenon, as he had never, to his knowledge, actually *had* parents.

"Nice to meet you," Hellboy said with a nod. But he did not offer to shake her hand. Not with the hammer.

Abe held out a hand to the professor, who shook it with a more powerful grip than might be expected from a man his age. Then he shook hands with Pernilla as well. "Just call me Abe."

"I apologize if this seems rude, but what *are* you?" the woman asked, pushing her dark curls back away from her face.

"That's the hundred thousand dollar question," Abe replied. "I'll let you know when I find out."

An awkward moment passed, there in the foyer, as Pernilla closed the door and Hellboy and Abe moved further into the house. After a moment, Professor Aickman suggested they move to the parlor and led the way deeper into the house. As he walked, Abe focused once more on the hole in the old man's hand.

"It isn't polite to stare," Pernilla Aickman whispered at his side.

Abe looked up at her, stricken with a rush of guilt. "Sorry. It's just . . . well, it's amazing to me that he can still . . . use it."

"That's all right," Pernilla said warmly, a lopsided grin on her face. "If you can forgive my rudeness, I am certainly willing to forgive yours."

"It's a deal."

The trash bag had been torn away and lay on the floor. Hellboy sat on the sofa, but leaned forward so he could lay Mjollnir on the table in front of him for the Aickmans to examine. Both were nearly speechless as he and Abe told them about the discovery of the corpse to the far north and the lightning. They spoke Swedish to one another in frequent bursts, and then apologized for excluding the others before lapsing into Swedish again.

Hellboy had never seen anybody get so excited over a hunk of metal. And working with the Bureau, he seemed to always be around people who got excited about strange hunks of metal. They moved around the room, grabbing various books, both new and archaic, and conferring again, until the parlor looked as though its furniture and bookshelves had been ransacked by thieves. There were maps and scrolls as well, and a light breeze came from the open windows along with distant jazz to riffle the papers.

"Well, of course it is an extraordinary find," Professor Aickman said at last, a light in his eyes that made him look far younger than his years. "Perhaps one of the most important and explosive archaeological finds in history. I should like to see the corpse, of course."

"If you want to go to the university tomorrow, I'm sure Professor Aronsson would be more than happy to give you a look," Abe told them.

"Amazing," Pernilla murmured. "It's simply incredible."

Professor Aickman paced the room in contemplation. He walked to the bookcase on the far side of the room beside the wide fireplace, stepping over papers and texts without even glancing down at them.

"I'll want photos. And we can visit the site to compare notes with the man from the university. We shall have to try to take a sample of the metal, of course. Do an etching of the symbols on the hammer to determine their meaning—"

"It's Yggdrasil," Hellboy said, then felt a rush of annoyance and frustration. He had spoken almost without meaning to, the knowledge and the words coming up through him. Not that he wouldn't have shared that information, but he felt uneasy and even slightly embarrassed by the strange tics in his behavior since he had picked up the hammer.

Aickman froze. He looked around slowly, eyes wide, as if he feared the room had suddenly become haunted. Tentatively he started back across the floor and stumbled over a thick leatherbound volume. Pernilla shot up from her perch by the table and grasped his arm, steadying him. Her father shook her off and stared at Hellboy, then bent over to look at the hammer again.

"Why, *yes*. Of course it is," he said, but there was something now in the timbre of his voice that made Hellboy uneasy.

"You all right, Professor?" Abe asked.

The old man only stared at Hellboy again. "How did you know?"

Hellboy shifted on the sofa and sat back, drawing Mjollnir into his lap out of necessity. He did not like its weight there, or the feeling that grew stronger and stronger inside him, that the hammer was somehow listening to them. Not listening, of course, because that was just stupid. But maybe aware.

"I just did," he replied. "I've been having these, I don't know, daydreams. More like nightmares, though. Seeing things in my head. And I had this urge to check out a spot only a few miles from where they found . . . the dead guy. We went, and there was a cave there. Someone had taken something out of there that should have been left buried. Pretty sure it's connected, but I don't know how. Not yet. We were hoping you could help with that part."

Aickman looked suddenly frail and unsteady on his feet. He put a hand on the back of a tall chair to maintain his balance. Pernilla looked as though she might try to steady him, but she held back. Hellboy figured she was getting tired of the old man spurning her efforts to take care of him. Not that it was any of their business.

"Father, you ought to get some rest. We can continue in the morning," the woman suggested.

"In a moment," Aickman replied, staring at Mjollnir again.

"We think there may be some sort of trace memory attached to the hammer that Hellboy's picking up on," Abe explained. "I spoke to our field director at the Bureau, and she thinks it's woken some sort of psychometry in Hellboy that he didn't know he had."

"Psycho-something," Hellboy muttered.

"Just with this one object?" Pernilla asked. "There's no real precedent for that. Psychometry is usually an inherent ability. Either you have it or you don't."

Hellboy was getting a bit creeped out by the way Aickman was staring at him. The old man had not taken his eyes off him while the others were talking.

"Perhaps there are other things at work here?" Professor

Aickman suggested. "It could be no more than an echo. Or it could be something more purposeful."

"What the hell does that mean?" Hellboy asked, growing edgy.

The old man quivered slightly and lowered his head. When he raised his gaze to them again he seemed somehow far, far away from that room. Almost as though he had remembered some appointment he was late for.

"My daughter is correct. I must rest now. But please, if you do not yet have other accommodations, spend the night here. There is a great deal more for us to discuss, and I will want to go to the university first thing tomorrow."

Hellboy glanced at Abe. He didn't want to stay in this creepy old bastard's house. Aickman had always been a little off center. Sure, they needed his help, wanted his input, but he would rather not sleep under the same roof with a guy who almost got him eaten by a giant mythological werehound. On the other hand, though Professor Aronsson had offered to put them up at the university, it had gotten late, and he wanted to get an early start in the morning.

Abe shrugged lightly.

"Please. It will take me only a moment to make up your rooms," Pernilla insisted. "It's a very large house. Plenty of space. And it's no trouble."

A clock ticked on the wall and invaded Hellboy's sleeping mind.

Tick-tock. Tick-tock. Tick-tock. Ticktickticks. Ticktickticks. Even in his sleep, he frowned. That was not right. *Tick-tock,* that was the sound the clock made. And it chimed every damn half hour too, which was annoying, and roused him slightly each time. That other sound insinuated itself into his unconscious mind—not the clock, but an intermittent chittering noise.

He rolled his huge bulk to the side, bed creaking underneath him. The hammer, still clutched in his right hand, slipped off the bed and thumped loudly to the floor, dragging his arm with it.

His eyes snapped open. For a moment he only lay there, tired and waiting for sleep to claim him again, mentally cursing the damn hammer for being so inconvenient.

Ticktickticktick.

The sound again, and now he was wide awake. It was definitely not the clock. Hellboy turned and slowly raised himself up from the bed, nerves on edge, muscles tensed. But he was not surprised. He had sensed something wrong tonight, and in the back of his mind had been expecting something odd to happen.

Then he saw it, sitting on the window sill, snapping open nut shells and nibbling at their innards. A squirrel.

Hellboy relaxed, feeling a bit ridiculous. He shook his head and sighed, began to settle back down on the pillows. "Shoo, buddy. You chew too loud. Go bother someone else."

"He is fleeing, Hellboy. You must stop him. The fate of Midgard depends upon it."

With his eyes wide, Hellboy bolted upright and stared at the squirrel. He pointed at the rodent with the hammer.

"Say that again."

"*You must stop him,*" the squirrel said, staring right at him.

Hellboy stared at it, and then something clicked in his mind. Something familiar. "Oh, crap. You're Ratatosk, aren't you?"

"*Hurry,*" the squirrel said.

Then it turned and fled out the window, leaping to a nearby tree branch and disappearing into the night. It took Hellboy only a moment to realize that there was only one person the squirrel could have been talking about.

"Aickman," he muttered as he got out of bed. "You son of a bitch." Without pajamas, he had self-consciously worn his pants to bed. Now he was glad as he ran out into the hallway, hooves cracking the wood floor in a couple of places.

"Abe!" he shouted.

But he did not wait for his friend. Instead he ran for the stairs and went down them two and three at a time, holding the ornately carved rail with his left hand, the hammer swinging at his side. It was dark downstairs, and there was very little light, and no more music, coming from outside. Hellboy raced through archways and past antiques on the first floor, did not even pause at the book-strewn parlor. If Aickman was truly fleeing, he would not be lingering there.

The thick oak front door was open just a crack.

"Damn it," Hellboy muttered.

As he passed a broad stretch of glass, he saw movement in a splash of light outside. Hellboy went to the window and there, out on the sidewalk, he spotted Aickman hurrying away along faster than a man his age ought to be able to go. There was a hitch in his step, no doubt, but he moved away from the house with stunning alacrity, such that his departure could not be confused with something as innocuous as nocturnal wandering. He had a destination in mind. Professor Aickman was running to something.

Determined not to let the old folklorist abandon them, Hellboy went for the door and threw it open. Flashes of silver gleamed off distant streetlamps and a razor-edged blade whistled through the air and sliced his left shoulder. Other blades—long and thin as fencing swords but unnaturally sharp—danced toward him.

Hellboy raised the hammer in his huge right hand and blocked them. One thrust at his chest and stung him there, in the middle of his breast bone, and he took a step backward, peering into the darkness, eyes focused only on the glimmer of silver on the swords. It was as though they came out of nothing, as though these weapons were wielded by the night itself . . .

Then something leaped in at him . . . several dark, leathery somethings. Lanky, bony things with long, tapered talons for fingers and glowing eyes of stunning, dark, frozen beauty. They drove him to the ground and others emerged from the shadows of the foyer to claw at him, hissing.

They were going for his eyes.

CHAPTER FIVE

Even buried beneath blankets and dreams, Abe was cold. Though he slept, there on the broad mattress, bordered by the ornate posts of the bed, his unconscious mind continued to investigate the phenomenon of the chill he had been feeling ever since arriving in Scandinavia. In the landscape of his dreaming mind, he stood on a broad, flat plain with nothing but brown scrub grass as far as he could see. No snow, nor any other precipitation. But no water, either. In the depths of sleep, Abe's brow wrinkled, his mind troubled at this absence.

The sky was clear and robin's-egg blue, the sort of sky that comes once a year, if that often. At its apex, the sun hung directly above, blindingly bright, washing the ground in a kind of burnt hue. He ought to have been sweltering, but Abe shivered with an icy breeze that blew across the barren plain, rustling the scrub grass.

Abe Sapien had never been what one would call a sensitive. He was one of a kind, no doubt. He had proven himself a more than capable field agent for the Bureau, with some talents they taught him and others that were unique to him. But he was not, by any means, psychic. In truth, he had never even really been particularly curious about what it meant to be *sensitive* to the

whorls and eddies of thought and emotion that lingered in the ether.

But he did not understand why he had felt so damned cold, and that troubled him.

On that scorched but chilling plain, he stood and gazed at the horizon, felt his skin drying out, felt the yearning for water. And he heard the thud of hooves in the distance, heavy footfalls. Hellboy was near. Abe could not see him, though there was nothing for miles around, but he could hear his friend shout his name.

Hellboy . . . Abe thought.

His dreaming mind was focused on the waking mystery, and so was not far from the conscious surface. He opened his eyes without a start, without even the confusion that normally accompanies waking. The echo of Hellboy's voice calling his name still resounded off the sage and knowing wood of the halls and doorways of the Aickman home.

Abe heard the pounding of Hellboy's hooves downstairs and almost without thinking he shot his hand down to the floor to snatch up his pants. He had left his shirt on for warmth, and now he slipped his pants on even as the sounds downstairs subsided for a moment.

Then, as he stood, he heard Hellboy shout again, though the words were not intelligible this time. Abe had shut the window tight, not even a crack to let in fresh air, and now he felt parched in the stuffy room. On the bedside table was a glass of water his hosts had been kind enough to let him take to his room, and he drank it down now in three gulps.

Wiping his hand across his long, thin lips, Abe rushed from the bedroom. The corridor was dark but some light filtered in from the windows. As he ran for the stairs he glanced further along the hall and an apparition appeared, a pale gauzy thing that made his mouth go dry once more and made him falter, nearly stumbling over his bare feet. The long claws on his toes scratched wood and he reached out to steady himself on the balustrade above the stairs.

The apparition flew closer and resolved itself there in the darkness. It was Pernilla, ebony hair falling around her marble flesh, body draped in a silken shift and gown. For a moment longer, Abe could say nothing, so stunned was he by how very like a specter she seemed.

Then there came more shouts from below, and a crash.

"Your father?" he asked.

Fear was etched in the lines of her face. "I checked his room first. He's not there."

"Stay here."

Abe started down the stairs, hand on the carved

wooden rail, studying the shadows at the bottom. His eyes were keener than others', but there was nothing in the dark there. Nothing he could see.

A whisper of silk made him glance back. Pernilla followed him, unmindful of the railing, moving down the steps as if floating. Abe was about to admonish her, but she looked at him then and there was a silent communication between them, a moment of understanding when their minds seemed to touch.

"Watch the shadows," he said.

But the horror that waited below was no longer hiding in the shadows.

They moved so fast, flailing limbs and blades flashing, that Hellboy could not even tell how many of the little weasels there were. Five . . . maybe six. Even that might be wrong, given the way they seemed to merge with the darkness in the foyer of the old house.

A reed-thin sword sliced through the air and clanged off one of the stumps on his forehead where his horns had once been. Though it did not cut him, it sent a spike of pain into his head.

"Thanks," he muttered. "And me without Excedrin."

One of them leaped on his back, and Hellboy tore it off, threw it across the room where it crashed out the window through which he had seen Aickman fleeing. The glass shattered, shards exploding into the night, reflecting the moonlight off jagged edges.

He swung his tail at another of the things. It slashed the thick hide of his tail, the blade slicing a gash there just before his tail cracked its skull against the wall. The thing collapsed to the ground, head split open, and shadow leaked out, a black mist that enveloped the thing's entire body. And then it disappeared.

"What the hell?" Hellboy said, staring at it, even as he backhanded another of the things.

His attention diverted, the things moved in. One blade sliced across his thigh while another slipped just under his ribcage. Sharp as it was, its point could not go very far through the muscle there. But it hurt like a son of a bitch. It shouldn't have—after all, that was what made him such an effective field agent for the BPRD—he was incredibly durable; hard to hurt, even harder to kill.

Shouldn't have, but it did.

Hellboy raised the hammer and brought it down in a sweeping arc. As he did, a kind of exhilaration rushed through him, filled him up; his right arm felt as though it were no longer even in his control. It was, in that moment, as if that ancient war hammer rushed toward his enemies of its own accord. Hellboy swung so hard that the hammer obliterated the head of the nearest creature, its decapitated body tumbling toward the floor as the hammer shattered the torso of another.

Three of the creatures remained and they backed away from him in horror, staring at the hammer, whispering its name in an ancient, guttural tongue.

"Mjollnir."

Hellboy raised it again and the three hesitated, backed up. Hellboy glanced at the open door, at the dark night beyond. *Aickman*, he thought. *Damn it!* The old folklorist clearly knew more about what was going on here than he let on, and these greasy little monsters had not arrived here by coincidence. The hammer knew them. Fighting them was . . . familiar.

Again he swung Mjollnir, advancing on the creatures. One of them was crushed under that blow and the other two scattered to either side. Their glowing crystal blue eyes widened and they looked almost pitiful, but the sting of their blades was still fresh in his skin.

"Hellboy!"

He turned and saw Abe rushing down the hall with Pernilla Aickman trailing behind, their hands clasped as they ran. Abe came to a halt at the edge of the foyer, stopping the woman as well. The things hissed at them, even more on edge, eyes darting around as they tried to figure out their next move.

"Where's my father?" Pernilla asked, her accent thicker now that she had panic in her voice.

Abe looked up at Hellboy abruptly, his focus off the creatures. Then he crouched and picked up one of the long, thin blades and tossed it to Abe, who snatched it, wide eyed, from the air.

"What am I supposed to do with this?" Abe demanded.

Hellboy stared at him grimly. "I'm going after him. Watch yourself."

Abe glanced dubiously at the blade in his hand, then at the weasels. He nodded once. "Under control."

Aickman, Hellboy thought again. He could mash weasels all night, but what he needed was knowledge. Information. Once more he turned to the door, but now he ran toward it. The weasels would either follow him or go after the others, but Abe would have no trouble handling the two that remained.

As he rushed out the door, the remaining weasels tried to jump him. Behind him, Hellboy heard Abe shout at them and attack, diverting their attention. Then he was out in the cold Stockholm night, hooves clacking on the stone steps, then on the cobblestones. This was supposed to be a part of the world where the sun never really went away, but this night was as dark as any he had ever experienced. The sickly glow of the streetlamps did not stretch far enough, their influence like distant beacons in lighthouses along a rocky coast.

A silence fell over the Aickman home, broken only by the ticking of the grandfather clock against the far wall and Pernilla's hitching breath. Abe did not notice his own breathing, but he was surprised to find that after their dervishing attacks upon Hellboy, these creatures were not winded at all. That was a bad sign.

The two intruders stood off to the right, crouched side by side, their slender blades at the ready. In that moment of indecision, Abe could see that they had not come there to attack himself or Pernilla; it was obvious that the creatures did not want them to follow Hellboy.

Their eyes glowed a bright crystal blue that ought to have been beautiful to see if it were not set into the long, cruel, almost jaggedly thin faces of these creatures. At first Abe had thought they were naked and hairless, but he found as he looked at them more closely that they were neither. Both of the creatures had black hair that was slicked back across their skulls as though oiled, and they wore clothes of some sort of leather, some stretched and treated animal skin, with black iron buckles and buttons, but no zippers. Just as they seemed almost to disappear in deep shadow, so too did their carriage—the way they bent over all the time and never attacked directly—create the illusion of nakedness. Their skin was not much different from the texture of their garments.

Pernilla broke the silence, the standoff. "What have you done with my father?" she asked in thick English. Then, with a step forward, she rattled off more words in Swedish.

Probably the same question, Abe figured. And it was a good one. The way it looked, these things had abducted Professor Aickman. Unless Hellboy could get him back, the only way they were going to get any answers was to capture one of these things.

The woman spoke through gritted teeth, her words choked with both panic and anger. She moved closer to them, slightly in front of Abe.

"Pernilla," he cautioned her.

Which was when the creatures moved. One of them darted for the door with that inhuman speed and agility. Abe might have been able to catch it, to reach the door and slam it shut before the thing could escape, but the other lunged at Pernilla with its blade in that very same moment. Its point whispered through the air with a subtle, deadly hush, and though she stumbled backward, the blade sliced down toward her throat.

Abe slipped past Pernilla and parried the creature's attack with a twist of his wrist. The thing became enraged and leaped at him, its blade flying through the darkened foyer, glimmering with dim light from the moon and the city outside, as though it were the ghost of a sword rather than the weapon itself.

Abe had talents and abilities he had brought to his work as an operative for the BPRD. He also had skills they had taught him, things he had found an aptitude for. This was not one of them. He was a decent shot with a pistol or a rifle, but swords were archaic things and he had only ever fenced once before, on a lark, with Professor Bruttenholm, who had seen one too many Errol Flynn films.

As the thing lunged for him again, Abe dodged quickly. That was his best bet in this fight . . . avoiding getting cut or stabbed long enough to get lucky. He managed to parry another thrust. The clang of the blades was tinny, not like the clash of steel at all, and he wondered what metal they were made of. The weasel lashed at him; Abe took a step back, turned away the point of the thing's blade . . . and it lunged in with talons raised and scratched at his sword arm with a hiss.

"Ow!" Abe snapped, fighting back the choice epithets that came to mind. He switched hands with the blade and advanced on the thing. It scuffled backward on the floor, glowing blue eyes locked on him.

"Guess after doing this job so long I should expect dirty fighting from creatures of darkness," he said as he pressed his attack. "Call me an optimist." Anger made him foolhardy and his own blade flashed downward now, then across, forcing the creature to jump back, surprising Abe himself most of all.

It practically quivered with energy, whether anger or fear Abe did not know, and its gaze darted toward the

open door. For a second, the thing seemed about to bolt. Then Pernilla ran across the room and slammed the door shut tight. She bolted it for good measure and then turned to face the combatants, her back against the door. Again she shouted at the thing in Swedish, demanding, Abe figured, to know where her father was.

Its eyes were on her.

Abe slashed his blade down and cut its sword hand off at the wrist. Black mist poured out of the wound as it screeched in an earsplitting wail of pain and clutched its stump. It staggered backward, staring at him with wide eyes as though stunned that he had dared to hurt it. Abe followed, the point of his blade only inches from its chest.

"Where is Professor Aickman?" he demanded of the thing.

Pernilla came up behind Abe, one hand on his back in an intimate gesture of alliance. She said nothing more, only stared at the thing expectantly.

It began to gibber in a singsong voice, some language neither of them understood. Abe pressed the point of the sword against its chest, puncturing the clothing and the skin beneath, and that black mist swirled out.

"I'm going to ask you one more time. What have you done with—"

His words were cut off by a loud pop as the creature simply disintegrated—clothes and all—right in front of their eyes. One moment it was solid and the next little more than a fine scattering of black soot and a swirl of ebony vapor.

Abe sighed. "Now what?"

Hellboy turned left, away from the cathedral, in the direction he had seen Aickman hurrying. The old man had been hustling, no doubt about that, but Hellboy was certainly faster. Even with the odd, unnatural swiftness the man had revealed, Hellboy had to be faster. He ran along the cobblestones and passed through the first splash of yellow light from above. There was a buzz of electricity that wavered, the light flickering as he ran beneath it.

It went out.

Just one of those things that happens, Hellboy thought as he ran on toward the corner ahead. A couple of blocks away was the subway station he and Abe had arrived at earlier. As if he had Aickman's scent, he was suddenly sure that was the man's destination. Another streetlamp loomed ahead, somehow deepening the shadows beyond the reaches of its illumination.

Hellboy passed through the pool of its influence, eyes adjusting to the dim glow and then to the night again. When he was swallowed once more by the shadows, there was a sudden skittering on the cobblestones, an eerie, clicking counterpoint to the heavy clack of his hooves upon the street.

The darkness came alive with motion. For a moment he was uncertain if they were the same creatures he had fought at the house, but then he saw the flash of thin silver blades all around him and he knew they were. Weasels. Whatever the things were, they were a damned nuisance. One of them leaped in front of him and he swung the hammer *through* its chest, so that its corpse was hung on his wrist a moment, and Hellboy had to shake it off.

Hellboy shuddered as he knocked the others out of his way with a blow of his left hand. The hammer was suddenly heavier in his grip, and yet it seemed to tremble with a power of its own. *What the hell is this thing?* he thought.

They continued to attack, lunging and loping about like slender, deadly monkeys. But these things were taller, of course. Most of the time they were crouched, but when they stood to their full height they were easily five feet. Their blades cut the night, stung him, but he ignored them now. Weasels were trying to keep him from catching up to Aickman, that much was clear. *Why*, he had no idea.

But there was only one way to find out at the moment.

Hellboy ran. Blades cut his arms and legs; a silver point scratched his face. When they got in front of him he ran them down, trampling them under his hooves or crushing them with Mjollnir. But he did not slow, did not fight them as they wanted.

At the corner, he turned left and saw Aickman alone on the sidewalk a little more than a block ahead. Beyond him, at the end of that second block, was the subway.

"Jeez," Hellboy said aloud, still baffled by the old man's speed.

A wave of sudden cold rolled down the street and it felt as though the air itself had frozen. Hellboy breathed in and felt ice in his lungs. A few flakes fell around him, tossed by the breeze, and it was as though the sky itself had conspired to slow him down as well. Hellboy ignored it. The cold would not deter him, no matter that it seemed to cut him deeper than these creatures' blades ever could, down to the marrow, so that his very bones hurt.

He did not slow.

With his sights set upon Aickman, he ran after the man. He could see the white wispy hair under the dim glow of a streetlamp halfway up the next block, and he picked up speed. Now the creatures lunged for his legs, tried to throw themselves under him to trip him up, willing to be shattered against the cobblestones for their trouble.

He gained.

"Professor Aickman!" he shouted, his bass voice resounding off the buildings he passed.

Lights went on inside several homes, but he did not see

a single door open, a single face at a window. He wondered if they knew better, the people of the northland, than to look out their windows at strange sounds late at night. There were parts of the world where people understood that sometimes it was better not to know what lurked unseen in shadow. Perhaps this was one of them.

Hellboy lashed out, cracking skulls, breaking bones, but still the things kept pace with him, even dancing ahead of him, like dogs nipping at the heels of a paperboy on a bicycle. What he wouldn't have given for a bicycle right then.

He closed the gap. When Hellboy hit the block Aickman was on, the one with the subway station at the end, Aickman was three quarters of the way down it. Now he lashed out at the things with less interest. They cut him, they struck him, one of them landed upon his back. When he ripped its sword away and tossed it aside, the thing tried to choke him. Hellboy ignored it, focused on Aickman.

"Aickman, don't screw with me again!" Hellboy roared.

But he should have known better. The truth of it was, in a way, he had. Aickman had not been someone he would have put his trust in, but he could not have predicted that the man was wrapped up with the weirdness in the Arctic Circle. He tried to work out the odds of that in his head, then realized they were better than he would have imagined. After all, he himself had come to Aickman for his expertise. It stood to reason he might not have been the only one.

Cursing loudly, he saw Aickman go down into the open entrance to the subway. Hellboy was nearly there himself now, and he picked up speed. His hooves struck the sidewalk hard enough to turn small divots of the stone to chalk dust and he had left a gruesome Hansel-and-Gretel trail of injured weasel creatures behind him, the dead ones having disappeared in a puff of black mist.

He reached the opening to the subway station. Aickman had been slowed by the long, steep stairwell that descended far beneath the city—necessary, as the subway traveled under land and water alike. The folklorist was less than a third of the way down the stairs.

Hellboy started down.

Another wave of cold swept up at him from underground. Frost formed all along the walls, and ice covered

the fluorescent lights for a few seconds. Then they began to explode in a chain reaction of tiny pops that plunged the deep stairwell into true darkness.

Something hit Hellboy's legs from behind. Then the weasels were all over him, more than before. Dozens of the things, maybe more. They seemed endless, and they drove him down to the steps and piled on top of him, and now he could feel their talons raking his flesh, trying to tear him open. But their claws were not as sharp as their swords. For that he was grateful.

"Off!" he grunted. "I don't have time for a weasel pig pile."

They were smothering him.

All but his right hand. They stayed well away from Mjollnir. He swept the arm up, cracking bones with the war hammer. He bucked against the things, gathered up all his strength, his muscles almost crackling with power, and he shook the weasels off him with a bellowed war cry that had not been heard on earth in millennia.

Mjollnir whirled. Hellboy spun around, clutching it in both hands now, and he used it as a bludgeoning scythe that erased the creatures it struck from the face of the world, tearing into them, so that only a black mist remained around him to mark their passing. It quickly dissipated, but as it did he heard the click of feet upon the stairs as the survivors fled in all directions.

His eyes narrowed, he peered into the darkness, started down the stairs again. Nothing moved there, in the cold blackness. The walls were still frozen, but they had started to melt, water running down to the stairs. At the bottom, where the steps finally opened up into the subway station itself, the lights were still on.

But when he reached that place, there was no sign of Professor Aickman, or of the things that had attacked him.

His fury surprised him, rose up through him to shatter his usual calm, and Hellboy brought the hammer around and struck the wall of the subway station. Shards of broken tile flew and the hammer caved in a two-foot stretch of the concrete. From somewhere deep in the tunnel came a horrible banshee wail, the scream of ghosts or the shriek of a passing train. It could have been either one.

"Oh, that's perfect," he whispered to himself. "Have a tantrum. That'll solve everything."

Unnerved by his own behavior, and by all that had happened, he turned to start up the stairs again, only to find his path blocked. The two figures who stood at the bottom of the steps were not weasels, however. They were broad, thick-bodied things with brown skin, marks like huge freckles scattered across their faces. Stumps of men, they seemed, long wiry hair clumped together with iron rings. One wore a thick beard and carried a war hammer similar in shape but much smaller than Mjollnir. The other had only a patch of stubble on his chin and his

hands lay across his belly, fingers gripping the handles of twin daggers he wore on either hip.

Hellboy rolled his eyes. "Dwarves. You've gotta be freakin' kidding me. Where's Snow White?"

The one with the daggers bowed his head. "The snow is white all across the Northlands," he said in the same ancient tongue Hellboy had spoken in two days before. Yet in Hellboy's mind, it was as though two voices spoke, one that rough, antique language, and one translating, the two voices intertwined. "We have come to aid the thunder-bearer in any way possible."

"Good for you. I'm sure he'll be thrilled. Any idea where Professor Aickman went?"

The two stout half-men frowned deeply.

"Didn't think so. Tell the thunder-bearer I said hello, will ya?"

He started for them, Mjollnir slightly raised, expecting them to stand aside. But the dwarves only stared up at him gravely, their eyes heavy with expectation.

Again, the one with the daggers bowed just slightly. "But you *are* the thunder-bearer."

Hellboy sighed and hung his head.

"Crap. How did I *know* you were gonna say that?"

CHAPTER SIX

Hellboy had no particular love of cities, and yet if pressed he would have had to confess that he found Stockholm fascinating. It was comprised of islands and peninsulas, bridges and sub-Arctic rivers. The Swedes had built for their capital a city that was a conquest unto itself, a conquest of the land and the ocean and the elements.

For a place so remote, it held a presence on the world stage far in excess of what might be expected. And yet up close there were sections of the city with an old European beauty that seemed to defy its global reach. The financial and commercial organs of Stockholm might be located elsewhere, but the old town section of the city, Gamla Stan, was still its heart. The echo of ancient times still resounded along its cobblestoned streets, from palace and cathedral to the homes and shops of those Swedes who chose to make this place their home. There was a purity here in Gamla Stan that most of the city lacked. It was a place where the old gods were still remembered, where myth had been built into every wall.

By day, the winding, narrow streets of Gamla Stan were alive with light and laughter, as both locals and tourists enjoyed the many shops that were lined along the cobblestones. Even at night there was purpose and energy as people filled the neighborhood's nightclubs and cabarets.

But in the long hours before dawn when very late became very early and the night seemed at its darkest, Gamla Stan seemed haunted by the whispers of its old gods. Boutiques, art galleries, jewelry stores . . . each shop window was filled with shadows. Gamla Stan seemed bled of all life, a place where the plague had come through and touched the foreheads of the people with its scarlet fingers. It was a hollow place, then, a place out of time, where the world had ended and these buildings stood as a grave marker for humanity.

Hellboy chuckled nervously as he glanced around at the shop windows, the clack of his hooves echoing off stone and mortar and glass. He knew the city was only sleeping, that it would awaken. But he had always felt that sleeping cities seemed to have an awareness of their own. And perhaps they did.

"*Twilight Zone*," he muttered.

The two dwarves—the Nidavellim, or whatever they were called—walked behind him at a respectful distance of about six feet. The bearded one with the small war hammer was called Brokk. The other, with the chin patch and the daggers, was Eitri. They had made introductions down in the subway station, and then Hellboy had bade them a good night and left. He had to walk and think. It was not really like him to be so contemplative, but then he had been doing a great many things that were unlike him in recent days.

Mjollnir felt heavier than ever in his grasp.

So he had walked and felt a sort of restless stirring both in his massive right fist and in his heart. He worried that the influence of the hammer was taking root, and he wondered what that would mean.

Yet despite his wishes to the contrary, he was not alone. Though he had said good night, Brokk and Eitri followed him. Hellboy was tempted to shoo them away; though they had guts to just tag along like that. Still, he knew that he would want to speak to them eventually, even soon, and they knew it too. So they followed, and they waited patiently, and the first words out of his mouth were "*Twilight Zone.*" He figured the Nidavellim were expecting something more profound, but then he felt the urge to hit something with Mjollnir and realized that the last guy to bear the thunder, or whatever, probably hadn't been exactly a sage himself.

"You confuse us, thunder-bearer—," Brokk said.

Hellboy shot him a withering glance.

Brokk bowed slightly. "Apologies. Hellboy. What do you mean by these words?"

"Just that it's kind of eerie out here, this time of night." *I keep expecting Rod Serling to walk out of an alley*, he wanted to say, but that would only have confused them more. And the truth of it was, anyone looking out their window just then—maybe an old lady with lots of cats and terrible insomnia—would have seen him walking down the street with two ugly, dark-skinned little men draped in primitive clothes and bearing archaic weapons, and thought just about the same thing. Or they would have if *Twilight Zone* had ever been popular, or even broadcast, in Sweden. He wasn't sure about that.

Brokk and Eitri continued to follow patiently until at last Hellboy stopped in front of an empty store front between a leather goods shop and one that sold musical instruments. He tried to fold his arms and was reminded with a heavy thump of the hammer in his hand. Self-conscious, he lay Mjollnir on his shoulder to rest his arm and gazed at the two Nidavellim expectantly.

"All right. Let's pretend I'm the thunder-bearer. Who were the weasels?"

Eitri frowned deeply. "Weasels?"

Brokk cleared his throat and put his hand on the head of his own hammer, which he had slipped through a loop on his belt. "They are Svartalves."

Understanding dawned upon Eitri's face and he nodded. "Yes. Svartalves." He said it as though it was supposed to mean something.

Hellboy sighed. "And?"

The dwarves looked perturbed. Brokk stroked his thick beard. Eitri became agitated, blowing out a long breath as though he were growing annoyed with Hellboy's ignorance.

Not that Hellboy cared. In fact, if Eitri didn't get the grumpy look off his puss, Hellboy might be tempted to give him a closer look at Mjollnir.

"Look," he said sharply. "Morning's not that far away and I haven't had nearly enough sleep. I need my beauty rest. You two dog me around talking about being helpful. But you're not all that informative, are you? So I'll ask questions. You give answers.

"What the hell are Svartalves? Other than annoying little weasels with greasy hair and sharp tools."

Brokk nodded. "There are many darkling races in the nine worlds. We Nidavellim are metalsmiths and armorers, respected for our craft. The Svartalves have no craft and no art. They are carrion creatures who once fed off the leavings of the Aesir and the giants. In the millennia since the age of gods ended in blood and fire, they have lurked in shadow and fed off the refuse left behind by humanity, and sometimes on the dead."

The way he said it was so detached, so matter of fact, that Hellboy shuddered. "Can't wait to meet up with those freaks again. What about you guys? How do you manage to walk around looking like that without drawing attention?"

Eitri actually smiled.

Brokk narrowed his gaze, tilted his head to one side, and studied Hellboy for a moment. Then he shrugged. "We hide. Sometimes we hide where the humans are least likely to look . . . right in their midst."

"One of the first things our kind learned about humanity was this: they do not believe what they see. Rather, they see what they believe. And they don't believe in us anymore."

That seemed almost too simple an explanation for Hellboy, but he did not have the time or the inclination to press the matter.

"Okay. But why did Aickman take off in the middle of the night, and why did your little buddies stop me from catching up to him?"

The two squat warriors exchanged a dark glance. When they gazed up at Hellboy again, both Nidavellim wore the gravest of expressions.

"Thrym," Brokk said grimly.

Eitri nodded in agreement. "Thrym."

Hellboy narrowed his eyes, bared his teeth in a grimace. "Oh, well that explains everything. What the heck is Thrym?"

But the word resounded in his head, caused a flutter of something buried deep in his mind, the awakening of some awareness that he had not always possessed. *Thrym.*

He knew what Thrym was. Or, rather, who.

In his grip, Mjollnir grew so cold that it burned even that hand that could not be burned. Hellboy twitched as a memory surfaced in him, a memory that was not his own.

Thrym.

To the mountain had he come in search of Thrym the Hollow. Through the tallest forest and across battle-scarred plains, along the River Iving and then across it to the foothills of the peaks wherein the citadel of giants had been built. But Thrym was not to be found in Utgard.

The king of the frost giants was no longer welcome there.

Across the whole of Jotunheim he was scorned by giant and frost giant alike. Caverns carved of stone and ice housed the once king and his few remaining subjects now, and even they did not trust him. For Thrym had been a tyrant, legendary in his cruelty. And so, though the soulless king still taunted and raged at his enemies, he had no allies save those who were outcasts as well.

His hatred of the Aesir had given birth to a thousand campaigns, from the most outrageous attacks to the quietest murders. Though he was considered crippled even by his own, the Allfather would not countenance the mischief of Thrym for even another day. He sent his son to dispatch the deposed king, the hollow one.

The mountainside was crusted with ice and snow and the skeletons of trees, the jagged upthrust stones of the earth's fury.

It was a forbidding place, though not without its beauty. The caverns had been hacked from the earth with barbaric brutality. When the thunderer crested the steep face and reached the plateau just beneath those caverns, wind whipping his cloak of furs behind him, he found the ghoulishly screaming mouth of the main cavern guarded by two sentries.

Their eyes were white crystals, and icicles hung from their heads as though they were hair. A dusting of snow lay thick atop their shoulders and their fingers were tipped with jagged shards of ice.

"I have come for Thrym," he announced, Mjollnir cold to the touch in his grasp.

And then the sentries stunned him. They moved aside and turned their eyes away from the mouth of the cavern so as not to see what was to come. They were a cruel race, perhaps even evil, though evil was so hard to define. But what their king had become was an abomination even in their frozen eyes.

He passed the sentries and made his way within, encountering others who ought to have stood and defended their master but did not. At last, in the deepest recesses of the frosted stone, he discovered Thrym. He who had once been king of the Frost Giants lay upon his side, knees tucked up toward his belly, hands crossed on his chest. There had been a time when to look up at Thrym on the field of battle meant to peer into the clouds, but on this day he seemed severely diminished. The ice where he lay must have melted when he first reclined there, for now it had built up around him so that Thrym was all of a piece with the cavern itself. He a part of it, and it a part of him.

His eyes were open too wide and his head tilted downward so that streaks of tears and snot and drool had frozen in diag-

onal ribs of clotted, discolored ice that ran like scars across the side of his face, becoming icicles themselves, some pillars that went from floor to flesh, others incomplete stalagmites and stalactites of his hollow madness.

But Thrym was not silent. Low and resonant, like the deep cracking of polar ice, he cursed the Allfather and the alves and the Nidavellim and even all his brothers and sisters in Utgard. In savage detail he outlined his plans for the evisceration of his enemies, as well as their children and brides. And when blind, mad Thrym began to speak of draping himself in Sif's organs, the thunderer struck.

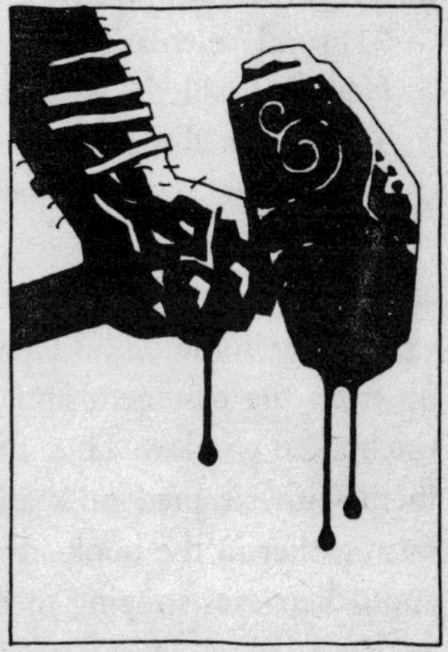

With a single blow of Mjollnir, he cracked the frozen skull of the hollow king. What spilled from within was brown and red, thick with a stench of rotten meat, and it melted the frost on the stone floor. An icy wind washed through that cavern, and Thrym was dead. When stories were told of that day, they would attribute an element of compassion to the thunderer's actions.

They would lie.

Thrym was a horrid thing, truly a monster. Killing him was an act of vengeance and honor, not of mercy.

Hellboy blinked, looked around the streets of Gamla Stan in alarm, Mjollnir raised as if to defend himself. Eitri and Brokk were beside him but they backed away, startled by his sudden movement. He could see their breath misting on the night air, ice particles glistening in it, and then he realized he could see his own as well.

"I remember," Hellboy said. Then he glanced down at Mjollnir and saw that the front of the war hammer had a dusting of frost upon it.

"Thrym?" Eitri asked.

Hellboy nodded. "Thrym. But how can it be Thrym?"

The Nidavellim explained.

With Pernilla's help, Abe had located a hammer and some nails. They had brought a broken table up from the basement and Abe had used it to board up the broken window. Then the woman had made cocoa for them with steamed milk and melted chocolate and they sat together in the book-strewn parlor and sipped at their cups, their eyes straying to the hallway from time to time as they talked quietly. The front door was locked up tight, but Abe's anxiety came not from concern that more of those creatures would return. Rather, he wondered how long Hellboy would be gone.

"He is your friend," Pernilla said, a trace of wonder in her voice.

Abe nodded as he sipped the delicious chocolate, a swirl of moist steam tickling his nose. "You find that strange?"

She lowered her gaze. "Forgive me. For my whole life the only thing I have known of Hellboy was that he was a monster who wished to take my father's life."

"Well, obviously he doesn't want to kill your father," Abe replied, scoffing at the preposterousness of it. "Though he might have the urge to slap him around a little. It ticks him off when someone else's greed almost costs him his life. He's funny that way."

"Of course I know that now," she said, shifting uncomfortably on the sofa. "I am grateful that he is willing to try to save my father in spite of that. Do . . . do you think they will be all right?"

Abe shrugged, glancing out into the hall again. "Hellboy's been through a lot of scrapes. He'll come back as soon as he can."

"And my father?"

"I wish I knew."

Abe felt guilty suddenly, as though he had wronged this woman somehow. Despite the lights in the corners of the room, her features were cast into shadow, framed by her hair, but it made her look vulnerable rather than mysterious.

"Tell me about your work," he said, a smile on his thin lips.

And so the conversation began, and slowly the world disappeared around them. Pernilla discussed her own research into comparative mythology and her desire to teach at the University of Stockholm, an amibition her father decried. He was growing old and claimed to need her to aid him in his own studies, but those efforts only frustrated her, for her father never included her fully. She was a research assistant and little more. Abe pointed out that they would be meeting with Professor Aronsson the next day, and that he might be willing to speak with her about opportunities at the university.

Pernilla smiled brightly and placed a hand across her

chest in a gesture so disarmingly unself-conscious that Abe could not help but laugh. He was pleased when she did not take offense. The clock seemed to fall silent, the minutes slipping rather than ticking by. His cocoa grew cold in the cup and the parlor seemed a world unto itself. When she had tired of talking about herself and her work, Pernilla studied him closely.

Shyly, she glanced away. "I fear you'll find me rude again, but I have to ask. What you said when you arrived, it seemed as though you don't know where you come from."

"Washington, D.C.," Abe replied, the quip an automatic defense mechanism. He regretted it immediately. She had been so open with him that she deserved more than that.

Pernilla blinked, regret in her eyes.

"Sorry," he said. "I know what you mean." And he told her what little he knew about the day decades before when plumbers had broken through a sealed door in the basement of St. Trinian's Hospital in D.C. and discovered the secret lab within, and the fluid-filled glass cylinder inside of which floated a seemingly lifeless figure. The label upon the cylinder had identified him as an Icthyo Sapien and had borne the date April 14, 1865.

Her eyes widened at that. "1865?"

Abe nodded. "That was the day President Lincoln was assassinated. That's where . . . that's where I got my name." He didn't like to think about that part, about the fact that a couple of whiskey-breathed, chain-smoking plumbers in a dank hospital basement had given him his name, as if they were his parents.

"It's a proud name," Pernilla said.

He smiled at that.

From down the corridor came the resounding echo of someone knocking at the door. Abe's gaze darted to the clock and he saw that it was a quarter past three in the morning. He and Pernilla rose at the same time and went cautiously to the front door.

"Who is it?" Pernilla called.

"The Big Bad Wolf," Hellboy replied crankily. "Open the door."

Abe sighed. "Sorry. He gets like that when he hasn't had enough sleep." He unlocked the door and swung it open.

Hellboy stood on the steps. Behind him, gazing up expectantly, were a pair of armed dwarves with dark, mottled flesh and iron rings tied in their hair. They were both armed and they looked almost startled as their eyes focused on Abe. The two little men bared their chipped and jagged teeth and their hands moved swiftly to the weapons at their hips.

"Good God," Pernilla gasped, and she put a hand up to cover her mouth. "Are . . . are they Nidavellim?"

The stumpy warriors looked very proud suddenly and straightened up. Hellboy frowned and glanced back at them.

"What? Them? Yeah. Brokk. Eitri. Meet Abe Sapien and Pernilla Aickman," he said. Then he focused again on the dwarves. "Guard the house. When the sun comes up, try to do it without drawing too much attention to yourselves."

They bowed their heads and withdrew down the stairs. Hellboy came into the house and shut the door behind him. As Abe locked up once more, Pernilla stared at Hellboy, gnawing on her lower lip.

"My father? You couldn't save him?" she asked.

"Save him?" Hellboy replied. Then he softened slightly and rubbed at the back of his neck. "Aw, I'm sorry. You thought? No. I woke up . . . well, the squirrel woke me up, but when I came downstairs I saw him taking off down the street. The Svartalves weren't taking him away. They were making sure I didn't stop him."

Abe was stunned by this news, but not nearly so much as Pernilla was. Though she was exhausted, she had still had some color in her cheeks. Now, suddenly, in the dim light of the foyer, she looked like a walking corpse, her flesh devoid of any flush or even emotion.

"Svartalves?" Abe asked, mainly to change the subject.

"Yep."

The amphibian hooked a thumb toward the door. "And those two guys? There a reason they're suddenly your bodyguards?"

Hellboy halfheartedly raised Mjollnir. "I'm the thunder-bearer."

"Ah, well, yeah, that explains it," Abe replied, not bothering to hide the sarcasm in his voice.

Pernilla still looked stricken, and though Hellboy had never been good with that sort of thing, he went to her and laid his left hand upon her shoulder very gently. His voice was tired and low and a bit like smashing granite with a sledge, but somehow, Abe thought it sounded soothing. He hoped Pernilla did too.

"I tried to catch him," Hellboy said. "There's a lot going on here, with the Nidavellim and the Svartalves and the hammer. Trust me when I say I don't want to hurt him, I just want to find him and see if he can help explain it all. But there's no way we're going to do that tonight. We all need sleep. Why don't we get some, and in the morning I'll tell you both all the crazy stuff that's in my head right now, and we'll go see Professor Aronsson, and then maybe together we can figure out where to start looking for your father."

There was a long moment when she just looked at the closed door as though she could see right through the wood to the street beyond. Then she nodded and touched the hand on her shoulder.

"Thank you," she said.

Pernilla slipped away from Hellboy and came to Abe. "And thank *you*," she said again.

"We're going to figure this out," Abe told her, though he had no such confidence himself. "You'll see. Professor Aronsson will help."

Silence.

All was perfectly, almost unnaturally silent within the home Karl Aronsson lived in upon the grounds of the University of Stockholm. It was close to the halls where he lectured and the offices where he met with students and the library the university was so proud of. But Karl never worked in any of those places. His research was always done in the study inside his own home.

A pop and hiss broke the silence. In the fireplace, the embers of the night's blaze still glowed and announced themselves from time to time. Karl had fallen asleep at his desk, face upon an open book, body splayed in the thick-legged chair that was comfortable beneath his bulk but terrible for his back. His breathing was light, no trace of a snore, and yet he was deeply, profoundly asleep, his arms crooked at the elbow and arrayed around his head like walls built to protect him.

Photographs had spilled from the top of the desk to the floor. A notebook filled with his scrawl lay open, awaiting more ink. The last words that had been written there were underlined three times. One of the words was "Thrym." There was a map there as well and circled upon it in green ink was the place upon the river Dalbard where the corpse had been found. The dead god and the hammer. The discovery of a lifetime for Karl Aronsson, and one that would change the way the world regarded history and mythology forever.

But that was not the only spot circled on the map. Another ring of green ink signified the place north of the river where Hellboy had led them to that cave, whose carvings Karl believed he had translated. If he was correct in his translation, the result was equally stunning.

A third location was marked on the map. This one within Stockholm itself. After rereading legends he had sifted through a thousand times, Karl had calculated distance and angle and pinpointed that one spot. It seemed impossible and yet eminently reasonable all at the same time. And after what they had discovered in the frozen north, what did it really mean any more to say something was not possible?

He had contemplated these things, these questions, for hours and eventually laid his head down upon the desk. Just to rest his eyes, just for a moment. Now he slept with a tiny smile at the corners of his mouth as the room grew cold in the absence of fire.

Another pop and hiss broke the silence as the glow of embers dimmed further. Karl started in his chair, snorting a bit. He shifted uncomfortably, his sleeping mind aware of the ache in his back from too many hours slouched across the desk.

But the hiss did not go away this time. In his dreams, Karl frowned deeply, troubled by the continuation of this sound. Then it was not a hiss, but a slow, deliberate scratching. The ache in his back and the foreign nature of this sound intruded at last upon his sleep, and Karl opened his eyes. He shivered a bit and sat up slowly, his mouth dry and his face a bit numb from lying on the hard surface for so long.

There came another hiss, but it was not from the cinders.

Karl turned and then froze, so astonished by the creatures who emerged from the darkness around him that he was unable to utter even a word. Here was yet another miracle, another myth come true. But these were not dry bones or a tomb devoid of artifacts. They were real, their powder blue eyes bright in the darkness of his study.

He stared at them until they tore out his eyes.

The last of the embers in the fireplace died with him.

CHAPTER SEVEN

The morning came too soon and Hellboy fought it for as long as he could. For some time after he had first groaned and slitted his eyes open to find invasive sunlight in the room, he shifted and turned and slept fitfully. Each time he woke he curled away from the windows and hoped that he could sleep a bit longer, that the next time he opened his eyes he would not feel quite so tired.

At last, late in the morning if he gauged by the angle of the sun through the glass, he found he could not force himself to sleep any longer. His eyes were dry and his head felt as though it were stuffed with cotton, but he rose from the guest bed with Mjollnir still clutched in his hand. Already it had begun to feel as though he had always held that hammer, and the familiarity bothered him. This was not something he planned to get used to.

Hellboy stretched and scratched at the back of his head, then went out into the corridor. The second floor seemed very quiet so he went downstairs, where he tried to ignore the damage in the foyer. Time to talk to Brokk and Eitri, see what sort of help they were willing to provide. But when he opened the front door, there was no sign of the Nidavellim. A few cars passed by on the cobblestoned street and Hellboy saw an old woman swerve as she stared at him while driving past. He stared back, and her car sped up.

An elderly man walking a dog that looked more like a wolf went by at the bottom of the steps and did not even look up. After he had gone by, Hellboy went down to the sidewalk and around both sides of the house. There was nothing to indicate a struggle, but the Nidavellim were gone.

Okay, he thought. *Can't count on those two.*

Though he wondered what had become of them and whether or not they would be back, he wasn't about to wait around for them. Back inside, Hellboy shut the door and walked deeper into the house. He glanced into the parlor but found it empty. With a frown, he began to wonder if Abe and Pernilla had left the house. As if in answer, he heard a metallic banging from the back of the house and followed the noise until he discovered the small kitchen there.

A small, slightly lopsided table was pushed against the back wall beneath a wide open window that looked out upon a slightly overgrown garden. The table was set for three. There were small pitchers of milk and juice, along with a small basket of thick toast.

Pernilla stood in front of the stove frying eggs in a pan. A fragrant mixture of sausages, onions, and peppers cooked in a skillet beside it. His tread was heavy, and Hellboy knew she could not have failed to hear him, but she did not turn as he entered the kitchen. He was about to break the silence when he noticed her shoulders hitching, and she wiped at her eyes.

Aw, Jeez, he thought, shifting awkwardly.

"Smells great," he said. "But you didn't have to cook for us."

Again her hand fluttered up, and she dabbed at her face. "It's no trouble. Abe is taking a bath. Would you tell him that breakfast is almost ready?"

For a moment he only stared blankly at her back. Then her words sank in, and Hellboy turned to go. In the hall he paused and turned to look at her again. The way the doorway seemed to frame her made him feel like an intruder, a peeping tom.

"Pernilla. We'll find him."

She waved at the air, still without turning. "Let us speak about it over breakfast. There are things you promised to tell us, and things you should know as well."

Hellboy frowned. *Well, that was cryptic,* he thought. But he could not hold it against her. Pernilla had a lot to deal with and she didn't need him hovering around while she was crying over her father's mysterious departure the night before.

Putting aside his curiosity about her comment, he went back down the hall and upstairs. The door to Abe's room was halfway open, and Hellboy knocked once and called his name before stepping into the room. A quick glance around confirmed that Abe was not there. His clothes were hung like a half-hearted scarecrow from one of the posts at the end of the bed. He did not particularly want to disturb Abe in the bath, but Hellboy was also in no rush to go back down to the kitchen and be alone with Pernilla again. Besides, she had asked him to let Abe know it was time for breakfast.

With some reluctance he went down the hall to the

bathroom and rapped on the door. "Abe. Pernilla says breakfast is almost ready."

As he waited for a response, it occurred to Hellboy that he could use a bath himself. He did not want to crack the tub, but thought that if he were careful he could manage it. Not that he ever really stank. Once upon a time a Bureau parapsychologist he worked with had observed that Hellboy smelled like dry-roasted peanuts. The guy had no idea why he would find such a comment insulting, and in retrospect Hellboy saw his point. There were a lot of worse things he could smell like. Still, the description had stayed with him. When he needed a shower, the way he did now, he always figured he smelled like a whole *lot* of dry-roasted peanuts. Stale ones.

Hellboy frowned and rapped at the door again. "Abe?"

He listened. No sound came from within that room. No running water, no movement. His mind flashed again to the front of the house and the absence of Eitri and Brokk. For the third time, Hellboy knocked. He counted to ten and when there was still no response he turned the knob and pushed the door open.

The bathroom was empty. Or, at least, that's what Hellboy thought at first glance. The tub was filled nearly to brimming with water but it was dark inside. Something shifted and the surface of the water rippled. Cautiously, Hellboy took a step forward and peered into the tub.

Abe lay submerged, gills fluttering slightly in the water, a look of peace upon his features. His eyes were closed and Hellboy wondered if he was asleep in there. The urge to retreat was very strong. He did not want to disturb his friend. At the same time, however, the trepidation he had felt a moment before remained. Now that the daylight had come, they should not waste it. There was a lot to talk about and a lot to do, and they ought to get started. Plus, Pernilla *had* sent him up there in the first place.

He tapped lightly on the edge of the tub.

With a sudden thrashing, Abe opened his eyes and sat up, gripping the sides of the tub. Water splashed out onto the floor. He calmed down a notch when he saw Hellboy, but only a notch.

"What is it?" Abe asked. "What's wrong?"

"Pernilla wants you to come down for breakfast."

Abe glared at him. "Breakfast? You nearly gave me a heart attack. Don't *do* that."

With a dry chuckle, Hellboy headed for the door. "You're just lucky she didn't come up looking for you herself. Next time, lock the door."

"So, at some point, the age of gods came to an end." Hellboy put the last bite of his toast into his mouth and let his words sink in as he ate it.

Abe had taken two servings of the sausage and onions but had left the eggs alone. Pernilla, on the other hand, had had nothing but a slice of thick toast and two cups of tea. Her flesh was even more pale than it had been the night before, though there was no sign now that she had been crying.

She did not smile, however.

"But the Svartalves and the dwarves?" Abe prodded.

"Nidavellim," Hellboy corrected. "But yeah. They stuck around. Made a go of it. Anyway, this guy Thrym was king of the frost giants for a while. He learned magic from some of the Nidavellim who knew that kind of thing, traveled the nine worlds picking up as much arcane knowledge as he could gather. He got pretty powerful, apparently. Of course, he wanted what they all wanted, which was to destroy the Aesir.

"Even though the darkling races always fought amongst themselves, Thrym figured he had enough allies in Svartalfheim and Nidavellir to make an alliance work. The Svartalves threw in with him, but the Nidavellim refused and most of the giants other than his own clan ignored him. He had some other allies, though, even one of the Aesir, according to what Brokk and Eitri said. No one knows exactly who betrayed him, but apparently someone cast a spell on his favorite mug. Except they called it a tankard.

"Anyway, when Thrym toasted the impending attack on the Aesir and drank, his spirit was ripped from his body and trapped inside that tankard. He didn't die right then, but he had no soul. By the time I . . . well, when the Aesir caught up to him to punish him for his plotting, he was killed pretty easily. They buried his body on Midgard. Word is that the Tankard of Thrym was buried far away from his corpse in a secret chamber somewhere."

Pernilla had grown even paler as he talked, and she dropped her gaze when he finished. Hellboy watched her with great concern, wondering what it was she was not telling them.

"So your bodyguards told you all this?" Abe asked.

"Most of it," Hellboy replied, but he did not elaborate.

"And now they're gone?"

"Yep."

"Maybe I wasn't paying attention, but I think I missed something. What does any of that have to do with the hammer, or the body, or the empty cave we found?"

At Abe's words, Pernilla hugged herself as though she was cold.

Hellboy shrugged. "The dwarves—"

"Nidavellim," Abe corrected.

"Yeah. They say the word on the street is that Thrym is back and the Svartalves are helping him again." He glanced down at the hammer that he held upon his lap. "According to them, the fates unearthed those remains the old fisherman found up north on purpose. The timing wasn't a coincidence. Mjollnir was supposed to be found so someone would have the power to stop Thrym."

"Makes sense," Abe said with a nod.

"Glad you think so. Can you explain it to me, now?" Hellboy asked.

Abe took a sip of water from a tall glass and stared into it a moment. Before he looked at Hellboy again he glanced at Pernilla, and it was clear that they both knew she was keeping something back.

"The chamber we found up there? The one the hammer led you to? What I figure is that the Tankard of Thrym was buried there. Professor Aronsson can probably confirm that if he can translate the symbols we found, but it stands to reason. If all of this is true, someone dug it up."

Hellboy made no response. Abe toyed with his water glass, but he also said nothing more. Several seconds ticked past, and the two of them looked at Pernilla. She seemed to have folded in upon herself, grown smaller there in the chair. At length, she let out a long breath and sat up, pushing her hair away from her face as she regarded them.

Then she nodded. "Yes. My father."

"You know that for sure?" Hellboy asked, though he did not doubt it at all.

"Not absolutely. But he only returned last week from a dig in the north. He was ecstatic, but wouldn't share many details with me. That isn't all that unusual, I'm sorry to say. He told me that he had recovered an artifact that would have an enormous impact on our field of study. He's spent a lot of time away from the house these past few days. I assumed he was meeting with colleagues, that sort of thing."

"Maybe he was," Hellboy said. "Just not the kind of colleagues you were thinking."

Pernilla closed her eyes and grimaced. Abe shot him a withering look and Hellboy shifted uncomfortably in his seat.

"Sorry," he said. "I don't meant to make light of it. It's just that—"

She gazed at him grimly. "Just that he's betrayed you before."

"There's that," Hellboy agreed.

Once again the kitchen fell into silence. After a time Abe rose and began to carry dishes to the sink where he rinsed them. Pernilla and Hellboy sat across from one another and she drank the last of what must have been very cold tea. Finally, she rose.

"Let me have a look at my father's papers. Then we'll go see your friend at the university."

Pernilla drove. Hellboy had to put the passenger seat all the way back and he was still cramped. Somehow Abe managed to fold himself into the backseat in such a way that he actually looked comfortable. They traveled mostly in silence, each contemplating all they had learned. Hellboy figured Abe wished he was back in the tub, where he could tune out the world. But he doubted there would be much opportunity for relaxation for any of them until they got to the bottom of this.

Edmund Aickman's papers were startling only in their utter lack of information. There was nothing in his journals or on his computer about the Tankard of Thrym or the dig he had completed in the north. There was no way to know who had worked with him on that excavation, but he had obviously not done it alone. Still, Pernilla had placed calls to several of his usual associates and none of them had been involved.

In the entire house, the only bit of information they had uncovered about the Tankard of Thrym came from a battered, faded leather volume of Norse myth written in Lappish. According to legend, anyone who drank from the Tankard of Thrym would be gifted with extraordinary power, instilled with the strength of the Frost King. Considering what happened to Thrym when he drank from it, Hellboy thought anyone would have to be pretty dumb to fall for that one, but he did not say that aloud. Of course, the legend did not match up to what Brokk and Eitri had told him. They hadn't said someone had the power of Thrym. They said Thrym was back.

Big difference.

It was yet another thing they hoped Professor Aronsson

could help them with. Which made it that much worse when they arrived at the university to find the area around his office cordoned off by police, prowled by tracking dogs, and populated by students who were quickly spreading the rumor that the professor had been murdered.

"This is bad," Hellboy said as they pushed through the students and faculty that were gathered outside the cordon.

Several people shouted in alarm when they passed by. A pair of uniformed police officers who stood by their vehicle spotted them and conferred quickly. One of them spoke into a radio as they approached, his eyes darting from Hellboy to Abe, but his expression revealing nothing. When they reached the police car, however, the officer turned his attention to Pernilla and they had a brief conversation.

"What's going on?" Abe asked.

Pernilla took a deep breath. "It's true. I'm sorry, but your friend is dead."

Abe touched her lightly on the arm. "There's no reason to think because of this that anything will have happened to your father."

"That's not what I'm afraid of," she said quietly.

Hellboy frowned, wondering what she meant, and then it hit him. The woman was not afraid her father would meet the same end, but that he had been in some way responsible for Professor Aronsson's murder. He would have liked to comfort her, but he had nothing to say to that.

Pernilla glanced up at him. "There is a Mr. Klar here from the government. Apparently he was expecting you to be here. The officers have orders to bring you to see him."

Though they made it clear she could stay outside, Pernilla accompanied them into the office building. Its exterior had a Scandinavian flair that the inside sorely lacked. It was cold and impersonal, the rooms and corridors no different from those in a thousand other buildings Hellboy had been in. Professor Aronsson's office had been on the first floor in the rear of the building and Klar was waiting for them when the officers led them to the spot. If it was possible, Hellboy thought the severe government man had cut his blond hair even shorter. There was no exchange of pleasantries, not even a hello, as the man gazed sternly at them.

"Who is your companion?" Klar demanded.

Hellboy bristled at his tone. "This is Pernilla Aickman. She's helping with the investigation."

"The folklorist you spoke of yesterday?" Klar asked, studying her, eyes large behind his thick, rimless spectacles.

"His daughter."

"And what of the man himself?"

Mystery and suspicion and the sudden knowledge that not all myths were fiction had dimmed the spark in Pernilla Aickman over the previous twelve hours. Now it appeared that meeting Klar was just what she needed, for Pernilla was clearly practiced in dealing with obnoxious bureaucrats.

"My father has taken ill," she said, meeting Klar's gaze with a steely glare of her own. "I have offered my help to these gentlemen and we thought we might benefit from the expertise of Professor Aronsson. Obviously, that will now be impossible."

Hellboy tapped Mjollnir against his leg, drawing Klar's attention to it. "So, what happened to him, anyway?"

Klar's lips pressed together in a tight white line. "Where were you and Mr. Sapien last night?"

"You're kidding, right?"

"I doubt he ever kids," Abe noted dryly. He wore sunglasses, and his jacket collar was turned up. He shivered despite the warm clothes.

"In addition to my aid, I also offered them my hospitality," Pernilla noted. "They were guests at my home."

For long seconds the quartet only stared at one another. At length, Abe slid off his sunglasses and put them into the breast pocket of his jacket, just above the patch with the BPRD symbol on it. Klar's eyes were drawn to the symbol.

"Let me remind you, Mr. Klar, that we were asked to come here to aid in the investigation into the remains you discovered north of Skellesvall," Abe announced. "I'm willing to bet Professor Aronsson's death is related to that investigation. But you know what? I'm cold and I want to go home. So if you'd rather not have our cooperation, we'd appreciate a lift back to the airport."

Klar scowled, seemed to be searching his mind for an appropriate retort, and then simply turned sharply on his heel and led them through the tangle of police and government investigators into Karl Aronsson's office.

"This way," he said.

Hellboy gave Abe a none-too-subtle thumbs up, and the three of them followed Klar. There was some jostling as several officers had to vacate the office in order to make space for them. When the place was clear enough that

Hellboy could get a look at the inside of the room, he winced. Though the corpse had been covered with a black plastic sheet, it seemed somehow misshapen under there, as if the professor's limbs had been twisted at all odd angles. There was a pool of blood that seeped out from beneath the sheet, dried brown at the edges but still bright red and moist closer in toward the body. Hellboy thought about wet paint.

Angular patterns of blood, likely the spray from severed blood vessels or the spatterings of the murder weapons, decorated the floor and walls and desk.

Hellboy frowned. "The desk."

He stepped toward it, careful not to trammel upon the blood stains on the floor. Abe and Pernilla came up behind him and Klar on the other side of the desk. The spray of blood went up the front of the desk, started across the top, and then the pattern was interrupted by a broad stretch of wood that was clear, only to resume with a final few splashes of dark crimson.

"Did your people take anything out of here?" Hellboy asked.

"Not yet," Klar replied. "We noticed this as well. It appears that whoever killed the professor removed whatever he was working on at the moment."

"We know what he was working on," Hellboy said. Glum, suddenly filled with grief for this man he had known only a few days, he looked back at Abe. "Think there's any reason to search the place?"

"Not really," Abe replied, hands thrust into his pockets. "If they're smart enough to have taken his notes, I'm sure they'll have taken the photographs and things as well."

Pernilla blanched. "So we've got nothing to go on. We don't even know where to start looking. You've got nothing left from up there except Mjollnir and the body."

At the mention of the corpse that had acted as a lightning rod on that frozen riverbank up north, Hellboy glanced over at Klar. "What about it? Did you learn anything from examining the body?"

His eyes narrowed and he studied them, obviously suspicious. "A preliminary autopsy on the remains revealed nothing out of the ordinary aside from the unusual size of the deceased."

"And how remarkably well preserved it is, given its age."

Klar did not even blink. "Tests were performed. There is no evidence to suggest that the remains are more than a century old. Easily explained if they were frozen in ice."

"Oh, for Christ's sake," Hellboy muttered.

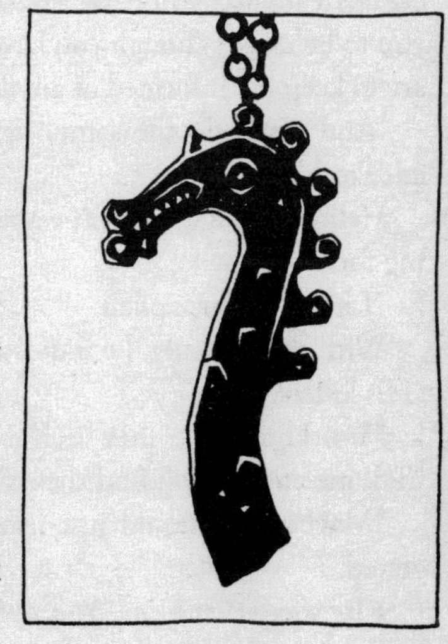

"We're not at a total dead end," Abe observed. "I mean, we can always go back up and take more pictures. And there's this." He reached inside his shirt and dragged out the heavy serpent pendant on its ancient chain.

"You've been wearing it?" Hellboy asked, surprised.

"Professor Aronsson took a picture of it. He said I

might as well hold onto it until they were ready to do metallurgical tests on this and the hammer."

"Both of which are property of the Swedish government," Klar reminded them.

"You'll get them when this is over," Hellboy said sharply. "I don't want this freakin' thing attached to my hand forever."

He raised Mjollnir and Klar actually flinched.

Pernilla stared at Mjollnir. "You said that when you were above the Arctic circle, you had a kind of intuition that led you to the place where my . . ." She glanced at Klar quickly, then back to Hellboy. "Where that excavated cave was found. Anything like that now? Any sense of where we should start to look?"

"Look for what?" Klar asked. He slipped off his glasses, and they dangled from his hand as he pointed accusingly at them. "You are hiding something. It may be that the government invited you here, but do not think we will allow you to behave as though you have no one to answer to. You are to keep me informed of anything you discover."

"And you'll do the same, right?" Abe asked, a cynical edge to his voice.

Hellboy shrugged. "You want to know what we're looking for?"

"I insist," Klar replied.

With the hammer, he indicated the corpse on the floor. "His killers."

"You know who they are?" Klar sputtered in disbelief. "Tell me and we will find them."

"Maybe you should just leave it to us," Hellboy suggested.

Klar sneered at him. "You *will* cooperate."

Hellboy glanced at Pernilla. "Miss Aickman. You want to tell him?"

Without any trace of amusement, she looked directly at Klar. "They're *Svartalves*, sir."

A myriad of emotions warred upon the man's face in that moment. He looked at first as though he wanted to laugh, and then as though he had been physically hurt by her words. At last, though, his face reverted to its usual, pinched, annoyed countenance.

"Elves?" Klar said, sniffing. "Professor Aronsson was murdered by elves?"

"Well, they're evil, if that makes any difference," Abe offered.

"And they have swords," Hellboy added.

Klar shook his head in disgust. "Get out of here. Stay out of my way. If you have any useful suggestions or information, you have my cellular phone number. Otherwise, stay out of my way. And you will not leave the country with those artifacts."

Hellboy turned his back on Klar. "Wouldn't dream of it."

CHAPTER EIGHT

Outside, they were ignored by the authorities and gawked at by the bystanders, who seemed to be waiting around for *something* to gawk at. Once they had moved beyond the cordon, however, and begun walking back toward the lot where Pernilla's car was parked, the campus seemed almost deserted.

Hellboy heard a cawing above him and looked up to see a pair of huge dark birds circling like vultures above him. He shielded his eyes against the sun and squinted, trying to get a better look. Abe and Pernilla had kept walking but now they stopped and waited for him.

"What are you looking at?" Abe asked.

"Those ravens," Hellboy replied.

"What? Where?"

Confused, Hellboy glanced over at Abe. His friend seemed genuinely baffled. With a shake of his head, Hellboy pointed up at the sky and was about to ask if Abe needed glasses. But the ravens were gone.

"Never mind."

"You're seeing things, now?" Abe asked.

"Guess so." Hellboy glared down at the hammer as though it could feel his ire. And the truth of it was, he was far from certain it could not. "Maybe I should just get a crowbar to take this thing off."

Pernilla went to him and touched the massive fist that clutched Mjollnir. "May I?" she asked.

When Hellboy lifted it, she examined his grip, ran her touch along his fingers where they clutched Mjollnir, along the hammer itself, and upon the edges and contours of his hand.

"What is it made of?" she asked. "It feels . . . warmer than I would have expected."

"Don't know."

Abruptly, Abe began to stamp his feet. He was shivering and had his arms wrapped around himself as though he was standing in the middle of a blizzard. The sun shone brightly down and, though far from hot, the day was pleasant enough.

"Abe?" Hellboy ventured. "You all right?"

He did not answer. Instead, he fumbled inside his shirt for the medallion and lifted the chain over his head. "This thing is like ice, all of a sudden. It's . . . it's freezing."

"Let me have it," Hellboy said, holding out his left hand.

Abe put the pendant into his hand, and Hellboy found that he was right. The metalwork serpent felt as though it had been carved from ice. The moment he was no longer holding the thing, Abe let out a long breath and began to calm down. After a moment, he unbuttoned his coat.

"Is that better?" Pernilla asked, concern etched into her features.

"Much," Abe replied, staring at the pendant in Hellboy's hand. "What do you think that was about?"

Hellboy did not reply. He was not even looking at Abe. Instead, he stared off to his right where a copse of trees grew up beside a grand structure that must have been one of the university's first buildings. Just within the shade of those trees stood an unnaturally tall woman in fur and armor, her long red hair pulled back in a thick braid. Her face was obscured by the shade, but he knew she was staring at him. In her right hand she clutched a proud spear made of strong oak with an iron tip.

Without a word, Hellboy started across the grass toward her. As he walked, he managed to slip the serpent pendant over his head. Its chain was so cold it seared the skin at the back of his neck.

Abe called after him, but he did not respond. Hellboy had the sense that his companions followed, but it was as though all of that happened in some dimly recalled dream.

Face to face with the woman in the shadows, he still could not see her eyes.

"I know you," Hellboy said.

"As well you should."

"Mist?"

"I have been called that."

"I cannot accompany you," he told her, uncertain where the words were coming from.

"You are already with us. This bit of you is only an

echo, the clang of the hammer perhaps. But I will collect even that when the time comes."

"Then why appear now?"

She gestured to the pendant around his neck. *"When you claimed the death-gift Eitri made for you, it brought me. Now I wait."*

Eitri, Hellboy thought. *Gonna have a few questions for that stumpy little monkey when I catch up with him.* "So you just hang around, waiting. I guess we can't expect any help from you."

A flicker of a smile appeared at the edges of her lips, and then she seemed to be swallowed further by the shadows. *"I am a simple servant and not given to idle gossip. You know who to ask if you wish to know what is whispered beneath the branches of the Ash."*

As cold as the pendant was where it now hung against his chest, so was Mjollnir warm in his grip. It seemed to stir of its own volition but he forced his arm to be still.

A hand landed on his shoulder and Hellboy spun, hammer raised to defend himself.

It was Abe.

"Hey. Are you okay? Maybe we should call Dr. Manning, try to get another team out here. I don't like what this is doing to your head."

Hellboy shook himself, understanding at last why Abe had seemed so cold all along. He touched the pendant at his chest but left it there. That was, after all, where it belonged. Abe and Pernilla stared at him, and the world seemed more alive, suddenly, the colors somehow richer than they had been moments before.

In the gray. In the shadows beneath the trees.

He looked over to where the spear-bearer had stood a moment before and was unsurprised to find her gone. "You didn't see her, I guess," he said.

"See who?" Abe asked. "Hellboy, I'm serious. I'm very concerned here."

Hellboy nodded. "Me too." Then he gazed up into the trees. "Ratatosk. Where are you, old friend?"

With a chittering sound, the squirrel popped his head out of the upper branches and gazed down upon them. After a moment, Ratatosk ran along the inner branches of the tree, scrabbled down the bark with his sharp claws, and then traveled along a lower limb. It sat up, staring at them, head jerking back and forth in the way that squirrels have.

Ratatosk chittered loudly as if panicked.

"The Svartalves," Hellboy said. "And the one with the essence of Thrym. Do you know what they plan? Or where we can find them?"

"Hellboy," Abe said. "I really think we should—"

"The reign of Thrym is to begin again," Ratatosk said, in that ancient tongue that Hellboy did not know, but nevertheless interpreted.

"What the hell?" Abe asked. He and Pernilla took a couple of steps back. "It talks?"

Surprised, Hellboy glanced over at them. He had assumed that Ratatosk would be like the ravens and the spear-bearer. But they had seen him, and heard him as well.

"Did you understand him?" he asked.

Abe scowled. "No!" he shook his head. "But I can tell it's talking to you."

"I didn't even expect you to be able to see him," Hellboy noted.

Ratatosk turned and began to scamper up the branch away from them. The leaves rustled as he went. Hellboy called after him and the squirrel turned and gave him an impatient look that was unsettling coming from a squirrel.

"I have appointments to keep," Ratatosk said crossly.

"You didn't answer my other question."

He glared at Hellboy with tiny eyes. "Where the children of Dain and Dvalin tramp upon his face, there were Thrym's bones interred. Find the body and you will find the soul."

With that, Ratatosk was gone.

Dain and Dvalin. The names were familiar somehow, but he could not figure out from where. He felt as though so many memories and bits of knowledge were just out of reach, and it infuriated him. Aronsson was dead, Pernilla's father had unearthed the soul of Thrym and thrown in with the weasels, and all of these freaks kept showing up to confuse him even more and not really offer any help at all.

A rage simmered within Hellboy. It had been born quiet as a whisper in him and now it began to rise up out of him as though the whisper had become a scream. He shook his head and stamped his hooves on the ground, and though Abe and Pernilla were speaking to him Hellboy did not hear them. He growled at the very air itself, at the mischievously cryptic messenger and the death-maiden Mist, whom he knew still lingered nearby.

Above, the sky went gray, clouds rolling in as if out of nowhere. The air grew thick and moist, and drops of rain began to fall. With a roar, he swung Mjollnir at the huge, ancient tree Ratatosk had scampered up into. Its trunk split as though struck by lightning and a huge portion of the tree cracked off and crashed to the ground beneath the limbs of its brothers.

Not far off, thunder rumbled across the sky.

Hellboy's chest rose and fell in deep, rapid breaths as he stood there, clutching the hammer. Then he blinked several times and took two steps backward, staring at the shattered tree. He glanced around quickly to see if anyone was coming and found Abe and Pernilla staring at him in surprise. There was genuine fear on the young woman's face, and grave concern on Abe's.

"Jeez, Abe," Hellboy said, slightly disoriented as he walked toward his friend. "What the heck's happening to me?"

Pernilla stayed back, but Abe came to him immediately and put a hand on Hellboy's shoulder. The clouds had begun to break up and the sun to burn through once more, but even with that warmth it was Hellboy now who felt cold.

"I don't know for sure," Abe replied. "But something tells me the sooner we get that thing out of your hand, the better."

Both of them turned to look at Pernilla. She seemed

somehow smaller, as though each new revelation caused her to shrink a little bit. All three of them were aware that the only way to put an end to all of this was to find her father, to stop whatever the ghost of Thrym had in mind. To destroy the thing or return it to captivity. What that meant for Edmund Aickman, none of them knew, but neither Hellboy nor Abe was about to start that discussion.

"The squirrel. Did you really understand it?" Pernilla asked.

Hellboy nodded.

"What did it say?"

He glanced at Abe, then up at the tree. Finally he regarded her again, this young woman who had spent her whole life buried in folklore and myth, only to have it come alive around her.

"The names Dain and Dvalin mean anything to you?"

Her eyes narrowed and creases appeared in her brow as she considered it. She whispered the names to herself a couple of times, and then her eyebrows shot up.

"Yes. There are four of them, actually. Dain, Dvalin, Duneyr, and Durathror. They're harts. Enormous ones, of course. Several myths claim they live around Yggdrasil, the world tree, nibbling at its branches."

Abe raised his hand tentatively. "Um, hearts?"

"Harts. Male deer," Pernilla explained.

"Ah," Abe said, a sheepish look on his face. "Got it. I think I knew that once, but I forgot. You remember what a doe is 'cause of the song. But not a hart."

"The song?" Pernilla asked, confused.

"Doe, a deer, a female deer?" Abe offered, just a little bit of the melody in his delivery.

Pernilla smiled at that, and some of the color returned to her cheeks. Hellboy was pleased to see it, but he was not paying very much attention to their exchange. *Where the children of Dain and Dvalin tramp upon his face, there were Thrym's bones interred,* those had been Ratatosk's words. The children of harts.

"You have a zoo here?" Hellboy asked. "In Stockholm?"

"A zoo?" she asked slowly, obviously confounded by his change in topic. "Well, not like the one in Copenhagen. If you really want to see a zoo, that would be—"

"That's not what I meant," Hellboy interrupted.

Abe stuffed his hands into his jacket pockets. "Good. 'Cause I remember the last time we went to the zoo in Copenhagen. The necromancer and that thing with the penguin heads? I'll die happy if I never have to go back there again."

"We're not going to the zoo," Hellboy snapped. Again the anger had risen in him, the readiness to spill blood that was so foreign to him. He took a breath and let the moment pass. "I could use a beer."

"Or, apparently, a cup of mead," Abe replied dryly.

Hellboy nodded slowly. "Sorry. All I want to know is, if I wanted to find a bunch of deer in Stockholm, where would I go?"

Once upon a time, Djurgården had been the hunting ground for the king of Sweden. A vast forest stretched across most of this island that made up the southeastern portion of Stockholm. A single bridge on the northern tip connected it to the rest of the city. It housed a great many museums and other historical buildings, and was among the primary tourist attractions in that glorious capital. But there were still oak groves dense enough that only the occasional band of hikers braved those woods, where the king's deer still ran.

That much, at least, they had learned from Pernilla while still at the university. She had offered to let them continue to stay at her father's house on Gamla Stan, and they had wanted to bring their bags from the university office where the late Professor Aronsson had held onto them. But all three of them had a sense of urgency now, and did not relish the idea of returning to Gamla Stan before driving out to Djurgården. Abe spoke to Klar and asked him to see to the bags until they returned for them; Hellboy would have gone in to speak to the man but he was afraid he might crush the little fascist's skull with Mjollnir.

Klar had reluctantly agreed, and they set off.

Most of the drive to Djurgården was made in silence. Pernilla turned on the radio for a while. It did not bother Hellboy at all, but there was only so much Swedish pop Abe could put up with, and he asked her to turn it off after a quarter of an hour or so.

A narrow strait separated the island from the rest of the city, and even as the car traveled across the bridge the forest appeared lush and green, beautiful ancient oaks that swallowed them up the moment they reached Djurgården.

"If I was gonna bury the corpse of a giant frost monster, this is where I'd do it," Hellboy said archly as he gazed out the window.

"It does seem strange that they would have buried him here," Abe said. "Not the location. I mean, here."

Pernilla kept her hands on the wheel, her eyes on the road. "Midgard. The human realm."

Abe nodded. "Yeah."

"Maybe not so strange," Hellboy mused. Flashes of memory, savage bits of history, ricocheted around inside his head, and none of them were his own. "This was their dumping ground. Our world. Landfill of the gods. And who knows what might have spilled over into this place when the crap hit the fan for them? The Nidavellim and the Svartalves . . . who knows what else is still around?"

The interior of the car was silent again after that. They drove along for several minutes and then Pernilla began to slow.

"What's wrong?" Abe asked.

"Nothing. I am just not sure where to go from here. There are several places where we are more likely to find deer than others, but how do we know where to look? We could wander until nightfall and only have begun to search."

Abe sat forward and peered around the seat at Hellboy. "Anything?"

Feeling foolish and self-conscious, Hellboy closed his eyes and tried to decide if he felt any sort of tug as he had above the Arctic circle, when some unknown force had led him to the cave where the Tankard of Thrym had been kept. Mjollnir seemed to tremble in his grasp, and it felt warm, even warmer than usual. But as to direction, there was none.

"Nothing," he said. "Sorry. I don't know what to—"

He opened his eyes, and he saw the ravens. They circled in the air off to the southwest, quite a ways away.

Hellboy pointed. "That way."

"You're sure?"

"No."

Pernilla took the next right, and they continued along an ever narrowing road until it began to loop back toward the east. A small path led into the wood from there, but a security chain was hung across the entrance. Hellboy assumed it was a passage meant for park rangers, or whatever the equivalent was in Sweden, but he did not spend very much time thinking about it. He climbed out of the car and snapped the chain off one of the posts with a single tug. Pernilla drove into the trees over a rutted, unpaved little road, and when the car was out of sight of the street, she pulled over and turned off the engine.

With Abe's help, Hellboy was able to get the chain strung again. It wouldn't hold up to inspection, but it was not going to draw attention, either.

As they began to walk down the path, which became more overgrown with every step, Hellboy heard a cawing above and glanced up. The ravens were impossibly large and sat opposite one another on thick tree limbs on either side of the path. For a long moment Hellboy stared at them, waiting to see if they would offer any other guidance. They did not.

"What?" Abe asked, coming up beside him.

Hellboy shook his head. "Nothing." A rustle of leaves and heavy wings came from above and he did not need to look up to know they had gone.

"You realize you are completely freaking me out," Abe told him.

"Sorry," Hellboy replied, and then he set off along the path again with Pernilla and Abe in tow.

The woods were dense and silent save for the rustle of the breeze in the leaves and the occasional sound of something moving in among the trees. Mjollnir still trembled in his hand, although the intensity of its quavering seemed to wax and wane.

The path ended and they kept walking, and perhaps an hour after parking the car, Hellboy came to realize that

the modulation in the humming sort of charge in Mjollnir might not be simple chance. He tested that theory by striking off several times from a central location and noting the subtle difference in the hammer's quiver. Once before he had thought of it as a sort of tuning fork. Now that impression came to him again. He just had to find the right frequency.

"What are we doing?" Abe asked.

"This way," Hellboy told him, ignoring the question.

Behind him, as he struck off into the woods, he could hear Abe and Pernilla talking. They were hungry and Pernilla in particular was quite tired. Hellboy did not blame them, but it had long since become early evening and in a few hours it would be dark. He intended to find what they were looking for before nightfall.

The forest floor was rutted and veined with thick roots and stones in some places. In others it was carpeted with a light grass that presented a tempting invitation to rest. Hellboy kept on. There was no further sign of the ravens and no further appearance by Ratatosk, but the thrum that passed through the hammer had grown so strong that his hand shook.

Twenty minutes after they set off in pursuit of his frequency theory, a deer crashed through the woods off to their left, running in the opposite direction. With the trees blocking much of their view, Hellboy could only get the vaguest impression of the thing's size, but he thought it had been rather large.

They all paused and stared after it.

"You do realize that was the first deer we've seen in here?" Abe ventured.

Before either Hellboy or Pernilla could respond, two more of them bounded through the forest off to their right. One of them paused a moment. In the shade from the canopy of branches above, it looked almost unreal, a part of the forest. Its wide black eyes studied them. Then, as suddenly as it had stopped, it ran on again.

"What are they running away from?" Pernilla asked.

Hellboy raised his left hand. "Wait. Listen."

A low hum seemed to build and roll toward them across the forest floor like slow, rhythmic thunder. It lifted and fell, sometimes harsh and others sweet and high. Slowly, quietly, Hellboy started forward again. After several more minutes of winding their way amongst the trees, his suspicion was confirmed.

It was chanting.

Mjollnir seemed now to pulse in time with its rhythm.

Though the night could not possibly have fallen, it

seemed to grow darker there in the woods of the Djurgården. The branches above threw the forest into darkness, save for slashes of sunlight that seemed only to make the landscape more unnervingly surreal.

Slowly, as quietly as they could, Hellboy, Abe, and Pernilla moved forward. Hellboy kept low, as most of the trees were not thick enough to hide him. As he crouched by a broad oak trunk, Abe tapped him on the shoulder and pointed upward.

The tree he squatted by had no leaves on its branches. It was dead. Hellboy craned his neck back to see that most of the trees ahead were also dead, their bark gray and split, little more than wooden skeletons.

Carefully they moved closer, sliding from tree to tree. Pernilla hung back, more cautious than the guys, afraid to give them away, though she was probably the stealthiest among them.

Hellboy froze, then, Abe only a few feet away, standing behind another tree. There was a small clearing ahead, not very large at all, but several dozen Svartalves were gathered there, kneeling upon the ground. Within a ring of stones a fire burned, tendrils of flame licking the air. The sky seemed to darken even further, and Hellboy wondered if that was magic or if the weather had changed, if there was a storm coming in.

With a whisper of motion, Pernilla crouched down behind Hellboy and tried to look past him at the chanting Svartalves. At the opposite end of the clearing, beneath the bare branches of a dead oak, Edmund Aickman stood with the Tankard of Thrym at his feet and a dagger in his hand. The old man seemed more withered than before, as though there was little more to him now than bones and shriveled skin, wisps of hair on his head. And yet there was nothing frail about him. His presence was somehow imposing and regal, and he stood calm and grave as he drew the blade across his palm, and his blood ran off his skin and splashed the ground. Most of it was caught by the tankard.

Aickman raised it and tipped it back, drinking his own blood.

Behind Hellboy, Pernilla hissed air into her lungs but said nothing. He thought she might have whimpered. Hellboy turned to gaze at her, raised his left hand, and lifted her chin. Pernilla's eyes were rimmed with red and tears streamed down her face. Her black hair hung down, framing her misery.

Damn it. We shouldn't have brought her, he thought. He had known it, of course, but how could they not have? They needed her knowledge of the area and her expertise as a folklorist. And, if he were truthful with himself, Hellboy had also hoped that she could somehow get through to her father. He still hoped it.

Despite the guilt he felt, he cupped her chin. "We need you," he whispered. "You and Abe are going to have to get to your father. If he's rational, fine. If not, he'll have to be restrained while we get him out of here, figure out if he's under Thrym's influence, and, if he is, how to help him. While you two are getting to him, I'm going to keep the Svartalves away from you."

Pernilla nodded slowly and glanced over at Abe. He gave her a grim thumbs up, careful not to make any noise.

Out in the clearing, the chanting halted abruptly. Hellboy glanced quickly around, afraid they had been heard, but the Svartalves were still focused on the task at hand. Each of them laid their swords across their oily hands and flayed open their flesh. Blood the color of rust dripped and ran and spattered to the ground, and the soil soaked it up greedily.

The chanting started again.

"All right," Hellboy said quickly, dropping his voice even lower, to a ghost of a whisper. "Let's hurry before they finish whatever malarkey they're trying to pull now."

He stood up, unmindful now of being seen. His heart thundered in his chest as the anticipation of the battle washed over him. He raised Mjollnir and started around the tree and across the clearing.

With a lurch, the ground began to shake, a tremor reverberating through the earth beneath them. Hellboy staggered backward, his hooves punching dirt. Abe and Pernilla held onto one another.

An enormous crevasse opened in the center of the clearing. The Svartalves scrabbled away from the crack in the earth, some of them stumbling, thrown off their feet by the tremor. More cracks appeared, smaller, beneath the dead trees.

Hellboy grabbed hold of a tree as the ground bucked and shifted under him. Not far from where he stood, dirt flew and was scattered across the ground by some sort of eruption.

A giant, skeletal hand, little more than intricate bone structure and dry, flaking strips of flesh, thrust from the earth and grasped at the sky.

CHAPTER NINE

The ground bucked and heaved, and Hellboy listed across the clearing as though it were the deck of a ship. His hooves punched loosened dirt and his momentum became too much for him, the extra weight of the enormous war hammer in his right hand making it impossible for him to regain his balance. The forest floor convulsed, rose as though a hill were being born from the womb of the earth, and a skeletal knee shot up through the dirt. Hellboy fell and began to roll down this newly formed hill, even as the rest of that leg broke free.

He tumbled end over end and slammed into a monstrous, skeletal arm that had thrust from the earth. It stank of fresh-turned graves and gardens left to rot. But along its length were also patches of icy frost, places where strips of flesh were still attached.

Across the clearing, a second hand erupted from the ground, and the entire forest seemed to rumble with the strain of the giant cadaver attempting to wrest itself from the clutches of its ancient grave.

In Hellboy's grip, Mjollnir burned enough to sear even that stone-like right hand. Against his chest, the serpent pendant was cold enough to sting his flesh. *Seconds,* he thought. *We were too late by seconds.* Now the question was, what was he going to be able to do about it?

He knelt, left hand against the ground to steady himself, and slowly rose. The ground still rumbled but he managed to stay upright. Fifteen feet away, the skull of the giant had begun to emerge from the soil. Sunlight slashed through the canopy of trees above and gleamed off smooth bone.

Hellboy raised Mjollnir.

As one, the Svartalves uttered an ear-piercing shriek of rage and then they began to come for him. Like spiders they scrambled across the uncertain ground, swords clutched carefully in their fists. Not spiders, though. Weasels. Their oily skin and dark clothing only lent to the illusion as they rushed at him. Suddenly there seemed to be more of them than he had noticed before, and he wondered if they had been lurking in the trees or out beyond the clearing. Twenty, perhaps thirty of the Svartalves bounded toward him.

With a cry of battle in an ancient tongue he did not even understand, he swung Mjollnir at the nearest of them. The hammer shattered its skull and it fell. Sword and corpse alike were swallowed up by the undulating ground.

Hellboy staggered back as a fissure opened in the earth. His tail snapped out and crippled a Svartalf. With his left hand he grappled for the gun in its holster at his side. Talons slashed at his fingers, scrabbled at his waist, and the gun was torn out of his grasp. He spun, kicked a hoof up to cave in the chest of a Svartalf, and then brought the hammer around in an arc that tore two of them apart in a spatter of inky mist.

In his mind he ticked through an inventory of the various things he had in the pouches on his belt. Talismans and wards, holy water, religious icons, several shuriken, and a couple of incendiary grenades. He had no idea if any of the magical artifacts would help, but the incendiary grenades would come in damned handy. One of the weasels leaped upon his back and another hung onto his right arm, trying to hold Mjollnir back. They threw themselves at his legs.

Searing hot in his hand, Mjollnir fell and the Svartalves were like nothing more than brittle, hollow shells. That black mist poured from them and they dissipated, leaving no corpses behind. Hellboy reached for the pouch at his left hip, inside of which were the two incendiary grenades he'd pocketed before this mission began. Even as he did, he glanced around, hoping to spot his gun in the midst of the tremors and the rush of Svartalves.

Swords whickered through the air. They cut his hand and he pulled it back from the pouch. A blade slashed his lower back and he arched it. A roar of fury swept through him and he tore the Svartalf from his back and tossed it at several others. One of them hacked at it with his sword, out of reflex.

Hellboy laughed loudly, triumphantly, a cruel bellow. It embarrassed him, for he had no idea where the laugh had come from. Then a wave of them swept upon him again. He was slashed and cut and he raised Mjollnir, but there were too many. The earth buckled and shifted violently under him, and again he lost his balance. He went down hard and they were upon him. A blade thrust into his side and he growled and arched his back, threw off several of the weasels.

A gunshot cut through the loud groaning of the shifting earth. *Abe*, Hellboy thought. He wanted to look around, to check on his friend and the Aickman woman. But another of the weasels lashed itself to his face and began to claw him.

"Hellboy!" shouted a gravelly voice.

It wasn't Abe. Hellboy tore the weasel off his face and rose to his feet, hammer swinging. He licked his thin lips and tasted his own blood from the cuts on his forehead and cheeks and glanced around. Perhaps three feet away, Eitri stood with a dagger in each hand. As Hellboy caught sight of him, the Nidavellim with the patch of stubble on his chin stabbed a Svartalf from behind even as he lashed out and cut the throat of another.

An unearthly howl split the air and suddenly Brokk was leaping out from the trees beyond the clearing, a hammer raised in both hands. His war hammer came down and crushed one of the weasels. A cold wind kicked up and loose dirt was swept into the air, blew into their eyes. Hellboy wiped at his face, swung the hammer again, and shrugged off the creatures.

Brokk and Eitri weren't alone. With an ululating war cry, five other Nidavellim charged into the clearing with swords, double-sided axes, even spears. Hellboy felt a surge of pride within him, a siren song of glory that raced through him like adrenaline.

"Destroy them!" he roared in the old tongue.

As the weapons fell and the Nidavellim and Svartalves clashed, he frowned. The ground had ceased its motion. For a moment he was almost thrown off balance by the sudden stillness of the earth. He staggered two steps as the dwarves and Svartalves battled around him, and then he looked across the clearing.

Thrym's left arm and right hand were free. The skeletal remains of the frost giant's legs were partially visible, jutting up from the earth with volcanic newness. They were completely still.

The giant's skull was free of the ground. Strands of hair and beard still were tethered to it, but otherwise it was all bone and enormous picket-fence teeth, some of them yellow and pitted. Loose earth spilled across that bony chin. In the hollow shadows of its eye sockets, twin lights burned a sickly yellow that spoke of dark tunnels and rotting corpses and madness.

As Hellboy stared at that horrible face, ice began to form on the skull, a slick coating that leaked from those eyes and spread like mercury across bone and fang.

And it hissed. "Thunderer." Its voice was like the outrush of fetid air upon the opening of some ancient crypt.

"Yeah, I'm here," Hellboy replied. One of the weasels slashed its sword at his chest, and he split it in two with the war hammer, then stared at the tainted yellow eyes of the giant again. "You want some?"

With a roar that was more a whisper, a throaty, gargled

rasp, the bones of the frost giant again bucked from beneath the earth. There were loud cracks and pops and Thrym planted his huge, skeletal fingers, each nearly the length of one of Hellboy's arms, into the ground. Then the corpse of the frost king hauled himself up out of the earth with a single thrust.

The darkling creatures that warred and slashed and drew blood atop his grave cried out and tumbled off and away from the clearing as he rose, tall as the trees. The soil began to slide back into the grave, and some of them were drawn down, under the earth, turned with the maggots that had feasted on the giant for millennia. Hellboy was nearly drawn down as well, but he leaped up and grabbed the limbs of one of the dead trees that had stood sparse and alone in that clearing.

The tree was young by comparison, though still hundreds of years old, and its roots had grown down and twined into the ribcage of the giant. It was not the only one, either. So when Thrym stood, dirt showered down around him but three trees remained, jutting like killing arrows from his skeletal chest, roots wound up in the bones, so bleached and gray that it was almost impossible to know what was bone and what was wood.

Hellboy hung inside the branches of one of those trees and did his best not to fall. Beneath him he saw Abe and Pernilla at the edges of the enormous hole that had been Thrym's grave. Abe had his pistol out, Pernilla behind him. The Nidavellim and Svartalves who had survived kept up their melee.

And thirty feet from Abe, old, white-haired Edmund Aickman held the Tankard of Thrym up in both hands and giggled like a child.

"Abe!" Hellboy roared. "Get the Tankard!"

Which was when the skeleton began to laugh and reach

its bony fingers to the tree upon his chest, trying to pluck Hellboy loose.

"Abe, please!" Pernilla cried. "You have to save my father. Get him out of here!"

The pistol felt heavy in Abe's hand. He felt a little ridiculous trying to protect Pernilla with all the nasties around. There were so many of them, and Thrym . . . they did not even understand yet how the bones had been revived, how to reverse the process. This was all in Hellboy's hands now. If he couldn't destroy the skeleton, they were in big trouble.

The Svartalves were vicious, and he had shot two of them already. One of the few things the Bureau insisted upon doing with agents, even unusual ones such as himself, was teaching them how to properly care for and fire a sidearm. He had had many occasions, over the years, to be glad of that. This was one of them.

Get the Tankard! Hellboy had shouted. As if it were that simple. But he had to try.

"Come on," he told Pernilla.

The wind had grown colder still, and frost seemed to drift like snow down around the clearing. Abe realized it was flaking off the bones, chips of ice whipping on the breeze.

"How can this kind of power be left in his remains?" Pernilla asked, shouting over the hiss of the giant and the screams of battle from the darkling creatures.

"Don't know," Abe replied. The gun was in his right hand and with his left he pulled her into a run. They skirted the edges of the enormous grave, working their way in and out of half-uprooted trees, feet driving into loose soil, and circling around toward her father.

Aickman held the Tankard up above his head, staring up at it as if making an offering to his god. Abe realized that in some ways that was exactly what he was doing. The old man didn't even seem to notice how withered he had become, like some pitiful, weathered scarecrow. It was as though the Tankard was supporting him, as though he dangled from it there in the unnatural wind that swept through the Djurgården, and without it he would be blown away like some dried husk of a thing.

"The Tankard's at the center of it," Abe told Pernilla. "Not to mention that little blood ritual the Svartalves just did."

"But if drinking from the Tankard allowed Thrym to possess my father . . . what is the point of resurrecting this empty corpse?" Pernilla asked.

The horror and confusion in her voice galvanized Abe to further action. He was not a fool, not going to do anything stupid, but in that moment he would have given anything to spare the woman all of this. Nothing good could come of it. She was being torn apart inside, and all because her father was a greedy, mischievous old bastard. Whatever terror she faced, whatever impossible evils strode the earth before her eyes, Abe suspected that at the core of her, Pernilla Aickman would be most deeply scarred by this truth about her father. Whether she acknowledged what he was or not, she could not fail to see it.

For it was right in front of her.

When Pernilla screamed his name, Abe glanced back

and saw that several of the Svartalves had broken away from their battle with the Nidavellim and given chase. *Trying to stop us from reaching Aickman,* Abe thought.

He stopped short, boots skidding on the loose dirt, nearly stumbling on an exposed root.

"Get that Tankard," he told Pernilla. "No matter what happens, that's the key." Then he leveled the pistol and pulled the trigger. He shot the first one through the head and the second one twice in the chest, but even as they melted into the air in a sifting black fog, the third was upon him. Abe fired at it, but the bullet went wild, and the Svartalf slashed down with its sword.

He ducked away, dove for the ground, gun hand trapped beneath him. Even as he rolled over, trying to pull the gun up again, he knew he was too late. He saw the slick, oily skin of the Svartalf and it occurred to him that Hellboy was wrong. These things weren't weasels. They reminded Abe more of seals with that glistening sheen about them. Its eyes narrowed, and it grinned cruelly and brought the blade down.

A spear thrust through its chest from behind, shattering bone and tearing flesh. The sword fell as the Svartalf dissipated. Behind it stood a dwarf with iron rings in its hair and beard and a deep scar on its face that had left it blind in one, white, rheumy eye.

"Thanks," Abe said, leaping to his feet.

The Nidavellim offered a curt half-bow, then raced back toward its fellows with the spear in both hands.

There came a cry of such heartrending despair that Abe at first thought Pernilla had been killed. When he spun around he saw that she was uninjured, for the moment, but whatever attempts she had made to speak to her father had failed, for she was on the forest floor with the old man, grappling with him for the Tankard. Even as Abe watched, the professor used his unnatural strength to break her grip and strike his daughter with a backhand that echoed through the clearing.

"Damn it," Abe muttered.

Then he ran for them, trying to figure out how he was going to stop Aickman from hurting Pernilla without having to shoot the old man in front of his daughter.

Thrym's breath was like a blizzard. Horns of ice had formed upon his bare skull and the jaws of the dead thing screeched like carrion birds as they opened wide. The frost king raised Hellboy up in one bony hand and tried to drop him into its gaping maw. A mouthful of swords opened and though there was no gullet, no stomach for him to eat with, this soulless shell of Thrym tried to eat Hellboy.

"Not a freakin' chance," Hellboy snarled.

With a thrust of one hoof, he cracked one of the monstrous skeleton's fingers. It gave him space, and that was all he needed. He clutched his left arm around the giant's unbroken fingers and swung Mjollnir, dangling above those razor-picket teeth. The hammer shattered several of those teeth and shards of bone and ice flew. A piece of Thrym's jaw broke off.

It shuddered as if more surprised than hurt, and the foul glow of yellow in the dead orbits of that skull glared down at him. Hellboy felt frozen suddenly, and he glanced around to find that ice had begun to form all over his body. He kicked out, thrust out his arms, and the ice shattered. A few more seconds and it might have enveloped him. Already it was growing across the skull, reconstructing more of a face over the bone.

Again Hellboy lashed out, cracking the ice tendrils that seemed to be growing like vines across his legs and back.

Another finger cracked, and then he was falling from Thrym's hand. For a moment the world turned upside down and his stomach lurched. Hellboy flailed at the air, the weight of the hammer tipping him downward, and as he tumbled he caught sight of the huge grave yawning open beneath him.

Then he struck the limbs of one of the trees that jutted from Thrym's ribcage. Not the same one, this was larger. Branches cracked and snapped off, and dead limbs scraped against his arms and chest. Though disoriented, Hellboy lunged, reached out with his left hand, and grabbed a thick branch near the trunk.

It broke.

"Gaaa!" he shouted in surprise and frustration.

But then the broken branch swung him down into the fork of the tree trunk, and, though the wood creaked loudly, and despite its age, it held. He heard more gunshots below and swore under his breath, gritting his teeth as he slid around in the joint where the trunk was split. His jacket snagged on some outer branches, and they snapped as he tugged it free.

"That's it," he muttered. "I'm all outta patience."

With a grunt of exertion, he pulled himself up on top of the horizontal tree trunk. Thrym stood in place and gazed around at the ravaged clearing, at the Svartalves and Nidavellim in combat. His yellow eyes glowed with menace as he scanned the ground carefully, but slowly, as though he were drunk or just stupid. Hellboy voted for stupid.

Though true dark was still some small way off, the night was coming on, evening crawling across the sky with a bank of clouds thick enough that the day had surrendered early. With the flecks of frost falling like snow in the clearing and the frigid wind that swirled around the resurrected giant, it was as though winter had arrived early.

Hellboy knelt on the trunk and crawled along it to where it met the giant's ribcage, where the roots disappeared into the skeleton, twined with bones, wooden tendrils wrapped around ribs and wound like vines all the way back to Thrym's spine.

"You should have stayed dead, old king!" Hellboy roared in the ancient tongue.

He stood up on the trunk of the tree just as Thrym began to move. The giant lifted his huge, skeletal feet and stepped carefully in the ruined earth. Hellboy grabbed hold of one of Thrym's ribs to keep his balance. Those empty sockets with their sickly flames flickering gazed down at him, and Thrym paused. Again he reached up to try to pluck Hellboy from his chest, as if the giant had almost forgotten he was there.

"Uh-uh, Spanky," he snarled, in his own language this time, and with all the pique he could summon. "You're sleepwalking out here, and you're not gonna get me twice. Time for you to go back to that little eternity dirt nap."

Clinging to the giant's rib, he raised Mjollnir. "Or didn't you see the freakin' hammer?"

Hellboy swung it down and the war hammer struck the precise spot where the roots of the tree met the frost king's ribcage. There came a series of cracks, one upon the other, like cannon fire, as tree trunk and roots and two of Thrym's ribs snapped.

The long dead king of the Frost Giants opened its mouth of swords and uttered a shriek of pain that was like a ghost itself, not a wail so much as the crashing of surf against the shore. Thrym reared back, the ice cracking where it had formed upon its skeletal arms, trying to connect the bones the way tendons and muscle should have.

Hellboy fell with the shattered tree and two long shards of the giant's ribs. Much as he tried he could not right himself in the fall, and so he struck the ground on his back at such an angle that if it were not that the earth had been so churned up by the disturbance of Thrym's grave, he would probably have broken his neck.

Groaning, Hellboy rolled onto his stomach and tried to push himself up to his knees. His vision was slightly blurred, and he knew he had struck his head. He shook it and blinked, and waited for his eyes to focus. When they did he frowned. The object in front of him was familiar, but he had been so jarred that, as though waking from a particularly fantastical dream, it took him a few seconds to recognize it.

His gun. "Look at that. Sometimes luck does run my way."

He stood up, hurried toward the gun—not that it would do any good against Thrym, but he was glad he had not lost it—and picked it up. As he slid it into its holster, he turned, thinking to try to get Abe and the Aickmans to safety and then come back at Thrym when they were safely out of harm's way. He'd come back and just shatter the giant's kneecaps, use Mjollnir to cut him down to size. Remind him he was supposed to be dead. Unfortunately, Hellboy had always found that reasoning with dead guys was pretty much a fool's game.

He spotted Abe across the clearing, saw a skirmish on the ground and realized it was Pernilla Aickman wrestling with her father. Hellboy shuddered at the macabre sight. Then he heard a grunt and a shout of pain off to his left, and he turned just in time to see one of the Nidavellim fall dead at his feet, torso sliced open from groin to gullet.

Then the Svartalves were upon him again. The dark things moved like shadows now as the clearing became darker, and they chittered like vermin as they came at him. Fewer, this time, and some of the Nidavellim still lived to oppose them. But even three or four of the weasels were enough to distract Hellboy in that moment, and he could not afford the interruption.

"You . . . try . . . my patience, Thunderer," Thrym rumbled, words like cracks in ice.

The enormous skeleton bent down then, bony fingers lunging toward the ground where Pernilla Aickman grappled with her father. Abe swore loudly and fired several rounds at the giant's face, but the bullets scraped bone and either lodged there or ricocheted.

"Abe! Grab her!" Hellboy roared, knocking aside one of the Svartalves and starting to run across the clearing toward them.

But he need not have worried. Abe grabbed hold of Pernilla and hauled her to her feet, then the two of them dove between two tall, lush oaks just as the skeletal fingers of the giant closed around Edmund Aickman. The old man cackled madly, shouting in Dutch, as he raised the Tankard up toward the giant's deadly, jagged maw. Thrym laughed, lifted the shriveled little man higher, and shook him with hideous glee.

The Tankard fell to the ground and all of the combatants there in the ravaged wood froze and stared at it a moment. Abe shouted at Hellboy to get it, but before he could even move Thrym stepped on the Tankard, driving it into the soil.

The icy horns on the giant were mere silhouettes now against the bruise-dark clouds in the evening sky. Thrym raised Aickman up, opened his jaws, and simply inhaled with the scream of a driving snow. The old folklorist had been looking around madly, scrambling, trying to figure out how he had dropped the Tankard. Now he stared up at the skull of the frost king and screamed.

And as he screamed, his eye exploded, sucked into the waiting maw of the dead giant. Then a stream of snow and sleet poured out of Aickman's mouth and his vacant eye sockets and his nostrils. It was as though the old man were vomiting ice into the giant's mouth.

Thrym laughed, and suddenly the voice was deeper. It shook the ground and reverberated in Hellboy's chest. The blaze in the empty sockets of the giant's eyes had turned from tainted yellow to blinding blue-white.

"Now," Thrym boomed. "We shall see what my kingdom has become."

He dropped Professor Aickman to the ground and something snapped in the brittle old man as he landed. Pernilla wailed and wept and Abe held her back.

“No!” Hellboy shouted.

Slowly, with a creak of bones and ice—ice that even now began to cover more of the giant’s body, filling in the gaps between his bones—Thrym turned to glance down at him again.

“Not now, Thunderer. But when I am ready for you, then we will have the battle so long denied us. And I will freeze your blood and strip your bones.”

“Yeah? Where do you think you’re going?” Hellboy called. He raised Mjollnir. “You woke up for this fight? Come on and get it, then!”

Thrym laughed again. "I did not rise for you. But you stand in the way. So you shall die. Soon. When my kingdom is whole again and my brothers bow down before me."

With that, Thrym turned and lurched through the trees. Where before he had been moving with almost painful slowness, now he was swift. Hellboy screamed and ran after him, hooves punching the loose soil. He lost his footing once but did not fall. By the time he had reached the opposite side of the clearing, there was only the distant pounding of the giant's footsteps to reveal his location. And even those sounds were receding.

Thrym was gone.

Hellboy turned and stared across the clearing again. Some of the Nidavellim still lived, but he could not see if Brokk and Eitri were among them. The Svartalves were gone, having scattered into the forest in pursuit of their master. On the other side of that massive grave, amidst a scattering of fallen ice shavings that lay across the ground like snow, Abe stood with one hand on Pernilla Aickman's shoulder, where she knelt by the broken form of her father and cried.

Mjollnir felt heavy in Hellboy's grip, as though it longed to destroy something, to shatter bone and crush skull.

"All right," Hellboy growled. "Now I'm really ticked."

CHAPTER TEN

The breeze had turned warm. Above the clearing, now devoid of trees, the sky had seemed low and gray only moments before. Now it was crystal clear, a deep blue velvet night scattered with pinprick stars. At the edges of that ravaged land where a dead myth had risen as a monster, had been born and torn from the earth, snow still lingered on the leaves of oak trees.

Melting snow. It dripped and slid down leaves and fell in wet slaps from limbs to the ground. In minutes, it would be gone. And as the thin shroud of snow withered to nothing, the life began to go out of Edmund Aickman.

Pernilla knelt on the ground, dampness soaking through her pants, and held her father's head propped upon her lap. He hardly seemed himself now, and she had to fight back a feeling of revulsion that swept through her. Part of her did not want to touch him, did not want to allow that this man might be her father. The skin of his face was slack and jowled like an old dog, folded and newly smooth, save for where the white stubble had grown on his chin.

In her arms his body felt like paper and bones, and something broke when she settled him down there on her lap with a sound not unlike a piece of chalk being snapped in two. The breeze rustled what little remained of his hair, not much more than spiderwebs now. His eyes were shot through with red from broken blood vessels and dark circles sagged beneath them.

He stared up at her, but she did not think he could see her.

At first she called to him in Swedish, and then in Danish, and finally she only whispered the kind of hushed nothings that one utters to calm a child, or to comfort the dying.

Pernilla was aware of those around her, of course, just as she was aware of the flutter of birds' wings above. Abe stood behind her, one hand on her shoulder, a silent comfort, lending her his strength. She could not imagine what it was like to go through life in this world looking like he looked, knowing he was not human. Yet in so many ways he was far more human than most of the people she had known in her life.

Across the clearing, Hellboy stood and gazed off in the direction Thrym had fled. Pernilla had glanced up at him only once, but there was something about the way he held himself there in the starlight that seemed different, even in the few days since they had met. There were no words from him now, neither to soothe her grief nor to lighten her spirit. As far as she knew, he had never been boisterous. Now he was grim and silent.

Several yards from where she knelt with her father, the Nidavellim were down on one knee, heads bowed out of respect for her, as an acknowledgement of those among them who had died and of the death that was about to occur. She flinched as the thought crossed her mind, but it was inescapable. Her father was about to die.

He gazed up at her with damp eyes, but there was no focus there, no indication that he actually saw her. The warm breeze blew her lush raven hair across her face, but Pernilla shivered with the chill that came from within her. Her skin felt tight and her eyes burned with tears that she tried to force away. Her belly ached as though someone had punched her there repeatedly, and her throat closed up, her mouth dry.

She pinched her lips together and fought the urge to run away, to flee from what was happening right there before her eyes. She could not do that to him, could not leave him when he most needed her to be there for him. So she cradled his head in her lap and stroked his face, and she began to croon to him, high and sweet, voice cracking with emotion, unmindful of the others who gathered near her in the clearing.

Images flashed through her mind, the sorts of moments from her childhood that she supposed most people had. This bruise or that scrape, her father cooing to her and kissing it better. Reading to her in that deep, sonorous voice as she drifted off to sleep. Carrying her on his shoulders through the streets of

Gamla Stan, into shops where everyone seemed to know him and want to give her a candy or ruffle her hair. But intermingled with those were other memories, of accompanying him to libraries and lectures and to exotic locales all over the world where one artifact or another might be unearthed. The thrill of discovery, the search for the truth in history.

Yet all along, he had held within him the avarice that had led to this day, the greed that had caused him to betray Hellboy those years ago. A seed of dark desire within him that had been represented for decades by the large hole through the center of his hand, the one burned there when he tried to claim the gold of King Vold. But even that horrid reminder had not been enough to prevent him from falling victim to his greed again. Edmund Aickman had taken a draught from the Tankard of Thrym out of his lust for power and wealth, and by doing so he had invited evil into his body. It had drained him, leeched the life from his body, far too powerful for his frail human shell to contain. Now it was going to kill him.

And he had no one to blame but himself.

Pernilla could not stem the tide of bitter tears that streamed down her cheeks. She could taste them as they traced the edges of her lips. Her father, she had only recently learned, was not a good man. But despite his failings, he had been a good father, and to her, that mattered so much more.

She whispered to him again and he began to shiver and to murmur something, and just in case he was speaking to her, Pernilla lowered her ear to his lips. It was gibberish, though, nonsense words, or else a language she had never heard before.

His breath was warm against her ear.

Then he twitched, once, and his breath came no more.

"Oh, God, Daddy," she sighed, chest hitching as though she would also cease to breathe. She spoke the words in Swedish, but Abe seemed to understand, for at that moment his hand slipped off her shoulder and he took a step back from her.

For long minutes there was only silence. She hung her head and wept fiercely. After a time, Pernilla stood and let her father's body slump to the damp ground. When she looked around she saw that all of the snow—the impossible frost that had swept down upon them—was gone, as if it had never happened at all, as if this dead, towering evil had not thrust itself up out of the earth. But it had, and the grave it had left behind was there as testament, even if she had not seen it herself.

Abe stood just a few feet away. His wide eyes seemed damp as well, and she wondered if he had cried for her, cried for her father, despite what the man had done. The gills fluttered at his neck and she knew she ought to be repulsed by him. Instead she felt only grateful.

Hellboy had come up behind Abe while she was not looking, and he stood there now, stoic and apparently unmoved. That was not fair, she knew. His features were severe, and she had not known him long enough to read the limited range of expressions he seemed to have. Pernilla walked toward them, barely sparing a glance for the Nidavellim nearby. They were impossible creatures, but it had been a day for the impossible, several days in fact. She felt a rush of contempt for them, and though they had helped, in her mind she lumped them together with the Svartalves and with Thrym, these darkling beasts out of myth.

They didn't belong in this world, and they had cost her father his life.

No, she thought. *He brought it on himself.* She had to keep reminding herself of that. But it did not assuage her burning hatred for Thrym. Not at all.

"Where did he go?" she asked, glancing from Hellboy to Abe, and then back again.

Hellboy shrugged. "No idea. North. Other than that, he moved too fast for me to follow. I'm sorry."

Pernilla nodded, jaw set. She wiped her hands across her stinging eyes. There were no tears left to weep, not tonight. But she was certain there would be more.

"Thrym shouldn't be hard to track," Abe told her. "It's early yet. People are going to notice him."

"Only until he gets far enough north," she replied. "And if he can swim, he could get out of the city unnoticed. Where do you think he's going?"

Abe glanced at Hellboy with what might have been a frown. His features were hard to read as well. Hellboy glanced down at the war hammer fused to his hand and shrugged.

"I don't know. I . . . I'm not getting any intuition on it." Hellboy shifted uncomfortably on the churned earth and turned to gaze at the two Nidavellim who were in front, the same two who had guarded the door the night before. "Any ideas?"

Brokk and Eitri, those were their names, master forgers of their race. They bowed their heads. The one who seemed younger, Eitri, put his hands upon the hilts of the twin daggers in his belt.

"Let us begin to search," Eitri said. "We may be able to follow the trail. If not, there are darklings who dwell within this city and around it, some of our race, and some of the alves, as well as others whose race is unknown to us. Word may pass amongst them."

"Go," Hellboy told him.

To Pernilla it sounded like a command, and the way the Nidavellim responded, she imagined they took it as one. Eitri stared for a long moment at the serpentine pendant around Hellboy's neck, and then he and the others ran toward the edges of the forest where Thrym had disappeared perhaps ten or fifteen minutes before. They would never be able to catch him, that was something they all knew. But they might be able to track him.

"You'll be going after him, then?" she asked, eyes on Abe now.

"As soon as we have a lead."

"I want to bury my father," Pernilla told him, the words hurting her, voice breaking with each one. "Then I'm coming with you."

Neither of the BPRD operatives argued with her. She waited another moment to make sure they would not, and then she walked up to Hellboy. She laid a hand on his chest and gazed up into his eyes. They were inhuman, those eyes, but there was still a warmth and gentleness in them.

"Will you bring him back for me?" she asked.

Hellboy nodded and went to her father's corpse. Even with Mjollnir in his hand, it was simple for him to lift the dead man.

Then they began to walk back through the forest, Hellboy carrying her father in his massive arms like a sleeping child. But Edmund Aickman was not asleep. And as far as Pernilla was concerned, he would not be truly at rest until Thrym was destroyed at last.

In the basement of Riddarholm Hospital, Fredrik Klar pinched an unlit cigarette between his lips and thought about God. He was the Prime Minister's man, and proud of that fact. Klar had earned a reputation over the years for his ability to handle sensitive operations, particularly in conjunction with foreign governments, with diplomacy and alacrity. Three successive Prime Ministers had retained his services, and that was a feat. When Parliament named a new PM, most of the last fellow's most trusted operatives were reassigned. But not Klar. They needed his expertise and particularly his calm.

Keeping that calm had never been more difficult than it was at this moment. It had been difficult enough, having to cooperate with Hellboy and that malformed creature, Sapien. But Klar had been forced to choose obedience to his employer over his own ego many, many times. And so, though he felt free to keep a firm rein on Hellboy, particularly as long as he held that hammer, Klar cooperated as best he could.

In his time as the Prime Minister's man, Klar had seen a number of strange things, freakish oddities and monstrosities. Things that should not exist, but did. None of them—even Hellboy—had made him doubt for a moment his faith in God.

Now he stood behind a glass partition and gazed dully

into a glistening steel and tile autopsy room, and wondered just exactly what the hell the doctors were cutting up in there. Klar was in a small foyer that contained two desks, each with computer stations, heaped with files on various autopsies that had been done recently in the hospital. Behind him was a door out into the main corridor that ran through the basement of the Riddarholm. His associates waited there for him, impatiently, he imagined, likely talking amongst themselves, sneaking out to have a smoke or grab a sandwich. It would have been far better if he could have waited there with them.

Instead he was here, locked into a death room with a cadaverous myth. A glass door was set into the partition, and he could see nearly everything the pathologist and his assistant were doing. The room had two large steel autopsy tables, air vents that cycled the odors of rot and formaldehyde upward and out, metal tables upon which surgical instruments were displayed, and drawers filled with various slides, trays, tubes, and jars, so that samples taken could be properly preserved and labeled.

The corpse was so huge that a hospital gurney had been brought in and set against the bottom of the autopsy table to support its legs. Klar imagined that the weight of its torso might have collapsed the gurney. When it had been placed in the room, even the solid steel struts beneath the autopsy table had groaned.

What the hell are you? Klar thought, staring at the skeletal remains, the strips of leathery flesh that still clung to the bones, peeling at the edges. He took the cigarette out of his mouth for a moment and stared down at it. The urge to light it, to let its poisonous smoke curl down into his lungs with that comfortable familiarity, that deadly, burning weight, was almost too much to resist. But there was no smoking here. Not ever.

Klar snapped the cigarette in two and tobacco spilled onto the floor. He left the broken butt on top of the nearest desk and approached the glass partition more closely. The skull was easily twice the size of a normal human head, the hands like those of a gorilla, the femur as thick around as a lamp post.

Against the black screen of his mind's eye he could still see the lightning striking out of the sky, scarring the clouds as it touched a tendril down to that ancient war hammer again and again.

The hammer.

Klar gritted his teeth as he thought of it and shoved his hands deep into the pockets of his suit jacket. That hammer was the bane of his existence. The PM wanted it back. As far as Klar was concerned, he hoped that it could never be removed from Hellboy's grip. For it was the hammer that bothered him most of all. Without it, the cadaver was merely a collection of enormous bones, a freak of nature dead and buried a hundred years or so.

But the hammer . . . that made it possible for many to begin to believe that the skeleton belonged to something more than human, to a being who could not possibly have existed. For if it were real, if myths walked the earth, and magically forged weapons were used to slay giants and serpents of unimaginable size . . . if the gods were more than legends . . . then what of his faith?

Klar took off his glasses and wiped them on his jacket before settling them back upon the bridge of his nose. This was taking too long. The two doctors had been scraping and cutting at the remains for hours. Though there were no windows here, he suspected that if he could step outside to where the hospital overlooked the breadth of the Riddarfjärden, darkness would have fallen by now, turning the waves black.

Klar wanted to go home. It was getting late and Margarethe would be putting their Victoria to bed soon. A tentative smile flickered at the corners of his mouth as he thought of her, his little girl, named for the Crown Princess and just as pretty.

With a sigh, his impatience having gotten the better of him, Klar reached out and rapped his knuckles on the partition. Dr. Tegner glanced up and frowned at him from behind his safety glasses. In his hand, the bone saw whined loudly, its blade a spinning blur.

Klar raised his eyebrows and held up both hands to indicate his frustration. Tegner clicked off the bone saw and called out to him. Even through the closed door, Klar could hear him.

"Nobody said you had to stay!" the doctor called in Swedish.

Petulant, knowing he was too tired to still be hanging around there, Klar rolled his eyes and leaned on the desk. He reached into his jacket and pulled out his cigarettes, shook one out. A quick glance revealed no smoke detector in the glass-enclosed foyer. He fished out his lighter and lit up.

The smoke curled in the air above him and the cigarette's tip burned orange and black. Klar took a long drag and blew it out, then looked into the autopsy room again. Tegner had the bone saw shrieking again, but was staring at him through the glass.

Klar smiled at him and gave a short bow, magnanimously sweeping his right hand out to indicate that, by all means, the man should continue. Childish behavior, he knew, but it felt good.

Dr. Tegner shook his head and turned to the remains again.

The skeleton sat up.

Tegner cried out in alarm, and the bone saw dropped to the floor, whirring blade chipping the tile. His assistant, Dr. Milles, tried to catch the instrument tray that had been resting on top of the massive corpse. Scalpels and shears clattered to the floor, and Milles screamed like a little girl.

The withered husk slid off the table. A flap of dessicated flesh on its cheek hung from the bone as it glanced about the autopsy room with dark, hollow orbits where eyes ought to have been. Fine, wiry hair floated down from its head, more of it falling away with each new movement. One of its skeletal hands clasped suddenly to its chest with a rattle of bones, and the other clutched at the air, stared down at its empty hand as though it could not believe the hammer was not there.

Klar muttered a silent prayer, and all the fear churning in his gut turned to ice, freezing him there in that spot.

Dr. Tegner turned to him and screamed his name. Klar took a step back, afraid that the shout might draw the thing's attention to him. That motion broke his paralysis and training kicked in. He had faced the impossible, the unnatural, before. Whatever this was, it could not be what the late Professor Aronsson had imagined it to be. Simply could not.

If he could convince himself of that, he would be all right.

The towering corpse opened its jaws as if to shout, but no sound came out. Teeth clacked together. Its mouth should not have worked at all. There wasn't enough muscle left tethering the bones together for it to have moved at all without falling apart. But it was moving nevertheless. Dark, horrible magic.

Milles ran for the door, hands flailing as he fled. The skeleton lashed out with incredible speed, and its bony fingers tangled in his hair and hauled him back. Again the doctor screamed.

He thinks we're the enemy, Klar realized. *That we took the hammer. That we did this to him, somehow.* But then the dead thing reached out for Dr. Tegner and ripped his face off. The man went down in a heap on the ground, bleeding and screaming but hideously alive. The skeleton glared down at Milles, grabbed him on either side of his head and swiftly snapped his neck.

It dropped the corpse.

The incessant pounding on the door behind him seemed so distant to Klar. His men were trying to get in, responding to the screams. They had dropped their sandwiches and forgotten conversations about their girlfriends.

Something rumbled in the air in the autopsy room and the glass partition shook. It might have been thunder. Condensation beaded up on the inside of that window and the tiny wisps of hair on the shambling thing's head stood up as though electrified.

It glanced up at Klar, empty eye sockets dead but still somehow filled with contempt. And it started toward him.

"Oh, please, no," he whispered as he backed toward the door, thinking of his daughter.

He reached out, grabbed it and pulled, only to find it locked. Whimpering, he threw the lock and hauled the door open, then stood aside as his men flooded in. The first few men through the door staggered to a standstill, horror widening their eyes and catching their breath in their throats. Others followed.

The skeleton shattered the glass partition with a single blow of its massive bony fist. Huge shards of glass rained down like glittering guillotines in that glaring, pale fluorescent light.

"Destroy it, you idiots!" Klar screamed.

He was filled with anger at these fools who just stood there, although he himself had been frozen there gape-mouthed only moments before. Now he reached beneath his jacket to draw his weapon from its holster under his arm. It was a Heckler and Koch VP70, nine millimeter semi-automatic, eighteen rounds in the magazine.

The thing stood boldly in front of them and lifted its chin with an arrogant swagger that conjured images of the proud warrior it might have been in life. Klar shook those images from his head. It was a monster, a dead thing.

"There is only one God," he whispered. "You are just a soldier. And your time was long ago."

Klar lifted the VP70 and held it in both hands. With a twitch of his finger upon the trigger, he fired six rounds. The thing staggered backward as bullets chipped the dense bone of its skull. One punched right through an empty eye socket and sent shards flying as it burst out the back of its head. Another cracked off teeth as it disappeared into its maw.

More glass shattered as it stumbled back into the autopsy room. His men followed suit, now that the moment of their initial terror had subsided, and drew their weapons. The small room echoed with gunshots, too loud and close, slamming pressure against his eardrums in that enclosed space.

The dead thing's skull and ribcage were obliterated

under the hail of bullets. Someone fired at its legs and the bones cracked. It went down and they kept firing until nothing was left of its head but pale shards that might have been the remains of an antique china tea set.

It twitched once and went still.

The gunfire ceased, but its echoes still ricocheted about the room, pounding his ears. Klar simply stood there, the Heckler and Koch too hot in his grip, and stared at what was left of the body they had found on the banks of that river far to the north, beneath the striking lightning. Where had it come from, this corpse? Why now? Though he believed in one God, he could not help but think that the dead thing's appearance at that time had not been mere happenstance. And now they had destroyed it. If they had not, it might have killed them.

But if his intuition was correct, and it had returned to life with some purpose, what now? Then such thoughts were driven from his mind, by another, more overpowering. *The Prime Minister is not going to be happy.*

If these remains truly belonged to another race, even to some ancient tribe that split off from humanity millennia past, it was one of the most important scientific finds in history. But the bones dated only a century old. Klar nodded as the structure of his report to the PM began to form in his mind. Despite what it would mean for theology and anthropology, this thing could not be what appearances suggested. Tests had proven it could not.

Klar smiled. If it was not the genuine article, its destruction would not cost him his job. Not as long as he managed to get the hammer back from Hellboy.

On the other hand, given that he did not know what tests upon the hammer would reveal, in some ways it might be better if Hellboy never returned the hammer. Klar would have to see what could be arranged.

"Clean it up," he ordered his men. He holstered his weapon and wiped a hand across his forehead. Then he gestured toward the two pathologists who lay on the floor. Milles had died instantly, but Tegner was dead as well, probably of shock. "Cover them up while I try to explain what happened here. Let me see. Dr. Milles was in league with black marketeers, tomb raiders who wanted to steal this archaeological discovery. He attacked Dr. Tegler, who fought back, broke Milles's neck. In the process, the remains were destroyed."

Several of the men turned to glance at him as though he were out of his mind. Klar put his hands on his hips.

"I suppose you've got a better idea?"

None of them said a word. Klar nodded, still working the details over in his head. After a moment, he went back out into the foyer. The door to the corridor was ajar and he went to close it. The last thing he needed was unwanted witnesses, and given the noise they had made, people were sure to arrive soon to investigate.

He pushed the door. It stopped abruptly several inches before it could close.

Klar frowned and hauled it open. Just outside the door stood a tall, red-haired woman clad in armor and thick furs. Though he could see her dark eyes, the rest of her face seemed somehow out of focus to him.

"*I have come to claim the shell,*" she declared in a voice like the whistle of the winter wind.

Oddly enough, Klar did not really even notice the wooden spear until its metal tip punched through his chest.

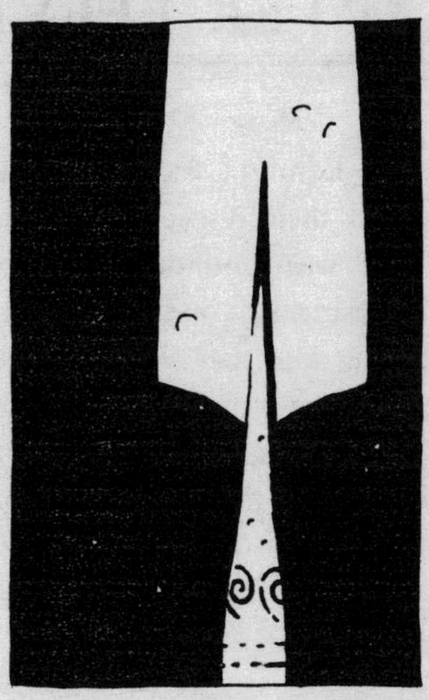

CHAPTER ELEVEN

On the day of Edmund Aickman's funeral, Hellboy and Abe paid their respects before the ceremony, when nobody else was around. At the cemetery they waited in the limousine, just one in a long line of vehicles parked in a snaking line that stretched up through the graveyard. The windows were tinted, but Hellboy had his rolled down a few inches, and the sky didn't look much different with or without the tint. It was not the black of approaching thunderstorms, but the persistent, stubborn, steel gray that refused to break for sunshine, but neither would it deliver rain.

A shroud.

That morning, the day of Edmund Aickman's funeral, the sky was a death shroud.

Hellboy sat in the back of the limousine, taking up most of the rear seat, with Abe squeezed in beside him. Opposite them were Karin Ogilvie from the American embassy and Erik Wilton, who worked in some capacity for the Prime Minister of Sweden, though he mentioned the king frequently, as if that would hold more sway.

Wilton was on the cellular phone with Dr. Manning back at BPRD headquarters in the States. Miss Ogilvie watched him, rapt with attention. Hellboy fidgeted restlessly, his tail turned uncomfortably against the leather seats. Sometimes when he moved, it squeaked against the upholstery. For his part, Abe only gazed out the window across the well-kept lawn of the cemetery, to the gathering of black-garbed mourners who seemed somehow less than three-dimensional against that gray sky.

Abe wanted to be with Pernilla, that much was clear. Hellboy didn't think there was anything romantic going on between the two of them, though anyone who knew him knew he wasn't the most perceptive guy in the world when it came to that kind of thing. But he figured that wasn't it. It was just that Abe and Pernilla had been through a lot together in a very short time, shared some forced intimacy, and become friends. Now here she was burying her father, and she was surrounded by a crowd of people who had known her most of her life, who most assuredly loved her deeply, but who could never understand what she was going through.

Ancient myths come to life. Ragnarok. The hammer of the gods. How could she have a conversation with her great aunt or her third cousin about the bones of giants? The answer was, clearly, that she couldn't.

But Abe sat in the back of the limousine with Hellboy. After all, he and Abe weren't going to be any easier to explain to these people. Chances were none of them had ever met a paranormal investigator from America before.

So they sat in the back of the limousine and waited for the graveside service to be over.

Not the grief, though. That was going to go on for a very long time.

Hellboy had never known his father, but Trevor Bruttenholm had been the man who had adopted him, had raised and taught him. When Trevor had died, part of Hellboy had been interred along with him, an innocence he would never be able to retrieve. It was ironic, in a way, that he should think so much now about his adoptive father, for it had been Trevor who had first given him an introduction to Aickman. And the last time Hellboy had seen Pernilla's father—before this past week of course—had been at Bruttenholm's funeral. Despite the greed and pettiness, Hellboy felt himself mourning Aickman's death. Every time someone who had known Trevor Bruttenholm died, a little bit more of the man was erased from the world.

Hellboy frowned and glanced out the window, across the sea of gravestones, to where Pernilla stood by the priest on the lawn. *Selfish*, he thought. *Thinking about Professor Bruttenholm. She's the one who just lost her father.*

Erik Wilton flipped the cell phone shut and cleared his throat as he glanced over at them. Abe did not seem to notice, fixated as he was on the events outside the limousine. Or maybe he was ignoring the man on purpose. Hellboy thought that was entirely possible.

"What did he say?" Hellboy asked.

Wilton glanced at Ogilvie, and it was obvious they had known one another for a long time. The American woman sighed and offered a half smile, but Wilton did not seem pleased. He sat forward, a bit too far, uncomfortably close, and he stared down at Mjollnir where Hellboy had the war hammer on his lap.

"Dr. Manning has spoken to the Prime Minister directly, and the Prime Minister has heard from your Secretary of State, as well as a representative from Great Britain," Wilton began. His mouth twisted up as though he had swallowed something distasteful to him. "Apparently, in spite of how badly you've bungled this situation, in spite of the loss of the Skellesvall remains and the murders of Fredrik Klar and his team, not to mention the death of Professors Aickman and Aronsson, we are to continue to offer you whatever cooperation you require."

Hellboy did not smile. He did not have the heart to be amused by the man's discomfort today. He had not liked Klar at all, but Wilton seemed an all right sort. Put into the same situation, he doubted he would be handling it with any more grace than the Swede.

On the other hand, his ire rose at the insult. Wilton might not have meant to be offensive, but he was. Another time Hellboy might have brushed it off. But not now.

"Bungled?" he asked.

At the tone in his voice, Abe twitched and glanced over, his attention torn from the funeral proceedings for the first time.

The Ogilvie woman sat up a bit straighter. "Hellboy, I'm sure Erik didn't mean—"

Hellboy narrowed his eyes so that his brows knitted together. He lifted his chin as though he expected Wilton to try to hit him in a second. The urge for that kind of posturing came out of nowhere, but he could not deny it.

"You've got a cadaver between thirty-five and forty feet high wandering across your country right now, Mr. Wilton," Hellboy said. "It's been three days since Thrym tore himself outta the ground, and your people haven't been able to find a single trace of him beyond the city limits. After that first night, when he left Stockholm, nobody's seen a thing."

Wilton sniffed and crossed his legs. His wool pants hissed across the seat of the limo. "It doesn't appear you and your friend are faring any better."

Hellboy lifted Mjollnir slightly—only so that he could comfortably lean forward—but Wilton's eyes went wide and he flinched. Now Hellboy did smile, a hard look despite the humor in it.

"We've been waiting for Miss Aickman to bury her father, Wilton. Now that's done. We know what direction our target went, but nobody's seen it since, so the delay hasn't cost us anything. And it has gained us the expertise of a folklorist whose knowledge may be invaluable to our efforts. Our supervisor is aware that we've put off searching for Thrym until we can be assured of Miss Aickman's help. They're relying on us, and you can too. But unless and until you can do our jobs better than we can, why don't you keep quiet and out of the way?"

Wilton turned quickly to Miss Ogilvie, as though he expected her to come to his defense. The woman did not even glance at him.

"So you expect to leave soon?" the American woman asked.

"Soon enough," Hellboy replied. "Tomorrow morning at the latest."

She shook her head. "I don't understand. Do you already know where this creature has gone?"

"No. But we will. Call it intuition."

Abe had turned to look back out the tinted window again, so that when he spoke, his soft, almost foreign-sounding voice and clipped words seemed to be coming from everywhere and nowhere in the vehicle at once.

"There's a village on the Ume River that has completely disappeared. Only a little over a hundred people. But all that's left now are bones and ghosts."

"Sort of a poetic way to talk about a massacre, don't you think?" Miss Ogilvie asked.

"He's not being poetic," Hellboy replied. "The ghosts are there. You're welcome to go up and try to talk to them. Most of them are insane, though. Minds just snapped."

For a long moment Wilton stared at Abe, perhaps thinking he would face them. He did not. At length, the broad-shouldered Swede turned to Hellboy instead. "How do you know this?"

Hellboy turned away from him. In the cemetery, mourners had begun to drift en masse from Edmund Aickman's grave. The old folklorist had been laid to rest beside Pernilla's mother, and it seemed sort of a prosaic end for a man who sought to peer into the arcane heart of the world, no matter the cost.

"Did you bother to check what BPRD stands for, Mr. Wilton?" Hellboy asked. "We're the Bureau for Paranormal Research and Defense. It's our job to know crap like that."

Late the following morning, Hellboy, Abe, and Pernilla found themselves pressed uncomfortably close together in the cabin of a helicopter, searching the landscape below for a village of ghosts. All of them wore headsets that eased communication and cut down on the thudding noise of the helicopter's rotors. Modern helicopters were generally not as loud as they had once been, but this machine was the exception. Even with the headset covering his ears, Hellboy had a headache from hours of being pummeled by the rhythmic noise of the thing.

The BPRD had arranged for the Swedish government to continue to offer them support wherever possible. Mr. Wilton had instructions from his Prime Minister to do just that. But Wilton was a sneaky little twit, and so when Hellboy had asked for helicopter transport, instead of sending military personnel, the guy had actually arranged for a charter.

Asshole.

The pilot, Gustaf, had been mercifully silent for nearly the entire trip, and Hellboy had wondered more than once if it was because the guy didn't speak English, or because he was deaf from spending so much time in the chopper. They had flown on a small plane the night before to Sundsvall, then been transported by bus to the Ostersund. Pernilla had slept on the bus, but Hellboy and Abe had only managed a few brief hours of sleep early this morning, before Gustaf had arrived. They had flown north until they reached the Ume River, and then turned west to follow along its path.

The river rolled along beneath them, its ripples and rapids reflecting the sunshine back into the sky, catching them at times with its glare. In places it was impressively wide, and at others seemed almost narrow and placid enough not to be called a river at all. Many settlements existed along the Ume, but each time Gustaf began to slow above one of them Hellboy would glance out the window and then urge him on.

"Not here. Not yet."

Now Gustaf complained in heavily accented tones about running out of gas—apparently he could speak English after all—but he had more than enough to make it back to the Ostersund. For now. If it was much further they would have to let him set them down and continue on foot.

A little while after noon, Hellboy spotted it.

"Have a look down there," he instructed.

Gustaf nodded and brought the chopper in lower. His passengers all peered through the glass down at the village below. It was little enough to speak of. There was one road that followed the curve of the river, bisecting the little township, and several other smaller ways barely wide enough for two cars to pass one another. Several dozen homes were built up around a square at the center of the village, but there were only a few stone structures there, and those seemed long faded.

One of them had collapsed into the street, as though an earthquake had come by and somehow disturbed nothing else.

There were other signs of Thrym's passing, however, now that they looked more closely. Houses with their walls caved in, cars torn open, lying on their sides like discarded toys. There were fishing boats in the water, moored at the river's edge. Most of them bobbed there, unmolested, but several of them had been shattered against the banks of the river, pieces jutting from the earth at jagged angles.

As the helicopter circled, Hellboy saw that one of the boats protruded from the rear of a two-story house at the edge of the village that was furthest from the river.

"Set it down, Gustaf," he said.

The pilot shot him a wild look. Apparently he wasn't deaf, either. "You must be crazy. You don't want to land here. Something terrible has happened here. Don't you have eyes?"

"That's why we came," Hellboy explained. "Set it down. You can go as soon as we've got our gear."

For a long time, Gustaf just circled. He made as if he was looking for a place to land, but just about any street would do, or the riverbank for that matter. At length, he glanced back at Pernilla.

"What if the . . . the evil that did this . . . what if it's still here?"

"You'd see it," Pernilla assured him. "We want to stop it, Gustaf. To try to make sure it doesn't happen anywhere else."

That seemed to satisfy the pilot, for he swung the chopper around in one final arc and then set it down easily in the center of the village, not far from where the stone building had been demolished.

"I am not supposed to know why you are here," he said. "They told me not to ask questions. So I will only wish you luck."

"We'll take it," Abe replied. "Thanks."

Several minutes later they had unloaded their gear from the helicopter. Hellboy searched the street for a suitable vehicle and spotted a delivery truck a short distance away, in front of what appeared to be the only market in the little village. He made several trips, carrying all their gear over to it while Abe and Pernilla said their goodbyes to Gustaf, who had turned out to be both more reliable and more amiable than Hellboy had expected.

When Hellboy shook his hand—using his own left as always—Gustaf stared down at Mjollnir.

"That is impressive," the man said. "Where did you get it?"

"You're not supposed to ask questions, remember."

Gustaf smiled and nodded. Then, as if remembering how unnerved he had been while in the air, he glanced around anxiously and then back at his helicopter.

"You want me to come back and get you? Tomorrow? The day after?"

"Thank you, but no," Abe told him. "You did your job. We're not sure when we'll be back."

"Or if," Hellboy said, but so low that he didn't think anyone else heard him. He had been unable to stop the words from coming out, but he didn't want Pernilla to hear him saying it.

"Good," Gustaf said. "I wish you luck, but I do not want to come back here."

The man trotted back to the helicopter and climbed in. The rotors began to spin almost immediately, and moments later the machine began to lift off the ground, the air beating against the cracked road. Hellboy stood between his friends, watching Gustaf fly away, leaving them there in the midst of this dead community.

"We don't even know the name of this village," he observed.

"That's because everybody around here who could tell us is dead." Abe turned up the collar on his jacket. It was colder now that they had come further north, but not nearly as cold as it would be if their journey took them above the Arctic Circle again. And Hellboy had a feeling it would. Already there was a sensation in his right hand, a kind of tremble to Mjollnir that was becoming familiar. The hammer seemed to draw him further north, like a dowsing rod to water. If you believed in dowsing rods, that was. Hellboy wasn't sure he did.

Pernilla had wandered off toward the delivery truck. Now she stood in front of it, gazing at the rubble of the decimated building and around at the empty streets of the village, parked cars and houses with walls caved inward.

"Where are they?" she asked as Hellboy and Abe approached. "You said this place was full of bones, but I don't see any. No trace of the people at all. Where have they all gone?"

Hellboy shrugged. "Kinda noticed that too. I wasn't going to mention it."

"I'm more concerned about the whereabouts of your so-called bodyguards at the moment," Abe noted. "Weren't they supposed to meet us here?"

"Yeah. Let's get the truck ready. Make sure there's gas and everything. Then we can eat something, stock up at the market. If they haven't shown up by then, we'll go on without them. I'm sure they'll catch up before long."

Abe and Pernilla agreed to that plan, but while they went about their business, all three of them were restless and anxious. Hellboy noticed that the others spent as much time as he did glancing quickly over their shoulders and peering up at the windows of empty houses or into the ravaged interiors of those quaint-looking homes. Despite Hellboy's statements to Wilton, it had been the Nidavellim and not the BPRD who had located this place. Brokk and Eitri had sent a messenger with word of it, and of the ghosts here. The village was haunted, and even though they could not see the spirits of the dead, Hellboy and his companions knew they were there. It made them feel like intruders at best, and thieves at worst. They were going to steal the truck, after all, not to mention whatever additional food, clothing, and blankets they could add to their supplies.

No one would know or care but the ghosts of the dead.

Hellboy assuaged his conscience by telling himself that they were going to avenge these people, who had no use for such things now. But he still felt like he had been caught doing something very wrong. Robbing the dead was the work of vultures and other carrion beasts.

They unloaded all of the stock from the back of the delivery truck, things meant for this village and the next and the one after that. None of it was ever going to reach its destination unless they delivered it themselves, and there were, unfortunately, more pressing matters at hand. Then the truck was loaded up again, with their gear and the supplies and bedding they appropriated from the market and the houses around them.

When Hellboy had stowed the last of the packs—this one very gently, as it contained explosives—he turned to find Pernilla standing just behind him. Abe was a few feet away, in the middle of the street, gazing around at the buildings again.

"Not that I doubt you," Pernilla said, "and maybe it's late to be asking this question, but do either of you know how to start a car without the keys?"

Hellboy rested the war hammer on his shoulder, though the burden of never being able to put it down had lessened somewhat. He was becoming used to its weight, a fact that disturbed him more than a little.

"Abe can hotwire a car," Hellboy replied.

Pernilla raised her eyebrows and glanced over at the amphibian. Abe turned toward them, expressionless.

"A friend of ours taught me, another agent at the Bureau. But I've only ever done it once, and then it was luck and desperation and my fear of things with tentacles that made it work."

"Come on, Abe. Liz is a better teacher than that," Hellboy prodded. Then he smiled at Pernilla. "Anyway, it doesn't matter. The keys are in the ignition. Whoever our delivery man was, he didn't intend to be away from his truck for very long."

That solemn fact erased any good feeling they might have dredged up, and all three of them became uneasy again. Hellboy wanted to put the haunted village behind them.

"Let's go," he said. "The dwarves can catch up."

"You said that before," Abe noted, "but how do we know where to go from here? Despite his size, Thrym has not exactly left giant footprints to follow."

Mjollnir trembled in Hellboy's hand as he raised the hammer and pointed north with it. "A little birdie told me we're headed that way."

Abe was still for a moment, those wide eyes gazing back at Hellboy. At length, he strode up to the driver's side of the truck and opened the door. He began to climb in, then paused and looked back at Hellboy and Pernilla.

"Let's go, then, before Thrym gets so far away that you can't feel him anymore. Or before I decide to go home."

Pernilla sat between them in the cab of the truck. Abe was behind the wheel. Even without the hammer in his fist, Hellboy's right hand made driving difficult. It was a tight fit with the three of them up there, but Hellboy knew he would get claustrophobic, even a little nauseous, bouncing around in the rear enclosure, and though Pernilla offered to ride in back, they figured she would be even less comfortable there than squeezed between them.

The truck rolled through what remained of the village, and Hellboy considered it very lucky indeed that they were on the north side of the river. If they'd been to the south, they would have had to drive a hundred miles or more in either direction to find a bridge. The one that had existed here previously was nothing more than stumps on either bank now, the pieces of it having been swept away with the current.

The Nidavellim warriors were waiting for them at the northern edge of the village, where the last of the houses were spread sparsely along the roadside. Brokk, Eitri, and three others were ranged across their path. Abe braked and put the truck in park but did not shut off the engine. Hellboy rolled the window down but didn't bother to get out.

"Where were you guys?" he asked.

The Nidavellim gazed at him. Eitri stared a moment at the pendant around Hellboy's neck—he kept doing that and it was starting to tick Hellboy off, but now wasn't the time to call him on it—and then they approached the truck with caution.

"Garm did not attack you?"

"Who's Garm?" Hellboy asked, though the word rang true in his mind.

"The hound of Gnipahellir."

"Say that five times fast," Hellboy muttered.

But beside him, Pernilla sighed and covered her face with her hands. "Are you saying that Garm is . . ."

Hellboy had a feeling she was about to say something else. Maybe *real*. But what she said, after some hesitation, was ". . . alive?"

Brokk and Eitri nodded gravely.

"Who's Garm?" Hellboy asked again.

"He has gathered the corpses of the villagers," Brokk told Pernilla, his focus on her. "Thrym sucked their lives from them, the essence of them, and ate some of their remains, but most of their corpses he left behind. Garm has gathered the dead into a hall at the center of the village. Your . . . ," he paused, searching his mind for the word. "Your helicopter landed very near the spot."

"That explains a lot," Abe noted.

Hellboy leaned forward and rested his head on the dashboard. "Who's Garm?" he asked.

Pernilla used both hands to push back her raven hair and held it there, as though she might tie it back. She closed her eyes and when she spoke it was as though she had grown suddenly very tired. Hellboy thought she probably had.

"Garm was the wolf-hound who lived in a cave and guarded the entrance to Niflheim. A horrible beast who killed Tyr during Ragnarok—and I can't believe I'm talking about this as though it were all true."

Hellboy noticed Abe and the Nidavellim all staring at her oddly. How could she question what was true with Brokk and Eitri standing right there? A sudden image flashed through his mind, of a slavering beast tearing off the sword-arm of a valiant warrior. *Tyr. That was Tyr*, he thought.

Then he frowned. "I . . . remember. But Garm didn't survive. Tyr killed him before he died."

Abe glanced over at the Nidavellim. "Apparently not, since he's here, rounding up dead people like a squirrel gathering up nuts for the winter."

"But why is he here now, then? This isn't a coincidence. Thrym is resurrected, and then Garm, who's also supposed to be dead, shows up? Who's next, JFK?"

Brokk cleared his throat and rested his hand on his war hammer. "We have discussed that ourselves. Garm is not a husk as Thrym was. He must have survived between worlds or been trapped somehow here on this plane. It might have been nothing more than Thrym's passing by that roused him or drew him here, but it might have been the spell of the Svartalves. Magic that powerful always spreads."

"Wonderful," Hellboy muttered. "Just what we needed. Thrym's the Pied Piper for lost monsters. Let's just catch him and put him back in the ground before more of these beasts start showing up." He glanced at the Nidavellim. "You guys have any idea what other things might have survived Ragnarok?"

They shook their heads.

Hellboy sighed. "All right, get in the back. Abe, turn the truck around. We can't just leave the big mutt here to feast on whoever happens to wander into this place next."

CHAPTER TWELVE

With all the gear in the back of the truck there was barely enough room for Brokk, Eitri, and the other Nidavellim, and they grumbled as they climbed aboard. Hellboy ignored them. Things were pretty tight up front, too, and Pernilla hadn't squawked about being trapped between him and Abe. If she could deal with close quarters, so could they. Otherwise, they could walk.

Of course, it might have just been that they didn't want to be eaten by the giant wolf-hound. But the Nidavellim were proud warriors, and Hellboy figured none of them would admit to being scared of Garm. At least not yet.

Abe drove back to the center of town, and a kind of tremor went through Hellboy. A number of things were responsible for the strange frisson of anxiety he felt then. Part of it, he realized now, was Mjollnir. With the tug of Thrym's presence to the north almost crackling through the hammer's grip, he had missed the way it seemed to grow warmer as they approached the village center the first time. In addition to that, though, was the simple fact that he did not like to go backward. It was one thing to want to return somewhere, but he had always hated having to do work over again, or to backtrack because a job had not been finished correctly the first time.

Like this one.

The truck rolled into the middle of the village and Abe parked it, maybe on purpose, within a few feet of the place they had driven it away from, only with its nose pointed in the opposite direction. Abe slipped out of the cab and stood with his arms crossed. He sighed as he glanced around at the buildings. Pernilla got out behind him and turned to Hellboy, who clipped the door with the war hammer as he stepped out. The passenger window cracked from the impact and Hellboy swore.

"Let's get this done as quickly as possible," he said. "I don't know if Thrym called Garm up on purpose somehow to slow us down, but if he did, I'd rather not give him the satisfaction."

Eitri was the first of the Nidavellim to climb out of the back. They appeared to have had some trouble with figuring out how to open the door from the inside, but they managed. He had his twin daggers ready, brandished in either hand, and as the others climbed down they also pulled out their weapons.

Brokk was last. He gripped his war hammer—this sort of shrunken version of Mjollnir—and stepped up beside Hellboy.

"What is your plan, thunder-bearer?"

Abe did not even turn to look back at the Nidavellim as he replied. "He doesn't have a plan. We're going to go through whatever doors the place has, some windows if we can reach them, and kill the monster."

Taken slightly aback, Brokk turned to glance up at Hellboy. "A direct assault then?"

Hellboy slung Mjollnir onto his shoulder. "It isn't brain surgery."

Brokk nodded with satisfaction. "A direct assault. Worthy of Mjollnir."

"Glad you approve," Hellboy replied dryly. Then he looked over at Eitri. "Pick a couple of your guys to stay here with Miss Aickman, just in case any other myths decide they want lunch."

Pernilla spun around, a frown creasing her forehead. "What makes you think I'm staying here?"

Hellboy opened his mouth to respond, but hesitated. He gave her a sheepish look, unsure what to say. If he told her it was because he figured she would be safer that way, she'd probably accuse him of being sexist. And maybe she'd be right. He hadn't really thought about it enough to judge.

"Well, for one," he began, "you're not as durable as the rest of us."

She seemed about to rebut that, but then glanced around at the dwarves and at Abe and finally back at Hellboy, and she said nothing.

"Not to mention that you're the only one not armed," he added.

Emotions warred in her eyes. Hellboy tended not to respond to the sorts of things he saw going on in people's minds, the difficulties they wrestled with, but that did not mean he did not notice them. Pernilla had insisted she come along on this expedition and she did not want anyone treating her as though she were dead weight or excess baggage. He figured that was because she feared she might be just that.

The truth was, he was glad to have her along. Her expertise had already proven useful. And, as far as company went, she was a lot more pleasant to be around than a troupe of grim-faced dwarves looking for something to kill.

He started slightly when Pernilla stepped toward him, finger pointed at his waist. "You have the hammer. I don't imagine you are going to be using that cannon."

Hellboy glanced down and saw that she was pointing to the enormous pistol that hung at his hip, a temporary sidearm offered to him by the Swedes until he could permanently replace the gun he had lost. The leather of the holster creaked slightly when he moved, but he had grown so used to the sound over time that he often forgot it was there. He wanted to ask her if she had ever fired a gun, especially one that size, but the look on her face stopped him.

Hellboy reached his left hand down, unsnapped the holster, and slid the pistol out. She took it from him, tested its weight, sighted along the barrel, and then let it dangle at her side.

"Which building is it?" she asked Brokk.

The Nidavellim had watched this exchange in silence. Brokk pointed just up the street, to a squat stone building with large doors set into its face like a barn.

Pernilla turned to Abe. "Let's go."

Abe smiled and walked beside her. Hellboy hung back, let them get a ways up the street, and motioned for the Nidavellim to wait as well. After a moment he turned to Eitri.

"Don't let anything happen to her."

"I will see to it," Eitri replied with a respectful dip of his head.

"Good."

Hellboy started down the street, his hooves thudding dully on the ground. The Nidavellim fell in behind him, and Hellboy did not like the feeling. It was fine having them along. They were battle-hardened and determined, but they acted like puppies with a new master, and it was getting on his nerves.

When he reached the massive doors to the stone building, Abe and Pernilla were waiting.

"Quiet in there," Abe whispered.

"Yeah," Hellboy agreed. There were windows on the second story, but none in front. On the side, though, he could see a pair of very high windows. "It was probably an assembly hall. Maybe the local flea market or something."

"Could have been religious," Abe observed.

"Could have been anything. What do you call those buildings people used to have where ranchers could bring their cattle to sell them?"

"I don't know."

"Could have been one of those."

Abe raised an eyebrow. "Somehow I doubt there are a lot of ranches around here."

Hellboy shot him a dark look but Abe was impassive. Pernilla let the gun dangle at her side but already it seemed as though it was too heavy for her. Hellboy tried to pretend he did not notice. The Nidavellim stood ready for battle, weapons in hand, eyeing the front of the building.

"How do you want to handle this?" Abe asked.

"The three of us through the front. I'll take down the door. I'll split the munchkins up and send them around the side."

Abe nodded and both of them looked at Pernilla. After

a moment she nodded as well. Then Hellboy strode to the Nidavellim and instructed Brokk and Eitri to split their group in two, with Brokk taking one of them around one side of the building, and Eitri leading the remaing two the other way.

"When you hear the door go, come quickly," he told them.

"It will be done," Brokk assured him.

The Nidavellim split up and in moments they had disappeared around either side of the building. Hellboy went up to the massive doors again. He ushered Abe and Pernilla backward, raised the hammer, and brought it down in one swift, impossibly devastating blow. The wood splintered and the door cracked off its iron hinges. One side tore with a shriek of metal and dangled sideways in its frame. The other side fell back into the building and landed on the wooden floor inside with a crash.

Glass began shattering nearby, the sound echoing along the streets of the tiny village. The interior of the hall was striped in shadows, and pools of sunlight and dust swirled in the light. Hellboy had wondered how Garm was getting in and out of the building, particularly dragging corpses with him. Now he knew, for at the rear of the long building, its inside vaulted and cavernous as a church, there was a section of wall that had been broken away and the sun streamed in there as well.

Where the shafts of sunlight penetrated the shadows, blood streaked the wooden floor. But in the direct light of day which shone through that twelve-foot section of shattered wall, Hellboy could see the bodies. He slowed as he ran into the hall, nearly slipping on blood that was not quite dry. Abe and Pernilla came up on either side of him, as transfixed as he was by the sight before them.

It was a small mountain of the dead, a pile of corpses that spilled all around the floor at the rear of the building. Benches had been thrown aside and rubble was strewn about as well, but the real debris there was that of the dead. Some had been killed brutally, ripped to shreds, their bones gnawed on and flesh torn off. Others were husks, shells, little more than scarecrows of people, as if they had been long dead and buried and then only recently unearthed. Hellboy might have thought exactly that if not for the fact that their condition reminded him of what Professor Aickman had looked like at the time of his death.

Drained. Those were the ones Thrym had sucked dry

of life before moving on. It was not enough that he was king of the Frost Giants, that he was savage and cunning and incredibly strong. He was also a sorcerer and had used that power to drain these people of their lives. It was a hideous sight, among the most gruesome Hellboy had ever encountered.

The enormous beast that lay atop the mountain of shattered bone and torn flesh was worse. Its fur was matted with blood and when it shifted, the entire pile of human remains moved beneath it with a skeletal clacking. Though their entrance had certainly been noisy enough to give them away, Garm seemed oblivious at first. The great wolf-hound held a dead thing between its paws, a human corpse whose lower torso and legs were still intact, but whose upper body seemed to have been stripped of flesh, bone scarred by the monster's teeth.

The Nidavellim stalked toward the pile of bones, moving warily, on guard for a sudden attack by the beast, but Garm continued to ignore them. It gnawed on the skull of the dead man in its grasp, only to have the spine shatter and the head come off. It splintered in Garm's maw and the beast spat it out.

Hellboy felt the serpentine pendant grow cold against his chest again and Mjollnir seemed lighter than ever, as if rather than burdening him, it were pulling him on. Abe and Pernilla hung back a step or two behind him as the three of them started toward the mound, approaching cautiously, completing the circular enclosure the Nidavellim had begun.

As if only now aware of their presence, Garm dropped its massive snout over the corpse in its clutches and glared at Hellboy out of the corner of its eye as though he might want to steal its dinner. Then the massive beast took one of the dead man's arms in its mouth and began to chew, not ripping it off but gnawing on it with a pop and crunch of bone and the tearing of ligaments.

"That is really gross," Hellboy muttered.

Garm pricked up its ears and lifted its head, turning sharply to snarl at him. Its black lips curled back from gleaming, blood-stained fangs. Its growl was low and deep, a rumble that shook the pile of corpses under it and echoed across the cavernous hall.

"Somebody needs a Milk Bone," Hellboy said.

The beast began to rise from its perch, hackles going up. Brokk let out with some unintelligible roar that Hellboy figured was some sort of ancient challenge. Eitri banged his daggers together as if to draw attention to the blades, and the others shouted as well, trying to confuse or disorient the beast. Garm glanced around quickly and moved one step back as it took their measure.

It wasn't a giant thing, not like Thrym. But a wolf-hound the size of an elephant was just damn creepy to look at, particularly with the dark intelligence that was sparking in its eyes.

"Abe."

"Yeah?"

"Shoot it."

"Gladly."

Hellboy heard the revulsion in his friend's voice, but did not look away from Garm. The creature's eyes were locked with his own in a kind of stalemate and he wanted to draw its attention as long as possible. But in his peripheral vision, Hellboy saw the motion on either side of him. Abe had come up on one side, his sidearm leveled. He was a good shot; Hellboy had always envied him that.

On his left, Pernilla used both hands to lift and aim Hellboy's gun.

Garm grunted and sniffed at the air. The Nidavellim had moved to the bottom of the death mound but no further, and the creature ignored them.

"Fire," Hellboy said.

Abe and Pernilla shot at Garm almost simultaneously. Hellboy's gun was louder and harder to manage, and Pernilla got off two shots in the time it took Abe to fire almost an entire clip at the monster.

Bullets punched through Garm's fur, adding its own blood to that of its victims, trickling through its filthy fur. But the creature barely flinched with each bullet, eyes never moving from Hellboy.

"Crap," Hellboy whispered. He turned to Pernilla. "Leave."

"But—," she began.

"Go!" he snapped. He spun to glance at Abe. "Take her and get out of here."

Then they were moving, and Hellboy felt a kind of release go through them. It had been an experiment, and the big ugly dog had been cooperative enough to sit still for it. Guns weren't going to do a damn thing against it. Now they knew. No reason for Abe and Pernilla to be there at all.

Garm began to growl again.

"Play dead?" Hellboy suggested.

The monster stood up, massive paws sliding through bones that shifted and tumbled in miniature avalanches of the dead. It snarled, a red-tinged drool sliding from its lower jaw, and then it leaped from the tower of corpses and landed on the wooden floor, its body striped with shadow and slashes of sunlight from the windows.

"Didn't think so," Hellboy muttered.

Brokk shouted in his guttural ancient tongue for the other Nidavellim to attack. They let out a bloodthirsty war cry and ran at Garm, even as it began to lope toward Hellboy. Garm was too fast for them, but those who were closest caught up to the beast. Eitri punched both daggers into Garm's side and began to use them as pitons, slashing into the wolf-hound's body and climbing up its side as it ran. The Nidavellim's body shape was deceptive; they were much faster than they looked.

Another of the dwarves hacked into one of Garm's haunches with a double-edged battle axe. The weapon was torn from his hand as the monster continued to lunge for Hellboy, who stood his ground, hooves clacking on the wood. His tail swung in the air, curling with the anticipation of Garm's attack.

Brokk leaped into Garm's path, raised his war hammer. The creature stopped, claws scratching wood. With a shout of triumph, Brokk swung his hammer at Garm's chest, almost beneath him now.

Garm dipped his snout down and bit Brokk in two; threw back his head and gulped down the top of the dwarf's body, hammer and all, while the bottom half struck the ground, pumping blood onto the floor. Eitri saw this and shrieked in fury. He was atop the monster now, and he wept openly, screaming and driving his blades into Garm's flesh again and again.

The remaining Nidavellim attacked anew, swords and axes falling, hacking at Garm, gashing its skin.

The great beast shook them off as though they were insects. Its growl rumbled across the floor and dust fell from the ceiling, swirling in the sunshine. Garm stared at Hellboy and started for him again.

Mjollnir felt as though it was burning him. Which was impossible, of course. Hellboy's huge right fist could not be burned. Still, the hammer seared his palm and fingers, and he held it even tighter as he let loose a bellow of rage that echoed the war cry of the Nidavellim. He barely understood the words, but in his heart and his gut he knew the meaning of it. *To the death.*

Garm had killed Tyr.

Whoever Tyr was.

And the beast had killed Brokk.

Hellboy ran at it, tail curled up behind him. He cocked back his arm and swung the hammer. Despite its momentum, the great beast stopped short. The wolf-hound chuffled as though in amusement when Mjollnir cut through the air only inches from its snout. Then Garm was on top of Hellboy, shoving him down, pinning him to the floor the way he had the stripped corpse at the top of the pile of the dead.

Its drool slipped out and soaked into his long jacket, and where it touched his skin, it burned.

"Son of a bitch!" Hellboy shouted in pain.

Garm's yellow eyes seemed almost to glow as it glared down at him. "*The hammer. It isn't yours.*" Its voice was a low rasping growl, as though the words came from deep beneath the earth and had risen with the inexorable power of an earthquake.

"You can talk," Hellboy said, surprised.

"*Where did you get that*?" it snarled, the stench of death on its breath.

"That makes it worse."

Hellboy curled his left hand into a fist and struck Garm in the side of the head. The wolf-hound was thrown off balance and he took advantage of the moment, bucked against the beast and rolled away from it. Mjollnir slowed him down, however, and as he turned to attack, Garm was nearly upon him again.

Hellboy swung the hammer but the beast opened its maw, and its jaws closed around his forearm and the weapon clutched in his fist. Its teeth scraped the wrist of his right arm, of that mysterious appendage, but did not cut him.

"You want something to chew on?" Hellboy demanded.

He yanked his hand back and Mjollnir shattered Garm's teeth from the inside. The wolf-hound howled in pain and staggered back, staring at him warily now. Hellboy ran at it, raised Mjollnir, and leaped.

"Chew on this!"

Garm tried to dodge out of the way, but the hammer struck its back, shattering its spine, and the great beast went down on the floor, crashing into some of the benches that had still been arranged for people to sit on in the public meeting hall. The irony did not escape Hellboy, that the people of this village had had their last meeting.

The thing was still alive, though barely. Hellboy felt satisfaction at the echo in his mind of the hammer striking the monster's back, of shattering its teeth. That reaction depressed and disgusted him, and he turned and began to walk from the building, leaving the Nidavellim to finish Garm, to have their revenge for the death of Brokk.

If it was true that all of this was some kind of bizarre chain reaction from Thrym's resurrection, he wanted it stopped sooner rather than later. Not just because of the massacre in this village, and not just because he feared what could happen if more monsters like Garm started showing up—things that were supposed to have been dead eons ago.

He was doing his best to push the urges away, but he felt angry almost all the time, now. Enraged at nothing but the world around him, and wanting to lash out with Mjollnir, to have something more to fight, to destroy, monsters whose bones he could shatter.

It felt good, despite the burning of the hammer and the chill of the pendant against his chest. The craving for combat and destruction was delicious.

The sooner this was over, the better. But in the back of his mind, he wondered how long it would be before the presence within him, the essence of the hammer's previous owner, influenced him so much that he decided he did not want it to be over. That the more dead things that rose from the earth, the more ancient monsters somehow recalled to this world, the happier he'd be.

That scared him.

Abe stared at the open front doors of the assembly hall. He had reloaded his sidearm, and the texture of the grip was almost too rough on his skin now. He figured it was what people called an itchy trigger finger, but he'd never felt the sensation before. He wanted another crack at Garm, with or without the gun. Not because he felt particularly inclined to throw himself into the gnashing jaws of a wolf the size of their stolen delivery truck, but because of the remains inside that building.

People. Those were the people of this village. Not just remains. They had lived and worked here, gotten by with a kind of old-fashioned self-sufficiency that most of the world thought was extinct. Then this thing had just come along and eaten them.

That wasn't exactly right, though. Garm had not been here first. Thrym had been first, had killed most of the villagers, and left Garm to feast on what he left behind.

"We should go back in," Pernilla said anxiously.

Abe glanced over at her, saw the pensive look on her face, and reached out to lay a gentle hand on her shoulder. Together they stared back at the front of the building.

"No," Abe replied. "He was right. If guns weren't going to work, we were just in the way. There was this thing with a *djinn* and a bull one time in Calcutta when . . ." His words trailed off and he glanced at her. "Let's just say I learned the hard way that sometimes the only backup I can give him is to get out and be there to pick up the pieces if things go wrong."

There was a moment of silence between them that became awkward, and Abe removed his hand from her shoulder. Pernilla watched him and, though Abe kept his gaze on the front of the building, he felt her eyes on him.

"That must be hard," she said quietly.

"It is."

Shouts and roars came from within the building, but they moved no closer, only stood together, connected by the electric tension of the moment.

"This is so unreal," Pernilla said at last. "I mean . . . Garm is a myth. So is Thrym. Every time I think I've accepted this, I slip back into the insanity of it all. I feel as though my whole mind is out of focus, and the only thing keeping me from losing it entirely is the one certainty I can hold onto."

"What's that?"

"My father's dead," Pernilla replied, a hitch in her voice. "My father's dead and a myth killed him. That's the only focus I need. But it's still hard to accept that myths are real."

At last Abe turned away from the building. He felt almost silly with his gun in his hand, and so he holstered it as he gazed at her, hoping she could feel his sympathy, because expressing it would only embarrass them both.

"Some are. Some aren't," he said. "Even the myths that are true aren't *completely* true. But none of them are completely made up, either. I've had an inkling about that for a long time, but this solidifies it. Every myth started somewhere."

A loud thump interrupted them, and they spun to see Hellboy and the Nidavellim walking across the street toward the truck. The sound had come from the half of the door that was still attached to its frame. Hellboy had put it back in place, as if he could shut the horror of what had happened in there away.

The expression on Hellboy's face was grave, but the Nidavellim were even more grim. They were dirty and disheveled, their clothes and hair stained with blood. But there were only four of them. Abe scanned the faces and realized who was missing.

"Brokk?" he asked, as Hellboy passed him, headed for their vehicle.

Hellboy paused and glanced at him, eyes unreadable.

"He's dead. Drive the truck."

CHAPTER THIRTEEN

It was shortly before 7:30 A.M. when Tom Manning pulled into the underground garage beneath the unremarkable building that was headquarters for the BPRD. It was nestled on a gently rolling hillside in Fairfield, Connecticut, surrounded by trees and shrubbery so that it seemed almost part of the landscape, heavily influenced by certain Asian architectural styles. The BPRD offices were faily remote—not a single restaurant that didn't require a car to get to—but that was a decent trade off for the view from the top floors.

The weather was spectacular, and Dr. Manning had driven with the windows down, turning the radio up loud enough that when he stopped at a red light, he was embarrassed enough to turn it down again, thinking himself too old for such indulgences.

Still, he was smiling as he stepped out of the car and locked the door. He had gone for a short jog that morning in the neighborhood around his home and he felt invigorated. It was still summer, but several days of sweltering heat and crushing humidity had given way to a kind of harbinger of autumn, a hint of what was to come.

The second he got inside, he planned to open his windows wide, and then tackle the mountain of paperwork on his desk. If he played his cards right, he'd skip lunch, keep his beeper on, and then tell Kate Corrigan, his Assistant Director of Field Operations, that she could ring him if anything urgent came up.

Tom had a couple of Corona beers in the fridge at home, and a fresh lime to go with it. It was that kind of day, and at his age, they didn't come around too often.

He was whistling as he rode the elevator up from the garage, briefcase dangling in his hand. Dr. Manning used his key card to let himself into the corridor where all of the upper-echelon offices were. Several people greeted him in the hallway, and he smiled amiably. When he reached his own office, he slid the key card in again. The tiny light on the mechanism turned green, and he pushed inside.

Penelope, the young woman who had been acting as his receptionist while his assistant was out on maternity leave, was nowhere to be seen. Her desk had been abandoned, save for the open can of Pepsi that seemed omnipresent ever since the woman had been moved upstairs from communications. He glanced around, but saw no note, nor any pile of mail and phone messages that she would usually have waiting for him.

Must have gone to the ladies' room, he thought.

Without any further hesitation, he opened the inner door that led into his interior office, but he left it open behind him so that Penelope would know he had arrived. Tom strode across the office, dropped his briefcase on the chair behind his desk, and went to the nearest window. He unlocked it, and began to crank it open.

The door clicked shut behind him.

With a frown, Dr. Manning turned to find Kate Corrigan standing just inside the door. Her short, blond hair looked unkempt, as if she had just woken up, and she held a mug of coffee in one hand. Tom glanced around the office and saw paperwork spread out at the small coffee table in the far corner.

Kate had been waiting for him. From the expression on her face, Dr. Manning knew that the weather was about to change.

"Good morning, Tom," she said.

"Kate. What are you doing, getting here this early? I come in at this time, and have Penelope come in at this time, so I can get my work done before the shit starts to hit the fan."

She rubbed tiredly at her eyes. "Not getting here. Never left." Kate sipped at her coffee and sighed, then walked over to slump down in one of the two chairs opposite Dr. Manning's desk.

Reluctantly, he moved his briefcase to the floor and slipped into his chair.

"I was up all night working on that Crossley thing with the *draco volans.* Was all set to go home around 4 A.M. when I got a call from Barry."

Dr. Manning let out a breath and studied her curiously. There were dark circles under Kate's eyes, and no wonder. "Barry? He's not in Vienna?"

"I sent him to check up on the situation in Stockholm."

"Oh, right," Dr. Manning replied, a sinking feeling in his stomach. "And?"

Kate sipped her coffee, and Tom wanted to snap at her for it. She hesitated as if trying to figure out how to put words to it.

"It seems the Swedes haven't been completely forthcoming with us."

Dr. Manning sat back in his chair, wishing his own coffee cup was full. Wondering how long Penelope was going to be and how soon he might expect caffeine. And to think he had been feeling so energized just a few minutes ago.

"Elaborate."

Kate nodded. "Word is—and this is only whispers, mind you—that in addition to Karl Aronsson's murder, and the murders of the operatives that the Prime Minister had tasked us with keeping an eye on the . . . remains . . . the remains themselves are missing. Stolen, apparently."

Dr. Manning cursed under his breath and sat up straighter. "Hellboy didn't mention that in his report. Or, in Abe's report, because you know Abe wrote it."

"I'd say it's safe to assume nobody told them."

"Damn it," Dr. Manning said. "I wanted to have a look at those remains myself, or at least have some of our people examine them. Any word on who took them?"

"Not a one," Kate replied. "But the Prime Minister is apparently very unhappy. Also, Barry tells me we can expect a call from him fairly soon ourselves. Or, actually, you can."

"To tell me somebody stole the corpse of a god from them?"

Kate went to take another sip of coffee, and then scowled when she found that it was empty. She set the mug down on his desk and ran both hands through her hair. Tom had rarely seen her look so exhausted.

"Not exactly. Honestly, I doubt they'll ever tell you

that. Probably stonewall forever and then tell you it wasn't the genuine article anyway, which is what Barry says they're already telling each other, trying to convince themselves."

"Then why is the Prime Minister of Sweden calling me?"

Kate smiled, but there was no humor in it. "You'll love this. They had some people observing Hellboy and Abe. From a distance, of course."

"Spying," Dr. Manning said.

"Spying," Kate agreed. "Only they've lost track of our guys not far north of some village where the entire population, a couple hundred people, were massacred and some very strange things were found."

Dr. Manning sighed. "And of course they have no plans to tell us what these strange things were."

"Barry said something about a giant dog, but he didn't have the particulars. Anyway, they're getting near the Arctic Circle—the terrain is less than tropical up there—and the Swedes lost track of our team. The Prime Minister is apparently up in arms after the theft of the remains and the murders of some of his operatives. He's getting paranoid. Barry says word behind the scenes is that he's accusing Hellboy of stealing the remains, and of trying to smuggle the hammer out of the country. It's a national treasure, according to the Prime Minister."

"How can they say it's a national treasure if they insist it isn't what we think it is?" Dr. Manning spat, wide-eyed with frustration.

"That's what I said."

"And how can Hellboy have smuggled something out of the country when he's still there?"

"Again, what I said. Meanwhile, though, we may be looking at an international incident. Unless of course you can sweet talk your way around it. I'd suggest trying to convince the Prime Minister that they're right, that none of this is what we both know it is, that it's all a hoax, and that Hellboy's report to you indicates as much."

Dr. Manning shook his head. "You don't expect the man to buy that? He's a head of state, for God's sake. And people saw the dead giant walking through Stockholm. A lot of people, Kate."

Kate got up from the chair and started for the door. "Mass hysteria? He has to have something to tell the rest of the government if all of this slips through the cracks. He's going to need to cover his ass just as badly as we are. If you can make him realize that, maybe he'll play along. Meanwhile, I'm going home and going to sleep."

As she pulled open the door and turned to smile tiredly at him, the phone began to ring. Through the half-open door, Tom could see Penelope at her desk. She picked up the phone and chirped a pleasant hello, and a moment later she swiveled in her chair to look in at him, her eyes wide, impressed. She put the call on hold.

"Dr. Manning?"

Inside the open door, Kate glanced at her. "The Prime Minister of Sweden?"

"How do you *do* that?" Penelope demanded.

Kate turned back to look one last time at Dr. Manning. "Have fun." Then she walked out, headed home.

Tom Manning sighed, thinking of the two Coronas and the lime waiting in his refrigerator at home. "Put him through, Penny," he said with a sigh.

He had known it was going to be one of those days. But this wasn't the kind of thing he had in mind.

For two days, they drove north, drawn on by the dowsing-rod pull of Mjollnir, and aided immeasurably by maps they had found in the cab of the delivery truck. Hellboy slept outside at night, swathed in blankets from the provisions they had taken from the ghost town they had left behind. There was just enough room for Abe and Pernilla to sleep in the front of the truck, though cramped, and just enough room in back for the Nidavellim to get some rest as well.

But it was cold.

Summer could be quite pleasant in Sweden, but once you were above the Arctic Circle, even with the long days and brief nights, the echo of winter never faded. Though they were cold inside the truck, they were at least protected from the biting chill of the Arctic wind.

The maps helped them to divert from their path slightly in order to find villages where the truck could be gassed up. Most of the people they found there were Saami, the people of Lapland, who stared at Hellboy and Abe with a kind of fascination, but without horror. This did not surprise Abe very much. People who lived so far from what most would consider modern civilization had ties to the past, to their ancestors, that the rest of the world could never understand. Oral tradition amongst these peoples often included talk of myths, of gods and monsters. Even the most progressive among them likely still held a place in their heart where they believed such things, even if their minds and mouths denied it.

They paid for their gas and went on their way, and the Saami watched them go with the understanding that they now had a new story to add to the old myths, about the fish-man and the huge demonic beast with thundering hooves and a hammer worthy of the gods.

That contact was on Abe's mind quite a bit as he drove the truck ever northward into the mountainous terrain, closer and closer to the border between Sweden and Norway. It was early afternoon on the second day out from that charnel house of a village, and all was quiet within the truck except the bang and clank of the engine. The Nidavellim were grim warriors and tended to ride in silence, not bothering to emerge at stops until it was time to camp and prepare a meal. Hellboy had Mjollnir resting on his lap, and he tried to compact his body as much as possible to allow Pernilla as much room as he could manage. But he stared out the window, eyes ever on the skies, or if they passed through a stretch of forest, peering into the wood as they drove.

Sometimes Abe thought he saw the hammer tremble in Hellboy's hand.

Pernilla was tired and cold and Abe did not blame her. From time to time during the long hours in the truck she would nod off and lean her head first against Hellboy and then against Abe. He wondered when he glanced at her what sort of life she would return to. After her father's death she had not even taken the time to put his affairs in order, nor hers either. The house awaited her, empty, filled with his books and notes. He had seen grief many times before and knew that Pernilla was probably only running away from her own, that she had not really yet begun to deal with her pain. But though he had come to care for her, he would say nothing. It was not his place; not unless she brought it up first.

The front right tire struck a rut in the road, and Pernilla murmured in her sleep as they were all jostled. She shifted and lay her head against Hellboy again. Abe thought of the Saami and glanced at Mjollnir before returning his attention to the road ahead.

"How much farther do you think?" he asked.

Hellboy seemed almost not to hear him at first. Then he blinked and tore his gaze from the sky, turning to look at Abe. "I don't know. Can't be much further. Eventually we'll cross into Norway, and then it's not all that far to the ocean. So it can't be too much further or we'll run out of land. But I think he's a lot closer than that. The mountains are getting taller, and the air is colder. He'd feel at home here."

"We haven't seen anything else," Abe noted.

He considered elaborating, but Hellboy nodded. He understood what Abe meant, that after Garm there had not been any other creatures, things that had survived Ragnarok and been drawn somehow, either by the hammer or by the sorcery involved in Thrym's resurrection.

"You know what I don't get?" Abe asked, hands gripping the wheel tightly. "How did they all get here? The corpse with the hammer and Thrym's body, the Svartalves and the Nidavellim and Garm. If Ragnarok happened, it didn't happen on this plane of existence. I'm sure the Bureau would have a dozen theories, but one thing seems pretty clear. There's no record of the kind of devastation

Ragnarok would have caused, no record of these creatures showing up before, or their bodies being discovered. Nothing except the myths, and those are really ancient.

"I can believe the dead might go undiscovered, but Garm just got here, and the Nidavellim and Svartalves go around unnoticed. But they don't come from here. Not naturally. Why didn't they just go back to where they belong?"

Hellboy gazed at him a moment, his eyes orange in the slant of light coming through the windshield. Then he turned to look out at the sky again.

"They couldn't."

Abe frowned. "What do you mean?"

"The nine worlds collapsed. The land of the gods and the realm of the giants, even the netherworld . . . they caved in like a house of cards. That's how devastating the final battle was. Midgard . . . our world . . . was affected the least, but it depends how you look at it. Whatever was left of those other worlds, the fallout, I guess, is still here. Some of it merged with our world, other pieces are still outside this reality."

As he spoke, Hellboy's voice kept changing, growing even deeper and then returning to normal. Abe glanced at him several times, but his friend did not look at him again. A chill went through Abe and he shivered.

"You know a lot more about this stuff than you did a couple of days ago," Abe said slowly.

"The longer I hold the hammer and the further north we go, the clearer it all becomes in my head."

"Sometimes you don't even sound like yourself anymore. And I'm not just talking about your temper."

"Sometimes I don't feel like myself either."

"Any more hallucinations?" Abe asked.

"They're not hallucinations," Hellboy replied calmly.

As he spoke to Abe, Hellboy watched the ravens circling in the sky. The birds did not lead, now. He did not need them to, not with the pull he felt in the dense iron of the hammer.

The truck wound along a road at the base of a mountain range. Snow blew down off the mountains, and ice crystals formed upon the windshield. On the other side of the road was a line of trees, a dense wood that was scattered with white from a brief snowfall the night before.

Faces looked out at him from the trees.

"Stop the truck."

"What?" Abe asked.

"Stop. Please."

The vehicle shuddered to a stop. Pernilla woke abruptly, glancing around as though she had forgotten where she was and wondered how she came to awaken in a delivery truck in the frozen north with two such men. Hellboy ignored her as he stepped out onto the road, his hooves chipping ice. With Mjollnir raised and ready for battle, he marched across the small spread of land between the roadside and the woods, but when he reached the trees, there was no one there.

Hellboy stopped, a kind of deep, abiding sadness coming to rest within him, along with a profound dread. He shook his head once, then again. With his left hand, he made a fist and struck himself in the temple several times.

"Get *out* of my head!"

He took a long, shuddering breath and turned to stomp back toward the truck. Abe and Pernilla had gotten out to stretch, and Hellboy felt badly for his behavior. He knew that it wasn't fair to either of them, to his friend, or to this courageous woman he barely knew.

"Sorry," he muttered as he reached them.

Abe leaned against the truck, the mountain range behind it making them all seem so tiny and insignificant. "It's all right. We'll get to the end of this. This was as good a time as any to stop. We would have had to do it soon. We have a little less than half a tank of gas and no sign of any place up ahead that we could fill up. I suggest we go on by foot from here."

Pernilla still looked sleepy as she turned to him. "Is that really necessary?"

Abe shrugged. "We have provisions and equipment. We either go on foot now, or we don't have a truck to drive back when we're done."

Hellboy felt the heat of Mjollnir in his hand, and it pulled him toward the mountain. "It's all right. We're heading up now anyway."

They both turned to look up at the distant, snow-covered peaks. Then Abe looked at Pernilla.

"You can go back to the last village if you want. Take the truck. We'll make our way. It's going to be much harder on you than it will be on us making this trek. No one's going to fault you if you want to wait for us back there."

"No. I'll manage. Like you said, we've got provisions and equipment. I'll be all right."

"Okay," Abe agreed. He took a moment to digest that,

then glanced at Hellboy again and gestured toward the woods. "So what did you see? Svartalves? I've been wondering when they'd show up to try to stop us."

"No. Not Svartalves," he replied.

But he said nothing more. He was not sure how to explain to them that the faces and silhouettes he had seen in the woods belonged to Mist and her sisters, to the Valkyrie, and that they had come to claim his soul.

They found the first corpse eighteen hours later. The foothills had been easy enough to cross, and the pull of Mjollnir drew them through a narrow valley pass between two of the higher peaks in the range. Once beyond the pass Hellboy felt lured toward an adjunct mountain range where the peaks were linked with crevasses and hidden gorges but no real valley. There was only mountain, then, and they camped at the base for the night, and then picked up again in the morning, leaving the world behind.

The climb was steep and rigorous, and might have been impossible for Pernilla without proper climbing equipment had Hellboy not been along. Every few hours they paused briefly for a rest and a short meal. The snow was powdery on top, with a hard crust beneath. Even with Hellboy's bulk, his hooves did not sink very far, and he wondered how deep it was. There were bare places on the mountainside, outcroppings of rock where the wind whistled loudly and scoured the stone clean of snow cover. At such points, Hellboy went first, blocking his companions from the wind as best he could.

Despite the wind and the snow and the exertion of the climb, none of them complained. Pernilla's discomfort could be read quite clearly in her face, but she said nothing, only watched Hellboy and the hammer and nodded as though satisfied that they were on the right track. Several times she made comments about her father, and her determination to see Thrym destroyed for what he had done, but these were mostly to herself, as if she needed to remind herself why she had come.

In the early afternoon that following day it began to snow lightly. While he was aware that there was danger here, both from Thrym and from the elements, Hellboy was mesmerized by the beauty and power of nature. They were at the top of the world, almost as far divorced from human society as it was possible to get, and there was a certain wonder in that for him.

It was shortly thereafter that they crested a rise that fell away into a basin plateau thousands of feet higher than the foothills they had been in the day before, and they came upon the bloodied corpse of a Saami man.

"Damn," Hellboy whispered.

Abe and Pernilla crouched in the snow to examine him further. Hellboy narrowed his eyes and peered through the light snowfall, trying to get a sense of the landscape around them. The Nidavellim actually looked *up*, as well, though what they hoped to see, Hellboy could not imagine. Perhaps they imagined the corpse had been dropped from above by some great, monstrous bird. With the fresh snow, however, there was no sign as to how the man had been killed, or what had become of his killer.

The body was mangled, limbs twisted. The Saami man

was dressed in leather and fur, now stained with his blood, but the way he lay, there could be no way to tell which way he had been headed before he had been attacked.

Hellboy thought he knew, however. The magnetic tug on the hammer drew him northwest, and he believed that this man had been going the opposite direction, fleeing from Thrym, or whatever else awaited them further north.

Whatever it was, Hellboy suspected it was close.

As the afternoon wore on and soon became evening, they continued their trek along the mountain ridge. The storm increased in intensity, and soon the snow was falling thick and heavy, and they were forced to descend once more into a crag that ran between two peaks.

Though true darkness was still hours away, the storm had blackened the sky so it seemed almost as though night had already fallen. Eitri had taken the lead and slogged through the snow, which ought to have been harder for the Nidavellim, with their short legs, to navigate, but with which he had no trouble at all.

He tripped over the second corpse and fell nose-first into the snow, grunting as the pommels of his daggers jutted into his belly. When he stood, cursing, there was snow in his beard and on the iron rings in his hair. Eitri seemed ready to snap, desperate to have something to kill. Hellboy figured his grief over Brokk's death would be raw for a very long time.

"There are two of them this time," Abe noted. He glanced over at Hellboy, frowning. "Do you have any sense of what's going on here?"

At first Hellboy was not sure what he meant. In the many hours they had spent in the mountains, it had been easy for him to drift away from the weirdness of Mjollnir and its effect on him. Now he got it, though. Hellboy shook his head.

"It's gotta be Thrym. Part of what he's doing up here. But I've got no idea where these people are coming from. Maybe he snatched them from some village along the way and has been hoarding them for snacks."

Pernilla shuddered and put a hand to her mouth, apparently horrified by the image. But despite that, she knelt by the two corpses again. They were covered with a thick frost and their blood had turned to crimson ice where it had pooled upon their clothing. There was a male and a female, and the woman had an icicle of blood that ran across her face from a gash in her head and connected to the snow-covered ground.

"They've been drained," Pernilla announced, voice

sounding more and more detached every time she spoke.

"Drained?" Eitri asked, moving closer.

"Thrym is sucking the life out of them," Abe explained. "He did it back at that village where we met up with you."

"And he did it to my father," Pernilla said softly.

"Something tells me we're going to find more," Hellboy said.

They all turned to look at him then, strange silhouettes against the twilight curtain of snow. Pernilla stood up and brushed off the knees of her snow gear. Abe gazed at Mjollnir.

"Are we still headed in the right direction?" he asked.

Hellboy nodded.

"Then let's go," Abe said.

After nearly another hour had passed with the sky

growing even darker, Hellboy knew they were going to have to stop to camp soon. If they could find a cavern or even an outcropping under which they could take shelter, that would be best. It was obvious that the weather did not impress the Nidavellim at all. They could probably have gone on forever wandering those mountains in the storm. But Hellboy himself was exhausted and cold—frost had begun to form on the stumps on his forehead where he kept his broken horns filed down—and he had no idea how Abe and particularly Pernilla were going on.

In that short time they had found at least a dozen bodies, enough so that it no longer surprised them. They no longer bothered to even stop to examine the remains. Hellboy thought of Hansel and Gretel's trail of bread crumbs, and the macabre twist that put on the presence of the corpses in his mind gave him a chill that had nothing to do with the snowstorm.

As they crested a rise, Hellboy was determined to stop for the night. But when he had gotten his bearings, his hooves crunching through the crust of snow, he stared down into the basin plateau below, and he knew they had reached their destination.

"What is that?" Abe asked, eyes narrowed as he tried to make out the sprawl below.

"I think it's a village," Pernilla replied.

Hellboy shook his head slowly as he studied the dark shapes of buildings below, several dozen small houses and a trio of smaller central buildings. There had to be a road around here somewhere, a path that weaved in and out of the mountains so these people could get to a larger settlement when they really needed to.

But they weren't going anywhere. Not ever again. His eyesight was better than the others'. The dead they had found in the snow had come from this village, trying to get over the mountains to safety. There were probably more dead along other routes. But the rest were still here, in the rubble of this village, which had been all but destroyed save for two of the large buildings at the center.

"It was," he said. "Look again."

Pernilla squinted, and Abe actually took several steps down the cliff face. But Hellboy saw it clearly enough. The ruin of the village was obscured by what at first appeared to be a mirage. Transparent walls and battlements many stories high rose into the air, towers jutting up from behind massive gates. This fortress was no mirage, however.

"What is that?" Abe asked, mystified.

It took Pernilla another moment, but then she actually took a startled step backward. "How . . . how did I not see that at first? It is as though there's a whole city there. But then how can I still see the village too? It's as if the place has been swallowed by this other. Is it an optical illusion?"

Despite the fear in her

voice, Hellboy was no longer paying attention to her. His gaze had been drawn to the surviving Nidavellim, who had gathered close together, their weapons at the ready as they studied the sprawling mirage of towering walls and gates that loomed in the snowstorm below them.

"Hellboy, what's going on?" Abe asked.

The Nidavellim glanced up at the sound of his voice. Eitri nodded once at Hellboy.

"It is Utgard," the dwarf told him.

Hellboy nodded. "I know."

"No . . . wait," Pernilla interrupted. "You can't possibly mean that this is *the* Utgard. The citadel of the giants."

Hellboy only looked at her, then slowly turned to regard Abe, whose moist, dark skin was flecked with

snowflakes that melted almost as soon as they touched him.

"This? This right here?" Abe asked, an edge to his voice. "How can the city of the giants be here? Just plopped right down on some village that was here already. Never mind that, wasn't it destroyed during Ragnarok along with everything else?"

Once more Hellboy turned to gaze out at the sprawling silhouette, the image of Utgard that wavered in and out of reality with each rush of wind, each blast of driven snow.

"It isn't Utgard," Hellboy said, his deep voice carrying along the mountain ridge. "It's the ghost of Utgard."

CHAPTER FOURTEEN

Once, not long after he had joined the Bureau, Abe Sapien had spent six days trudging across the Australian outback with only an aborigine shapeshifter for a guide. They had been investigating an outbreak of nightmares that were driving people to madness and outright slaughter, and Hellboy had been dragged into the Dreamtime by a pack of dingoes. Abe didn't remember much of the story of what had happened to Hellboy there, because, by the time they were reunited and Hellboy gave him the details, he was so completely exhausted that all he heard was *blah blah blah.* As far as he was concerned, the only thing that mattered was that it was over and they could go home.

It was a close call, but he thought that he might be even more exhausted now than he had been in the outback all those years ago.

His feet were so cold they were numb, and he tried to pretend all those little niggling thoughts about frostbite and amputation were just silly jokes he was making to himself. Nothing funny about them, but otherwise he was going to start freaking out, and that would not do any of them any good.

Abe wrapped his arms around himself and shuddered as he forged his way through the storm. The snow had thinned and slowed, but it was still there, like a heavy curtain draped over them. *Not a shroud, don't think shroud.* He pushed the image out of his mind. His boots were weatherproof, so his feet were dry, but that didn't keep the cold out. He kept his eyes slitted against the snowfall and did his best to follow in Hellboy's enormous footprints.

They picked their way carefully along the ridge that overlooked the snug basin where the ghostly fortress stood. It seemed to have grown more solid as the minutes went by, but there were still times when he glanced down at it from a certain angle and the citadel of the giants disappeared completely in the screen of snow.

But Utgard was for later. Right now shelter was their top priority. His eyelids felt frozen and when he blinked they were sticky as if they wanted to freeze closed completely. Abe glanced back to make sure Eitri and the other three Nidavellim were still following. They waded through the deepening snow in grim silence.

When he looked ahead once more, Pernilla had stopped. She stood with both legs planted in one of Hellboy's massive footprints and she shivered, her teeth chattering. Abe went to her and put his arms around her for warmth, though he knew he wouldn't provide very much of that. His eyes ticked toward Hellboy, who was perhaps twenty feet ahead of them. He wanted to shout to him, tell him to wait, but he had no idea how far his voice would carry, and it would not do to draw Thrym's attention until they were ready for that.

But he needn't have worried.

Hellboy walked on a few more feet and then stopped. The wind drove the snow at him, it swept around him, and to Abe he looked like little more than a monstrous black silhouette against the night and the storm. His duster flapped around his legs, snapping like a flag in the breeze. Hellboy dropped into a crouch and stared at something ahead, then turned and waved to Abe and Pernilla to hurry.

"He's found something," Abe told her. "Just a little further."

Her eyes had a dull sheen to them, and he recognized it as both exhaustion and apathy. She was so tired now that she almost did not care if they died out there. But Abe knew that was only frustration and despair taking root, and it would go away the moment she had some respite from the cold.

"Come on," he said, and he slipped his arm around her and together they walked toward Hellboy.

He stood at the edge of a crevasse with walls of ice and stone. It was as though the largest of all giants had cleaved the earth asunder with a hatchet. The snow fell down into the black depths of that gash in the mountainside, and the wind pushed at Abe's back. He drew Pernilla a step away from the edge, for the pull of that chasm was too great, and a flutter went through him as he imagined them tumbling down into it.

"Dead end," Abe said.

Hellboy glanced at him. "Yep. But maybe also exactly what we need." He pointed along the crevasse to a place where the edge tapered downward, creating a natural ledge formation that led to a kind of plateau about a dozen feet down. "If it doesn't fall out from under us, and nothing explodes, we should be all right until the worst of the wind dies. If we're going to try to get the people who are still alive out of Utgard, I'd rather do it before dawn. I'm hoping the snow stops by then. If we can get a few hours' rest, all the better."

Abe smiled. Though he was obviously stressed, Hellboy sounded like himself. Lately it was impossible to predict if they were going to get the regular guy who rolled with the punches or the other guy. Hellboy had always liked to beat the crap out of things. If something got in his way, or gave him trouble, his usual solution was to whomp it with something heavy until it wasn't an issue anymore. He was hell on electronics that didn't behave themselves. Abe had lost two TVs that way in the time they had known one another.

But the other guy, the essence of this thing that had hitched a ride in Hellboy's head thanks to Mjollnir . . . that guy lived for the battle. He was brutal and a little crazy. Abe had heard stories about Viking berserkers, ruthless and bloodthirsty warriors who wore *berserks*, or bearskin shirts. There was the implication that they thought they took on the spirit of the bear to help them be savage in battle. But bears didn't have anything on these guys when it came to nastiness. From what Abe knew, they might not have been men at all, but some kind of thing somewhere between man and animal. In any case, if this entity that had hijacked Hellboy was any indication, it was no surprise that the Vikings had such a fierce rep.

"You seem . . . better," Abe told him.

Hellboy shrugged. "Got a mythological monkey on my back. But it's subsided for the moment. Can't even feel anything in the hammer anymore. Or in the snake," he added, gesturing toward the pendant around his neck.

"Now that we're here, maybe it's leaving you alone for a bit."

"Maybe," Hellboy allowed, but his jaw was set and there was a gravity about him. "To tell the truth, though, I've been thinking maybe I'm just getting used to it." He turned toward the ledge. "Come on."

For a moment Abe just watched him go. Pernilla slipped her arm through his and shivered.

"I don't think I like the sound of that," she said.

"Me either," Abe replied.

As they spoke, Eitri and the other Nidavellim gathered around them. Abe turned to the creatures, all of whom had been painfully silent since Brokk's death. They had lost others of their kind during the horrors of the past days, but Brokk had clearly meant a great deal to all of them, not merely to Eitri, who was his brother.

"We're going to take shelter down there for a while," Abe explained, pointing to the plateau in the crevasse.

Eitri grunted and frowned as he gazed down into the chasm. "There is very little room. We will remain here and alternate on sentry duty."

Pernilla frowned and reached out to place a hand on the Nidavellim's shoulder. "We'll make room. You really should get out of the wind for a while."

A kind smile appeared on Eitri's face, as if her gesture had warmed him for the first time since his brother's demise. "Thank you, Miss Aickman. But my cousins and I have weathered far worse than this. We will be all right."

Abe felt as though he ought to make a greater effort to urge Eitri to join them, but after a moment he decided against it. The Nidavellim could follow them down at any time if they wanted to. Right now it was imperative that he get Pernilla to as much shelter as he could find. Down in the crevasse they could light a fire without worrying that it would be seen. All they had was a trio of those flame-starter logs—which were stashed in Hellboy's pack—but it would give them a small bit of warmth and light for an hour or so if they spaced them out. That would be enough to discover if his feet were going to fall off from frostbite.

With Pernilla now behind him, Abe made his way along the gorge to where the natural ledge formation began. It was four or five feet wide—though much narrower in spots—and Hellboy was already nearly to the plateau below.

"Lay your hands against the stone face," Abe told Pernilla. "Like this."

He spread himself out against the rock wall and moved slowly along the ledge, and she followed suit. The moment they dropped below the edge of the crevasse, the wind was cut off. Abe could hear it whistling overhead, but the relief that flooded through him was almost euphoric. It was as though some great weight had been lifted from him. Thanks to the lack of wind, the temperature within that jagged slice in the earth was easily twenty or thirty degrees warmer than it was above.

Still cold. Still, in fact, ridiculously frigid—and Abe never wanted to feel that cold again. But liveable. His eyelids no longer felt like they might ice over at any moment.

"You all right?" he asked Pernilla.

She grunted with concentration as she traversed the ledge and did not look up, but a dry chuckle came from her lips. "Never better. All in all, I'd rather be on a Greek island basking in the sun, but right now this will do."

Several minutes later they had reached the broad plateau, which Abe now judged to be at least fifteen feet below the edge of the chasm. Hellboy had pulled out the starter bricks, and in moments the first of them was blazing brightly. It was too insignificant to pass for a campfire, but it would do. Within minutes they had gathered around the small flame and laid out their gear to try to sleep. Abe sat atop his waterproof bedroll and Pernilla lay snugly within hers, her face almost too close to the fire. Hellboy had also climbed inside his oversized sleeping bag—when it was all put together his pack was enormous and had to be absurdly heavy, but he never seemed to notice. He lay watching the fire, and its light made orange and black shadows flickers across his crimson skin.

Despite what Abe had been thinking earlier, Hellboy was too quiet now. It was disturbing. He had a sudden flash of the hotel room they'd shared in Washington D.C. right before leaving for this debacle in Sweden. Cable TV, macadamia nuts, and just hanging around. Both of them could be pretty stoic at times, but Abe thought that was part of why they were friends.

We have got to get home soon, he thought, staring across the tiny flickering fire. *And without that hammer.*

"Have you put any thought into how we're going to do this?" he asked.

Pernilla turned to study Hellboy across the flames as well. Abe had regretted allowing her to come along at least once every five or ten minutes since they had left Stockholm. But each time he thought about it, his mind would go back to that moment where she announced her intention to come along, and he could not think of anything they could have said or done differently to dissuade her without her hating them. And Abe did not want Pernilla Aickman to hate him.

Hellboy cleared his throat and scratched at the little patch of goatee on his chin with his left hand. In his right, Mjollnir lay heavy upon the ground. The hammer seemed to absorb the light of the fire rather than reflect it, and so it looked almost black there in the illumination cast by that small blaze.

"I'll take Eitri and the boys and crash the party. You two check those buildings still standing and get anyone who's still alive out of there."

Even with all his misgivings, Abe had to laugh. That was one thing that Hellboy and the spirit in Mjollnir had in common. They both favored the direct approach.

"Pretty simple plan."

"The best ones usually are," Hellboy said, eyes blazing red in the firelight.

Abe recreated the image of Utgard in his mind, but not only that ghost city. He tried to remember the layout of the devastated village that had been supplanted by the resurrected fortress.

"You'll have to get us in first, somewhere to the north. We'll be closer to the remaining buildings and as far as we can get from your attack. Then when you go through the front, you'll draw Thrym away from us."

Hellboy gazed at him. "Works for me."

"What if . . . ," Pernilla let her words trail off and seemed to consider them a moment. At length, she let her gaze move back and forth between them and her eyes settled on Hellboy. "What if none of them are still alive by the time the morning comes?"

"Then the fight gets easier."

Abe had heard the concern, the compassion in her voice. When Hellboy spoke, though, it was as though he had crushed those things. Pernilla shivered, but this time Abe did not think it was from the cold. She reached for her pack and rifled through it until she came out with a box of cigarettes.

"I didn't know you smoked," Abe said, trying to keep the distaste out of his voice. She didn't need judgment from him on top of everything else.

"They're for emergencies," Pernilla replied. "This qualifies."

He did not argue.

Hellboy turned over, his back to them now. At the base of his skull was a small black knot he created from what little hair he had, the sort of thing Abe only ever saw in martial-arts films. But it worked on Hellboy. And even if it hadn't, nobody was going to tell him it looked stupid. Well, except for Liz, who had threatened more than once to pull a Delilah on him and cut it off.

Abe sighed and reached out to grab the second of their starter bricks. Rather than just toss it on the remains of the existing, dying flames, he lit the corner of the paper and let it flare to life. He hoped it would burn more slowly that way. As he was about to set it down, Pernilla grabbed hold of his wrist.

"Hold on," she said. "Do you mind?"

He obliged, holding up the flaming brick for her as she lit her cigarette off it. She sucked on the filter and the tip of the cigarette glowed, embers burning. Abe put the brick down carefully, relishing the feeling that had returned to his feet.

"All right. Let's try to get a couple of hours rest if we can. The snow looks like it might stop soon."

"You, my friend, are an optimist," Pernilla replied, voice a tired rasp.

Abe smiled thinly. "No one's ever called me that before."

Pernilla took another drag on the cigarette, her knees drawn up to her chest. She let the butt dangle in her hand, there against her knee, and she returned his smile.

Then she screamed as flames shot from the end of her cigarette. Abe shouted in alarm and scrambled back from her. Pernilla held the butt pinched in her fingers, staring at it. Fire jetted from the tip and joined with the small blaze of the starter brick. It began to grow, to take shape and to roar with a low thunderous growl that was more than the hiss and pop of a fire.

"Throw it down!" Abe cried.

As if the thought had never occurred to her—and he realized that it hadn't—Pernilla dropped the cigarette and backed away further. By then, the roar of the fire-shape in front of them had grown even louder. Abe could feel the heat of it searing his face.

It had arms and legs and a head; it stood easily nine feet tall.

And it laughed at them.

"What the hell is this thing now?" Abe muttered.

Behind the fire-creature, Hellboy rose from the ground. "Hey!" he shouted. "You're screwing up my nap. You don't want me cranky, do you?"

Hellboy swung Mjollnir at the thing and it began to pass through the flames. For a moment Abe thought Hellboy's blow would just swing all the way around, harmlessly. But then, abruptly, the hammer struck something solid within that blazing creature's substance. It staggered back a step, but not far enough. The living flame that comprised it raged and enveloped Mjollnir and Hellboy's right arm, licking up toward his shoulder and racing across his chest as well, charring skin as it went.

The thing laughed again as Hellboy tried to tug his arm free, and the fire began to engulf his entire body. Abe ran to Pernilla, shielding her with his body even as he moved them both back against the wall of the crevasse, as far away from this thing as possible. He could see now that it had eyes of yellow mist and a gash for a mouth.

"*Foolish god-shell*," it roared, its voice the snap of burning wood. "*You are as dense as the true thunderer himself. Logi will consume you.*"

Hellboy snarled. "I remember you, Logi. You trumped my brother by deceit only. I have been burned before, Wildfire, and dragon's breath cannot last forever."

"But I am not dragon's breath. I am only myself. Eternal flame."

The fire crawled all over Hellboy and his jacket was ablaze now, a sheet of flame licking up toward the sky, snow melting as it neared him. Logi seemed to have enveloped him so that now Hellboy was almost inside him. He roared with agony.

Abe felt his skin prickle with the heat of it, but he had to help Hellboy. "There's something in there!" he barked. "You hit something before. Do it again!"

Pernilla's breath was warm on his neck and she panted in fear as Abe pressed her against the wall. He could hear her muttering to herself, nonsense words that he took, at first, for terrified ramblings. Abe watched as Hellboy attacked the thing, shouting in agony and fury as he burned. He raised the hammer and struck Logi, and the fire-creature staggered backward. The flames on Hellboy subsided somewhat, black smoke rising in places where the blaze receded. Hellboy struck him again, aiming for the head but hitting the mon-

strous thing instead in the chest. Something cracked loudly and yellow flames roared out of its chest cavity.

Logi cried out, enraged, and redoubled his efforts, using both hands to grab at his enemy once more. The fire blazed up around Hellboy again. Abe was frantic. He knew he had to protect Pernilla, and he knew that Hellboy could endure almost anything, that he could take care of himself . . . but this was too much.

"Start up toward the ridge," Abe told Pernilla.

"I can't. Not without my gear. I'll freeze up there."

Abe swore. "What the hell is this guy?" he muttered.

"Logi," Pernilla said, as though tasting the name. "Logi, wait, I've heard it. There's a story, one of the myths. Logi wasn't a giant, but he was a servant to the king of the Frost Giants—"

"To Thrym?" Abe asked.

"No. One of the others. He's fire incarnate. But the giants had to call him up from a source. He had to have a source, Abe."

"Your cigarette?"

They both glanced over at the spot where the cigarette had dropped. There was no sign of the burning ember of its tip. Near the edge of the plateau, above a drop that seemed to fall away into nowhere, Hellboy struck Logi with the hammer again and again, and though the creature seemed pained by them, the blows were not stopping it.

"It started there," Pernilla said quickly. "But look!"

Abe saw what she was referring to. Logi was far from the place where they had made their small camp, but skeins of fire stretched away from his blazing form, reaching back toward the single small starter brick, this chunk of chemicals and pulped wood.

"The source," Abe muttered. It would burn out in five minutes, maybe less, given the way the flames were fluttering now, burning faster as though Logi was feeding off them.

But Hellboy didn't have five minutes.

"Don't move," he told Pernilla.

A glance upward revealed that the Nidavellim were on their way down, but they would not arrive in time to be of any help. *So much for bodyguarding Hellboy*, Abe thought. It fell to him, then.

Silently, he pushed away from the stone face of the crevasse wall and ran out across the plateau. His boots slid a little in the snow, and he nearly lost his footing as he rushed toward the place where his bedroll lay sprawled too close to the fire. He noticed that the edges of the non-flammable synthetic were singed, but the fact barely registered as he reached the little fire-starter, the small log that was sputtering with flame. As he hauled back his foot, Logi seemed to sense him, and the fire-creature hissed and popped and began to wash toward him across the darkness.

Abe kicked the blazing starter brick as hard as he could. It sailed across the platform, bounced once, and then skipped out over the chasm below before dropping down, down into the seemingly endless darkness of that scar in the face of the earth.

Logi roared with fury as he was dragged over the edge. Impossibly long fingers of fire stretched into tentacles as he tried to hold on, but then the weight of the source became too much and he lost his grip, shrieking as he tumbled into the murk, as though someone had thrown a torch down a well. Abe stood at the edge and watched him fall until there was only the tiniest wink of light below.

"Abe," Pernilla said, and there was panic in her voice.

He spun and saw Hellboy on his knees in the snow perhaps a dozen feet away. Though it was dark now without the flames, Abe could see that his jacket was all but destroyed and the red flesh of his arms was puckered and seared, charred black in some places.

"Aw, damn it!" Abe rushed to Hellboy's side, but slowed as he got near his friend.

Hellboy seemed frozen, Mjollnir in his hand, his chest rising and falling as he took long, deep breaths. The stench of his seared skin was repulsive and Abe's stomach churned with nausea.

"Hey," he said, his own voice thick with concern.

Abe reached out to touch Hellboy's shoulder, but Hellboy abruptly turned and glared at him, slapped his hand away. Then he rose, far faster than Abe had ever seen him move, and Hellboy swung the hammer at him.

"Back, darkling beast!" Hellboy snarled. "I've had my fill of monsters today!"

If Abe had been a fraction of a second slower, Mjollnir would have shattered his chest, probably torn a hole right through flesh and bone. He shouted in alarm as he leaped away. Hellboy staggered slightly, shook his head as if to clear his mind, then sneered and started forward again. Abe rushed back toward Pernilla, wondering if they were going to have to run for the top of the chasm, and to hell with their gear.

Hellboy fell on his face, arms out at his sides. His flesh was still so hot after being burned by Logi's flames that the icy ground hissed loudly as heat met frozen earth. For several seconds, Hellboy did not move.

"Oh, no," Abe said quietly. Something began to feel

broken inside him. Again he moved toward Hellboy, more carefully this time.

With a pained moaning, Hellboy shifted. Abe stared at him in astonishment, noticing that his skin seemed to already be healing. That wasn't natural. Hellboy healed fast, but never this fast.

"Abe?" he croaked weakly.

"I'm here. You planning to take another swing at me?"

Hellboy rolled over on his back, too weak to do any more than that. His eyes were wide and childlike, and he looked not at all dangerous, but rather pitiful.

"Aw, Jeez, Abe. I'm sorry."

The sorrow in his voice was dreadful to hear.

Hellboy glanced down at Mjollnir, then lay his head back again and stared up at the sky. "All this time I've had this damned hand and I know it isn't really me, and sometimes that spooks me. But I've made it mine. You know? But this freakin' hammer? I'm going down there and killing that giant zombie with the stupid trees growing out of his chest and then if the hammer is still stuck to my hand, I'm cutting the whole arm off, I swear."

Again, Hellboy had returned to himself. This time, though, much as he wanted to be glad, Abe could not summon any relief. Hellboy was falling apart right in front of him, and there was nothing he could do about it.

On the ground, Hellboy lay and gazed at the sky, face illuminated by the light of the stars.

The stars.

Only then did Abe realize that the snow had stopped. The storm was over.

It was time to put an end to this.

CHAPTER FIFTEEN

Mjollnir was no longer luring Hellboy in one direction or another, but in some ways it haunted him more than ever. There was a presence inside him, lurking at the back of his mind; it felt like he was waiting in line for something with this rude, extremely impatient entity staring over his shoulder, urging him on. He felt like throttling the big barbaric bastard, but there was no way he could get his hands around the throat of some spiritual echo, especially when the only body it had at the moment was his own.

He led the way down the mountainside mostly to avoid having to look Abe or Pernilla in the eye. Guilt and embarrassment went hand in hand, and that had never been more true than tonight. It wasn't him; Abe knew that. But Hellboy still figured he owed his friend a bottle of tequila and a trip to the antiquarian book shop back in Fairfield.

If they ever got back to Fairfield.

The truth was, Hellboy had thought more than once about telling Abe and Pernilla to head back. Send the Nidavellim to protect them and just make them go home. And that was another reason he felt guilty; the only reason he hadn't done that was because he thought right about now Abe might take him up on the offer, and he did not feel like being up here at the top of the world by himself.

Not that he was afraid. No way. After the crap he'd gone up against and lived to tell the tale? Nah.

Well, maybe a little.

But there was more to it than that. He wasn't himself now. There was no way to know what he was going to do next. He had heard the expression "taken leave of his senses" a hundred times, but only now did he really understand what it meant. Of course, he doubted anyone he'd heard use the phrase had ever been talking about someone possessed by a myth. But that didn't mean it wasn't appropriate.

The presence that lingered inside his skull—and in that damned hammer—wanted to merge with him. Or, at least, that was the sense that he got, on the surface of things. Below the surface, though, he could feel that it wasn't really a merger the echo was looking for, but a hostile takeover.

So it was that they moved carefully down the mountainside into the basin where once a village had stood, and now there was only rubble and ghosts. The snow had stopped, and the night sky had cleared with remarkable speed. The air was cold and crisp, as though each breath that Hellboy drew into his massive lungs was comprised of tiny ice crystals. The stars made the newfallen snow glow a strange blue and provided more than enough light to see by.

Hellboy picked his way down the steep face of the mountain. His jacket had been all but destroyed. In with his gear he had an enormous sweater that had been knitted just for him by Anastasia Bransfield, the only woman he had ever referred to as his girlfriend. It had been years since he had spoken to her, and many more than that since he had seen her last, and still it pained him to have destroyed the sweater. In order to get it over the godforsaken hammer and his massive right hand, he had to cut the right arm of the garment along its length.

Hard-packed snow crunched under his hooves and the fresh layer of powder sifted in around his legs. His pack had not been a burden throughout their long journey, but now, though lightened, he was weary of carrying it. From time to time he heard Abe or Pernilla grunt with exertion behind him, but the Nidavellim made not a sound. They were coming nearer to the ghost walls of Utgard and knew better than to give themselves away.

As they descended, the wind whistling around them, the way became easier to navigate, and near the floor of that crag, they found themselves striding over foothills that put them briefly out of sight of Utgard. As they crested one such hill, Hellboy caught sight again of the narrow path that must have been the road to a larger settlement further along the mountain ridge.

At the peak of the final hill, they looked up. Hellboy was filled with both a cold familiarity and a terrible dread. The walls of Utgard were growing more solid as they drew closer, and they could gauge the size of the place now. The battlements of Utgard towered more than one hundred feet above them. Once upon a time they had been built of dark stone, and now they took on that aspect again, though from this distance the texture of those walls seemed to waver between solid rock and insubstantial mist.

"All right," Hellboy whispered as the others gathered around him. "Just like we talked about." He gazed grimly at Abe. "You and Pernilla stay clear of Thrym. Just do what you have to do and get the hell out of here. If you end up on your own, take whoever you can find and follow that track that heads west. I'm betting there's a Saami village that way. Might even be Norway this far north, I don't know. But if they've got any kind of road it's gotta be shorter than the jaunt we took to get up here."

Abe nodded, did not comment about the implications of Hellboy's instructions—that he might not be alive to leave with them.

Mjollnir began to grow warm again in his hand, and the serpent pendant became so cold against his chest, even beneath that sweater, that it was nearly stuck to his flesh. Hellboy hissed at the sudden icy pain and reached up to touch it. He pulled it out by the chain and let it hang outside the sweater.

"I should've left this thing back at the university."

"No," Eitri said sharply.

Hellboy, Abe, and Pernilla all turned to stare at him. Eitri and his cousins had been silent for so long that though he spoke quietly, that single word resonated in the air around them.

"What?" Hellboy asked.

Eitri gestured toward the pendant. "My brother Brokk forged Mjollnir, a gift of life to the thunder-bearer. I crafted that pendant, a representation of Jormungand, the world snake, the Midgard Serpent. The hammer was a gift of life. The pendant was a gift of death. He wore it at the end."

Even as he spoke, Hellboy knew the words were true. It was something he had known all along, but never thought about. He lay Mjollnir across his shoulder and touched the pendant, the fingers of his left hand aching with the cold in that metal.

"Great. I'm sure he thought it was very thoughtful. So why can't I take it off again?"

Eitri lifted his gaze to stare into Hellboy's eyes. "I think it is an anchor for the spirit in Mjollnir. If not that, then at least it is a negative to the hammer's positive. Think of it in that way. They complement each other, creating an energy between them that may be keeping the thunderer here in some way."

Hellboy stared at him. He wanted to cuss Eitri out. All this time, it might have been as simple as getting rid of the pendant to shake loose the hold Mjollnir had over him. It made sense in a way, considering that ever since he took the pendant from Abe the echo of the dead myth had resounded stronger in him, altering him more and more. But Hellboy also thought there was more to it than that. He had a feeling until Thrym was destroyed, whatever powers had brought the corpse of the thunder-bearer out where it could be discovered were not about to let their pawn walk away free.

He gritted his teeth but said nothing. If he raged at Eitri, he'd be no better than the belligerent spirit he wanted so badly to get rid of.

"All right," he said. "It stays. But when this is done, you can take it back."

Eitri nodded his head once in agreement.

Out of the corner of his eye, Hellboy saw Pernilla reach up to grab Abe's arm. It wasn't a gesture of warmth or friendship, but one of shock. Hellboy turned quickly to find that both she and Abe were staring off to the west toward the front gates of Utgard.

"Abe, what—"

"Get down," Abe muttered.

Hellboy didn't argue. All of them slipped back down the last hill, hiding themselves from the line of sight of anyone down on the plateau. Hellboy knelt in the snow and looked over the top of the hill, and he saw what it was that had stunned Abe and Pernilla.

From the frozen ground not far from the gates of Utgard, another giant was rising. Its skeletal, ice-encrusted arms had burst up through the earth, spilling snow and soil around it. The thing was hideous, a kind of spider-webbing of dry skin remaining as a death shroud upon those bones. In its right hand it clutched a huge sword, easily fifteen feet in length and covered in rust and crusted blood and dirt.

As they watched, astonished, it stood up from that frozen grave and walked toward the gates, which swung open to admit it and closed when it had passed. The moment it was gone Hellboy glanced around and realized that the earth all around the fortress had been cracked and broken, though the fresh snow had hidden most of the evidence of that.

Hellboy sighed. "Well, that can't be good."

"There's no way to know how many there are," Abe added.

"Nope. There isn't."

"What do we do now?" Pernilla asked.

Hellboy smiled to himself and glanced at her. "We could go home?"

Her withering gaze was as cold as the frozen mountainside. "That isn't funny."

His expression was grave again. Pernilla knew her father had been both part of the cause of this, and its victim. She wasn't about to turn around, and they both knew it.

"No. I guess it isn't. Sorry." He glanced around at the others. "Let's go."

Abe tried as best he could to shake his exhaustion, but like the cold it seemed to have settled in his bones. Their one small attempt at rest had been interrupted, and they were too far from anything resembling home, and much too far from help. This was it. The odds sucked almost as bad as the weather.

They worked their way east behind that last foothill for fifty or sixty yards, then slipped over the top and hurried down to the basin floor with only jagged upthrust rocks for cover. Inside Utgard there was only silence. Abe took the lead, then, sprinting across the open ground to press himself against the stone walls. Just as he came within a few feet of Utgard, he marveled at their solidity. This wasn't just big magic, it was *huge* magic. Nothing so simple as a ghost. Some haunted city that had turned up in response to Thrym's arrival, his calling of it, drawing it from out of the ether.

Then he leaned against it and inadvertently let his hand touch the stone and found that it was warm and moist, and it shot a kind of numbness up his arm that ached deep as the marrow. Abe shuddered and held out his unaffected hand to gesture to the others, to keep them from touching the wall. For he believed, then. Just that touch had convinced him.

This was a shadow out of time, the specter of a dead city, a phantom fortress. Abe had seen a lot of bizarre stuff since joining the Bureau—hell, sometimes he forgot that he was a pretty odd discovery himself—but nothing like this. When he glanced at Pernilla, he could see that she was also profoundly disturbed by their proximity to the place. It was more than surreal . . . it was unreal. Everything Pernilla Aickman knew about the world had been torn away in recent days, and it was nothing short of miraculous that she had not become completely unhinged.

Not yet.

But Abe saw in her eyes, now, that Utgard was haunting her. And he suspected that it would haunt her for a very, very long time.

"Come on," he said, reaching for her hand. "We can do this. It's almost over."

"How can you be so calm?" she asked, voice hitching.

"I'm not. There are times when it's helpful to be inscrutable. Nobody can tell when you're terrified out of your mind."

Abe smiled at her and Pernilla took a long breath. Then she nodded and they moved on, Hellboy and the Nidavellim pausing only a moment at the wall before hurrying to keep up. They made their way along the southern wall and then around to the east, as far away from the gates as they could manage. At a spot about a third of the way along the length of that massive structure, Abe stopped and waited for Hellboy.

"Here?" Hellboy asked.

"It'll do."

"You know this only works if nobody hears us breaking in. And now that we know Thrym's not alone in there, the odds of that are poor."

"I was just thinking about the odds a few minutes ago," Abe replied. "But there's nothing we can do about it now. If they hear us, then the plan changes." He shrugged.

Hellboy only nodded before taking a step toward the wall and narrowing his eyes, as though merely by studying it he could find the weakest point in its construction. After a moment he glanced at the Nidavellim and pointed to a spot on the wall where two massive granite slabs were fitted together.

"Here?"

Eitri stepped forward and studied the spot. "Yes. That is your best chance."

A change came over Hellboy then. His thin lips pressed together so that they seemed even thinner, and the still-scorched flesh on his arms cracked as he stretched himself out. Muscles popped as he raised Mjollnir, eyes flaring with a kind of primal strength.

He swung the hammer in a single massive stroke that rang loudly upon impact. The stones moved, cracked, shifted, and then several of the huge blocks crashed backward into the courtyard of the citadel of the giants.

With the echo lingering in the air they waited several long minutes to see if there would come any response from within, but there was none. At length, Hellboy looked over at Abe and gave him a thumbs up. Abe returned the gesture and then watched as Hellboy signaled the Nidavellim, and the warriors began the long trek around the ghost city to the front gates.

Pernilla slipped her hand into his, and when Abe glanced at her, she inclined her head toward the hole in the wall. He squeezed her hand and then, together, they entered Utgard.

The section of wall through which they had come had been well chosen. Utgard wasn't truly a city at all, of course, but its sheer size made it seem as though it was. Rather, it was a fortress, a citadel comprised of numerous huge structures—the living quarters for the giants—arranged in a rough rectangular shape. The outer walls had been built around these towers and battlements constructed atop them. In the midst of the citadel, however, was an enormous courtyard. Once upon a time, before Ragnarok and the collapse of the nine worlds, the implosion that destroyed all of Jotunheim, Utgard's courtyard might have been a marketplace or a field of combat for warriors who wished to test their mettle in rare times of peace. It would have been the place where feasts were held, weddings celebrated, and funeral ceremonies conducted.

Now it was a wasteland.

Abe and Pernilla slipped alongside a massive tower, perhaps the grandest of all. He suspected it would be the king's palace and feared that Thrym would emerge any moment. They stayed near the wall, in the furthest recesses of the fortress, but as they passed in the shadows and through the arches of the various towers, they glimpsed that courtyard, a frozen field of snow and ice, and the giants that lumbered across it. These were not ice and bones, but somehow had become enfleshed, incarnate. Only partially, though, and some more than others. One was sleeping out in the open, little more than a skeleton, but two others standing by the distant gates as sentries had the look of corpses who had been dead a month or less.

Abe spotted two more walking from one tower to another, a male and female who rumbled something to one another in a language Abe did not know. They were nearly whole, their flesh withered and sagging, but not dessicated in any way. They were edged with a gilding of ice and wore whatever strips of ragged cloth had not rotted off them in the ground, and the male had a horned helmet and a club.

Each of them carried a human corpse. The male lifted the dead villager to his mouth and crunched its upper half between his jagged teeth, then seemed to suck on the cadaver for a few seconds. He spat bones onto the ground and then used his teeth to peel the remaining flesh from the dead man.

Pernilla whimpered in horror and pressed herself against Abe, unwilling to look. But Abe could not turn away, revolted though he was. So he was watching when the giant *changed.* The resurrected monster's skin no longer sagged, and instead of looking withered, it now looked only weathered, leathery.

Quickly Abe glanced around at the other giants, in various states of decay, and he realized with profound horror how deep Thrym's magic reached. Not only had he resurrected all of these frost giants, but with each human life they took, each bit of human flesh they consumed, they became more complete, more whole. More alive.

No, not alive. They're undead. Giant walking dead things. It was bad enough with Thrym as a skeleton. Now he understood what Thrym had been doing all along, this entire trek northward. And he feared for Hellboy. But at the moment, he had a job to do.

"Nobody else is going to end up like that," he whispered to Pernilla.

Together they moved swiftly and silently along behind another of the towers. The giants varied in size, but the enormity of each tower was extraordinary. For long minutes they moved through the forgotten places of that fortress, and several times they had to circumvent the remains of some house or other, a dwelling that had been occupied scant days before and was now nothing but rubble. After a time they came around the edge of a tower to find a wood and stone building—a human structure—growing right out of the side of the thing. There was no seam, and both seemed very real and solid. The resurrected citadel of the giants had fused with the human building, which might have been the town hall or a church.

That three-story structure gave them greater perspective on the size of Utgard, which dwarfed the human building. From the mountainside they had seen three such buildings, though this had been the tallest. Now this fraction was all that remained. Abe wondered if the others had been supplanted by the citadel, the way a portion of this building was.

"We have to get in," Pernilla whispered. "If there are people still alive, they would have tried to take refuge inside there."

Abe agreed. The way the two buildings, one real and one somehow manifested there, were juxtaposed together, they could move quickly without being seen by the giants. The walls of Utgard were to their left and the last standing human structure to their right. There were windows, and, though he peered inside, it was dark within and he could not make out anything in particular. Through one, he thought he saw something move.

Then they had reached the corner. He peered around it and saw that there was only open courtyard beyond. One giant still slumbered on the frozen ground perhaps fifty yards away. The sentries seemed alert, but not particularly concerned about what might happen within the gates so much as what might come from outside them. There was no sign of Hellboy and the others, but Abe was not worried—it was a long walk around the circumference of Utgard.

He glanced along the front of that truncated building and saw that the door faced the courtyard. The sentries might see them, but they could not very well break a window. Shattering glass could bring them running, might even rouse the sleeper nearby.

Wordlessly, he took Pernilla's hand and they raced across the front of the building, exposed and vulnerable in the starlight. He could not erase from his mind the image of that giant stripping flesh from human bones the way a man would a piece of chicken. He hoped to avoid that fate for himself, and for Pernilla.

At the door, he tried the knob and it turned. It was a public building in a village at the top of the world, in the middle of nowhere. Of course it was not locked. It probably did not even have a lock.

Abe pushed inside, ushered Pernilla in, and then silently closed the door. When he turned, he flinched, horrified by what he saw. The inside of the building had been gutted. Where on the outside it was conjoined with the wall of the citadel, on the inside it was all torn away so that the giants could get at the people who had hidden themselves inside.

There were three still alive, a woman, a very old man, and a young girl who could not have been more than eight years old. They were huddled together under blankets, but there was frost on their hair and the blankets, and their breath fogged the air. They stared at Abe and Pernilla with wide eyes, astonished more, Abe thought, by their arrival than by his appearance.

The woman began to whisper to them, a fearful expression on her face. Abe didn't understand a word but it was obvious Pernilla did. He had no idea what she said to the woman, but immediately all three of them began to rise.

Tears sprang to the old man's pale cheeks and the little girl hugged herself to the woman's side.

"What'd you tell them?"

"That we're all leaving together."

"Is there anyone else?"

Pernilla frowned and repeated the question in that other language—Lappish, Abe thought it was. The old man wrapped a blanket around himself and walked through the rubble, the shambles that had been made of the interior, the upper floors having collapsed down upon the lower. Near the place where this structure met the citadel tower, he pointed to something beyond a barricade that might have been put there on purpose or might merely have been the way the floor above had crashed down.

Reluctantly, Abe followed him.

Behind that barricade was a pile of corpses, dozens of dead men, women, and children haphazardly thrown together and covered in frost. Icicles had formed upon them, and their eyes were wide and frozen as well. Between each corpse was a crust of ice that connected them all, and though he would have said had he been asked that he could not possibly imagine it, in his mind Abe could *hear* the sound they would have made when one of the giants came to break one off the pile to eat.

He staggered backward, his stomach convulsing, and nearly threw up. Pernilla moved toward him but he waved her back. "Let's just go," he whispered. "And when we get out of here, the Bureau is going to pay for a very long, very tropical vacation."

Several minutes passed as they gathered up what they could salvage from the debris to keep the survivors warm. Clothing and blankets and what little food they had set aside to try to keep themselves alive in circumstances that might have driven many to take their own lives.

Abe gestured to them to hurry, then, and he and Pernilla helped shoulder their burdens, placing some of their belongings in their own packs. At the door, Abe held up a finger and shushed them. His hand was on the knob when he thought better of it. With a frown, he worked his way across the room to a window that was relatively clear. It opened wide enough for them to fit through so he slid his pack out first and then climbed out after it.

He looked back in and beckoned for the Saami woman to follow. Pernilla would help them get through, and then come along herself. The woman lowered her belongings out the window.

The ground shook.

Abe spun toward the sound . . . toward the courtyard.

The sleeping giant had awoken and was staring down at him, bleary-eyed and curious.

The wind died as Hellboy stepped up to the front gates of Utgard with Eitri and his cousins in tow. The Nidavellim brandished their weapons in grim silence. They looked almost ridiculous, so small in front of that massive gate, and so few. But they were fierce and loyal and Hellboy would not discount them.

"Do not split up," he told them, staring at Eitri. "Stay together and kill one at a time. Bring them down to your level. Be swift and stay out of their reach."

Eitri gazed at him boldly. "We have killed giants before, thunder-bearer."

Hellboy nodded. "All right."

He turned and faced the gates, drew in a long breath, and focused on something inside of him, that indefinable thing he knew as himself. Whatever it was that had made him who he was now, not his birth or parentage, but his youth and his relationship with Trevor Bruttenholm and his friends at the Bureau. There was a lot more out in the world, he realized; a shame that these were the only things that defined him. But those were thoughts to be pursued another time. This night, he only needed to concentrate on who he was, on keeping his head.

In more ways than one.

The sky was clear above and the air was still, the wind seeming to hesitate as if wondering what he would do next. Hellboy raised the hammer and took a step toward the gates. He brought Mjollnir down in a furious blow.

From the cloudless sky, lightning flashed down and merged with the hammer, striking the gates simultaneously. All of Utgard shook and thunder rolled across the sky, deep and resonant. The gates of the ghost city crashed open, stone splintering and calving like an iceberg. Those huge doors slammed into the two giant, partially decayed sentries inside. One of them was merely staggered, driven several long steps from the walls. The other was thrown to his knees, and an enormous wedge of stone that calved off one of the gates landed upon him, crushing the sword-wielding giant's spine, sharp edge cutting right through him.

What flesh it had flaked away to nothing, leaving only cold, motionless bones behind.

Above, clouds began to roll in again, and lightning flickered and sparked behind them, as though the heavens

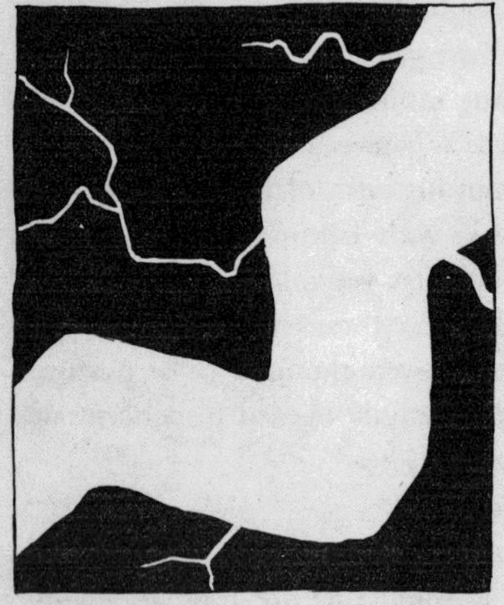

themselves were on fire. The rumble of thunder swept across the mountains, and the ground shook.

Hellboy ran through the gates of Utgard, hooves pounding the frozen ground, hammer raised high. The serpent pendant swung against his chest as he bellowed a war cry last uttered by the long dead legions of Valhalla. The wind picked up again, swirling down into the massive courtyard of Utgard, a broad open space larger than the village it had obliterated. Far at the other end of the courtyard, another giant stood in front of one of the citadel's towers and crashed a fist through a wall.

"Abe," Hellboy muttered. "Damn."

But it was too late for him to do anything for Abe. The guard who had been staggered by their entrance had snatched up a mace from his belt, a monstrous weapon whose iron head was at least three feet in diameter. It was not skeletal like the one they had seen outside. No, this one had the appearance of a more recent corpse, flesh pitted and dried. Like Thrym, it had its own horns, and its beard and hands seemed forged from jagged ice. The frost giants had some of that ancient ice in them, the frozen heart of Ymir.

"Quickly!" Eitri shouted. "Kill him before the others come!"

The Nidavellim did not wait for the giant to attack them. They raced at his legs, attacking with sword and axe. Eitri leaped higher than such a stout creature ought to be able to, and buried both daggers in one of the giant's legs. The dead flesh stank as it tore, but Eitri started to climb, hand over hand, blade over blade.

Mjollnir burned Hellboy's hand as he faced the giant.

"It cannot be," the giant muttered, its voice deep as the thunder. "You are dead."

Hellboy clenched his teeth and glared up at the thirty-five-foot monster. "At least I don't look it."

The giant grunted in pain as one of the Nidavellim hacked at his leg with an axe as though trying to fell an enormous tree. It stepped back, Eitri still hanging on with his knives, and brought the mace down, trying to crush the offending dwarf. The Nidavellim dove clear, but that was the moment Hellboy had been waiting for.

Again he shouted that battle cry. A barrage of lightning struck the walls of Utgard, blew a hole in one of the towers, and tore up the ground. Hellboy raised Mjollnir and lunged forward, his own leap far more substantial than ought to have been possible for him. He brought the hammer down and shattered the giant's wrist.

It roared with pain, staggered backward, and the Nidavellim hacked at its legs until it fell with a thump that shook the earth. Hellboy ran at it, hooves sliding across the ice, and leaped up to the giant's chest. The echo of the thunderer rose up within him; he felt the dead myth's savagery and bloodlust rushing through his veins, pumping in his heart. He was nearly blinded in that moment by the struggle inside him. Blackness began to swamp his consciousness, and he swayed a moment.

Cut the crap! he thought.

The presence that had festered within him tried to possess him, to control him. His hands shook and the unearthly substance of his right hand burned with the heat of Mjollnir. The serpent pendant was frozen solid to the wool breast of his sweater.

Hellboy screamed a blistering epithet, but this time, he spoke English. With both hands he brought Mjollnir down and caved in the giant's skull. It shattered, spilling

blood and rotting brain tissue onto the frozen earth with a hiss of melting ice. One of its horns snapped off and slid to the ground. The hammer no longer burned his hand. He would do what had to be done and draw on the strength locked inside that weapon, but he was going to do it on his own terms.

He could feel the thunder-bearer inside him, furious, but now focused on the external battle rather than the one within.

"Hellboy!" Eitri shouted.

But he did not need the Nidavellim's warning. He stood on the dead giant's chest and surveyed the courtyard. Tower doors had banged open and now the giants were coming, first two, then five, then seven, all in various states of decay. Not decay, Hellboy corrected himself. For they weren't rotting, but reconstituting themselves somehow.

Thrym was not among them.

Hellboy swore under his breath. For a moment the dead giants moved slowly, walking as though in a trance, staring at the Nidavellim and at Mjollnir. All but one of them was armed, several with swords, the others with axes and maces. Two were female, and they were perhaps more hideous than the others, with their twisted, thick-lipped mouths and sagging, withered, pendulous breasts. One of the females wore a thick cloak of fur and carried a morningstar ball and chain larger than any weapon Hellboy had ever seen. She had a scar across the left side of her face in a curling slash that ran beside her eye and then across her lips and jaw.

There was enough flesh on her that he recognized her. Even as she began to swing the morningstar, images flashed through Hellboy's brain and he put a name to that face. *Hyndla.* Though a giantess, Odin had been her father.

My sister, Hellboy thought. He shook his head, trying to clear it. Hyndla was not his sister, but that of the thunder-bearer.

By instinct, he raised Mjollnir above his head. The wind whipped against him, powerful enough that it shook him where he stood, there in the midst of the courtyard. He did not need to look to the sky to know that the clouds had begun to churn as though the heavens had become a whirlpool above his head. Thunder boomed and echoed and shook the walls and the ground itself.

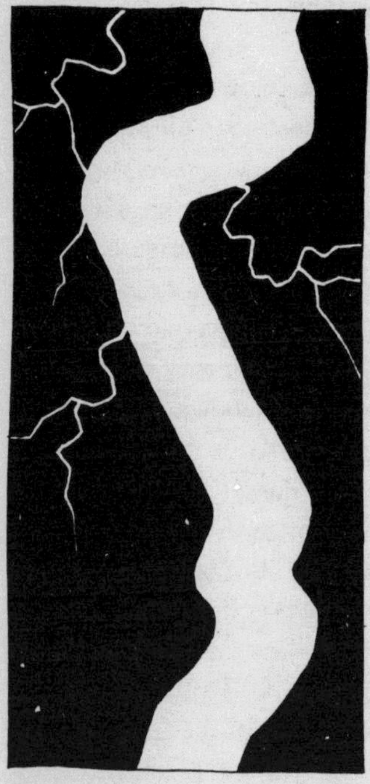

"Come, then," he screamed in that ancient tongue, the words coming unbidden to his lips, spoken not by Hellboy, but by the ghost in him. "Come to me, bones of giants, and we will all return to the grave where we belong, where all the nine worlds were meant to stay buried forevermore!"

There was one final word, one shouted so loud that Hellboy's throat burned with it, but there was no translation for it in his mind. It was a curse, an insult, a challenge, and at its savage utterance, the giants roared in return. They shouted, all together, a cacophony of war cries and taunts, and they rushed across the courtyard toward him. So large were they, however, that they bumped and jostled one another trying to reach him, trying to be the first to attack. They were not so stupid that they did not realize what they were doing, however. The ground shook with their massive footfalls and they began to spread out, to try to ring him in.

Hellboy raised Mjollnir again and with both hands brought it down. He struck the ground and the frozen earth cracked. Upon the moment of that impact, adrenaline surging through him, every nerve ending in his body crackling with tension, a fusillade of lightning flashed down from the sky far stronger than the first. It tore the ground up into long trenches of turned earth, shattered walls, and set stone afire.

Three of the giants—one of the females and two corpse-like males—shook and jittered as the lightning struck them. Fire exploded from their eye sockets and their hair was set ablaze. Electricity shot in blue-white arcs from their arms and torsos and seemed to tether them to the ground below. The two cadaverous giants glowed from within as the lightning refracted inside their rib cages like fireflies in a jar. None of them managed even to scream before the fire engulfed them and they tumbled to the ground, charred flesh and blackened bones.

Hellboy ran at the nearest monstrosity, a sword-wielding giant with two heads, one of them dumb and drooling with hollow eyes and the other cruelly grinning with sharpened fangs and a gaze of pure malice. It was the fastest, probably the strongest of those who served Thrym, and he realized he knew this one too.

"They called you Hraesvelg, before Ragnarok," Hellboy

muttered as he ran toward the two-headed giant, his hooves cracking the icy ground. "Now you have no identity. You are a memory with stolen flesh and rotting bones."

The world seemed to swim around him, to change, and Utgard took on more solidity. The sky looked different to him now, the air tasted of copper, a bloody mist surrounded him. He spoke of memory, but now he walked in memory as well. It was as though a veil had been torn aside and now he saw the old world, the land where myths had slain one another for sport and spite, until the day when the final battle had come.

Hraesvelg laughed, and the deep, sonorous boom of it was akin to the thunder. "I am a memory? Then what, might I ask, are you?"

"Just another dead thing."

Hellboy ran at Hraesvelg as the giant slashed down at him with that enormous blade. The sword cut a long gash in the ground, but Hellboy avoided its deadly descent. Despite his mindless, soft-skulled head, the giant's second head was cunning. When Hellboy dodged the blade, Hraesvelg reached down and grabbed him, snatched him up in one enormous hand.

Teeth bared in a growl, Hellboy shattered the giant's wrist with one blow from Mjollnir. The crack of bone echoed across the courtyard and the lightning tore the ground nearby. Hraesvelg roared in fury and raised his sword. Hellboy clung to exposed bone and rotting flesh with his free hand and hung on to the giant's arm. He got his hooves under him and then sprang with all the momentum he could muster. Mjollnir raised above his head, he leaped at the two-headed giant's chest and shattered it with Mjollnir, breaking bone and tearing muscle and ripping a hole where the monster's heart ought to have been.

Hraesvelg froze and tumbled forward, landed with both faces striking the ground. Hellboy was thrust up inside the darkling beast's gaping wound. The stench of dead meat was powerful and nauseating and his stomach heaved as he was enveloped in sickening fluids. It was pitch black there, trapped inside the giant's body. He raised Mjollnir and struck upward, tearing a hole in the giant's back; then he climbed up and out of it, using splintered bone as a hand-hold.

As he withdrew himself from that massive corpse, he saw that the Nidavellim were all still alive. Eitri and his cousins, with their heavy fur and mail armor covered in blood, had managed to kill one of the giants, severing its head entirely, and were now attacking another like wolves bringing down a deer.

The world around him remained a kind of fugue state, where the wind itself tasted of ancient worlds, carried the songs of Valhalla and the smoke from distant fires in the camps of the Aesir. Above, the two large ravens circled once more. Huginn and Muninn, the servants of his father. He knew them now. As he glanced around he saw still figures standing atop the walls of Utgard, beautiful women draped in long furs and carrying spears and swords and shields. Mist was among them, watching solemnly, awaiting the outcome.

The Valkyrie had been watching all along.

CHAPTER SIXTEEN

He stood atop the corpse of the two-headed giant and surveyed the courtyard. The Nidavellim were screaming in their own tongue, a kind of chant that they sometimes uttered in the heat of battle. There was no sign of the giant he had seen when they had first broken in, the one who had been tearing into the side of a building. And no sign of Abe.

Thrym had still not shown himself.

Only Hyndla remained, his sister, the crescent scar on her face gleaming wetly with each crack of lightning that illuminated the sky. She stared at him, still gently swinging her morningstar, the ball and chain clanking as they spun.

"Why are you here?" she asked, her gravelly voice almost soft.

"Because all of you are."

She swung the morningstar down and he leaped out of its path. It crashed to the earth, one of its spikes tearing through his sweater, slashing his back, and driving him down. He cried out in pain and snarled in fury. With a grunt of effort he shot to his feet again and turned to find Hyndla trying to pull the morningstar from the ground. The spikes on the mace ball were lodged in the frozen earth, but they were loosening.

Hellboy grabbed the chain and pulled with all the strength of the blood of Odin, which ran through him. Hyndla was tugged off her feet and landed on her chest on the ground. She tried to roll away, began to rise, but he was there, upon her, Mjollnir raised high. He shattered her shoulder first, then cracked her ribs, and finally he stood upon her heaving bosom and prepared to crush her skull.

Her gaze was distant and lost, her eyes as wet as her scar.

"Is this real, Thor?" she asked.

His heart was cold, his stomach tight, but his eyes were stung by the wind. Or perhaps only by the winds of fate.

"As real as it ever was, my sister," he replied.

Then he killed her.

Abe stood just outside the building, staring wide-eyed up at the giant towering over him. Never in his life had he felt a more profound desire to go home. A sudden image of Dorothy's ruby slippers appeared in his head, but he would have taken a wicked witch and flying monkeys over a bunch of zombie giants any day of the week. Had, in fact, now that he thought of it, managed just fine against a wicked witch and flying monkeys that time in Dusseldorf.

The giant roared, its lips peeling back from its teeth, the stench of its breath so powerful Abe could smell it all the way on the ground.

Then it began to shout, and he was glad he could not understand its words. Any second now other giants would arrive, but Abe wasn't all that concerned about the others. Just keeping this one from peeling the flesh from his bones with its teeth would be an accomplishment. After all those humans, he figured they'd all be fighting over some seafood.

"Abe!" Pernilla screamed behind him.

"Coming!" he replied.

He left the Saami woman's gear where it was, but they could not afford to leave his pack behind. Abe grabbed his unwieldly pack and tossed it through the window, just as the giant struck the wall above him with its fist. The stone wall shook and part of it caved in. The window shattered and the glass showered the ground.

Pernilla screamed his name again, and he saw her face through the broken window, those dark eyes wide with terror. He ran at the window, any sense of caution forgotten, and just as the giant reached down to try to grab him, Abe dove through. A shard of broken glass that jutted down from the frame gouged his arm, but then he was inside. He grunted and the breath went out of him as he landed on the floor, colliding with his pack.

"Go, go, go!" he shouted.

He hefted the pack and slipped it on his back, but even as he rose, Pernilla had gotten the three survivors moving. The woman and the young girl carried whatever they could manage, and they had blankets draped about their shoulders, but the biggest surprise was the old man. He was faster than he looked, and kept pace with the others. Abe realized he should not have been surprised. The man had survived this long.

With the weight of his gear a heavy burden upon him, Abe ran through the debris, praying he did not get his ankle broken. As he reached the other side of the room, where the frozen mountain of the dead lay in a grotesque diorama, he heard the voice of the giant rumbling above, and he paused to glance back.

The hole it had punched, high up on the wall, was blacked out by its face. It pressed an eye to the hole to stare in at them, shouting something in its old language.

With more speed than he would ever have credited himself with having, Abe drew his gun and shot the giant right through the eye. The bullet punched the huge orb and fluid spilled down through the hole. The giant screamed and reared back, then instantly began pummeling the wall, tearing it away, stones spilling down with a crash and a cloud of rising dust. The giant was enraged, screeching in a high, agonized voice.

From deeper within the tower of Utgard that lay ahead, Abe heard Pernilla calling back to him. With a grim satisfac-

tion, he gave the giant the finger, then raced after Pernilla and the others, leaving the monster behind. It was insane with pain and fury or it might have stopped trying to burrow its way into that smaller structure and instead run around to the tower entrance. Abe hoped it kept trying to dig its own door.

The arched halls of Utgard were so high he felt like a church mouse racing along the stone-slab floor of the main corridor in that tower. As silent as possible, he caught up with Pernilla, the old man, the little girl, and the Saami woman, thinking again how tragic it was that these three were the only survivors, and hoping that he could get them safely away.

As he reached them, Pernilla put a finger to his lips. She glanced around the corner and he knew there must be giants there.

Then from outside the tower there came a crash like a mountain crumbling and shouts of alarm and rage. Then thunder boomed through the fortress and the high windows revealed the zoetrope flash of lightning across the sky.

Abe smiled. Hellboy had arrived.

"They're going," Pernilla whispered, peering again around the corner. After a moment, she turned and nodded to him.

"Quickly and quietly," he told her, and she repeated it to the others in their own language.

Abe glanced back the way they had come. From down the massive hallway he could hear the shouts and the crashing as the now half-blind giant tore his way into the building. A shudder went through him as he remembered the frozen dead and the way the giants had eaten them. Then he followed after Pernilla and the three villagers. They moved in absolute silence, though there was chaos outside. It was not long before they came to an open passageway at the back of the tower that led them outside. In the shadows of the walls of Utgard, Pernilla and Abe hurried back the way they had come with a new burden and a new responsibility. It was slower going with the villagers along, but these three people were what they had come for.

They reached the hole in the wall at the rear of the citadel without incident, and fifteen minutes later they stood on the first ridge of the foothills leading back up the mountainside and watched the lightning crashing down upon the fortress from the sky, and they waited.

Abe gritted his teeth and listened and tried to see what he could of the melee below. He started back down after a moment, but Pernilla put a hand on his arm and shook her head.

"We need you here."

He gazed into her eyes, then reached up to touch her face, and he nodded. She was right, of course. If anything happened to Hellboy, it would be up to him to get them all back to safety.

The battle down there in that ghost-fortress was not for him, but for the myths: for gods and monsters.

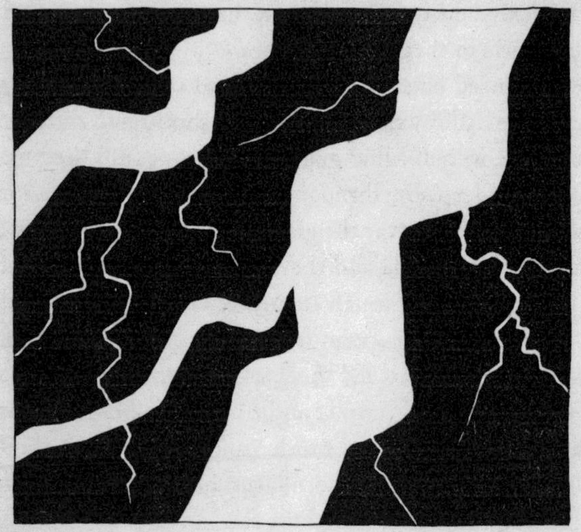

Gale force winds blew through the courtyard; the storm crashed overhead and lightning tore down the walls of Utgard, one bolt at a time. Hellboy felt larger somehow, like a giant himself in some way, as though he towered high above the creature he had once been. His chest heaved as he breathed in the cold, crisp air of legend, and he knew that the reason Mjollnir no longer felt hot in his hand was not because the hammer had cooled, but because his own body now burned with the same fire of battle.

Though the full weight of this conflict was upon him, the need to conclude it crowding nearly everything else out of his mind, still he found some reserve, some small place in the back of his head where he could retreat and gaze around himself in wonder, in awe, and in dread. For the shadows of

Utgard had coalesced now. Abe and Pernilla were not here, so he would never know if they could have seen it, but somehow he doubted it. Atop the battlements and below, lined against the walls in the shadows and arrayed amongst the towers, were all the warriors of Valhalla. These were shades only—not even ghosts, not the spirits of the long dead Aesir—and yet that did not matter.

All the dead of Ragnarok had come to witness this, the last battle of the old world, the true end. Jormungand the serpent reared its head high above the citadel and peered down within. No flesh to it, merely an echo, a whisper on the wind, yet a whisper he could see. Among the Aesir were trolls and light elves and dark elves. The Valkyrie were still there as well, thirteen of them in all, Mist and Host Fetter chief among them. Ratatosk sat attentive upon Mist's shoulder and gazed down upon the ravaged courtyard and its piles of giant bones.

The ravens flew above in an unchanging circle, never higher or lower, never faster or slower, inevitable and eternal as the passage of time itself.

Hellboy stood still, unshaken by the winds. The echo of ancient battles filled the courtyard, but he turned away from them now, from those ghosts of old. The Nidavellim had felled the last of the giants raised by

Thrym, though Hellboy could not be sure there weren't others. Eitri led his cousins across the frozen, churned earth to stand by him, and together the five warriors crossed the courtyard. The largest and tallest of the citadel's towers loomed ahead, untouched by the devastation of the lightning.

Before they had closed half the distance, an enormous shadow loomed in the entrance to that tower, a silhouette with horns and long fingers like talons. Things like massive rats scurried at its feet.

Thrym stepped out into the courtyard of Utgard. The king of the frost giants was covered with a frozen armor, a jagged crust of ice that was deadly sharp at the end of his horns and had formed upon his hands so that each finger was twice its natural length, a spike of ice. Two of the trees that had been twined in his ribs when he had first dragged himself from the ground had been dislodged at some point upon this long trek north, but the third and largest

remained. It protruded from Thrym's lower abdomen like the truncated vestiges of some half-born conjoined twin.

The frost king's eyes glowed a bright blue-white and steam leaked from their edges. When he spoke, the Arctic wind seemed to scream his words.

"Thunderer," Thrym said. "You have come only to die again. It is well. For the first time, it was not my hand that took your life."

The things that scurried about his feet were Svartalves, and until he saw them, those black, oil-slick beasts he had once thought of as weasels, Hellboy had nearly forgotten them. There were perhaps two dozen, no more, but they capered and sprinted now across the courtyard, eyes glinting with malice, stinging blades whickering across the wind.

"I had wondered where they had gone to," Eitri muttered at Hellboy's side. "I thought perhaps he had eaten them all."

Then the stout Nidavellim, proud and grave, barked a command to his cousins and they stepped forward to meet the onslaught of Svartalves. Swords and axes and daggers clashed and rang, and blood was spilled. The stench of it, fresh blood on this field of putrescent decay, set Hellboy's teeth on edge again.

Thrym. It was all down to Thrym.

He started toward the frost king, but the giant only laughed that wintry laugh and waved a hand. The ground began to rumble, nearly throwing him from his feet, but Hellboy rode the tremor, kept his balance. A huge, skeletal arm burst from the ground with volcanic force, its sheer size dwarfing any of the other giants Hellboy had fought thus far. Farther across the courtyard, another skeleton began to tear itself from the earth, and behind him, two more.

"No," Hellboy muttered. "No more screwing around."

Navigating the trembling ground, he ran at Thrym. He passed the Nidavellim, who were slaughtering the Svartalves, but one of Eitri's cousins let out an agonized cry as Hellboy went by, the dwarf driven to the ground under a twisting mound of Svartalves. He could not stop. Killing Thrym was all that mattered. That would put an end to it.

Thrym laughed as he approached, but it was a grim, throaty sound with the hiss of a blizzard. Then the frost king strode forward, crossing the ground between them in two steps. Mjollnir felt feather-light in his grasp, as if he were one with the hammer at last. He leaped a dozen feet into the air, swinging the hammer around his head, and brought it crashing down toward Thrym's hip.

The king of the frost giants, this dead thing filled with dark and mystic knowledge, slapped him from the air. His icy claws tore the wool from Hellboy's chest and back and gashed his flesh. Blood ran freely, spattering the icy ground as he struck the earth and rolled painfully. The serpent pendant was cold against his skin once more, but he barely noticed.

He staggered to his feet, Mjollnir hanging at his side, dangling limply for a moment. Hellboy shook his head, tried not to see the blood that was running across his belly and down his legs. Thrym reached down for him with both hands, and then he jerked back to awareness. Hellboy swung Mjollnir, shattering the frost king's left hand into massive shards of ice and bone and dead flesh, newly grown. But the other hand grasped him and held him tight.

The cold seeped into him instantly, slowing his mind,

dulling his thoughts. His bones ached so deeply that he wanted to tear his own flesh open to somehow relieve them of that lingering pain. His face and hands were numb and slack and his eyes began to frost over. Hellboy hung his head weakly and watched in horror as ice spread over his body, covering him in a thick frozen layer that enveloped him.

"That hurt," Thrym mused, gazing at his shattered hand almost idly as with the other he cast Hellboy in a block of ice. As he stared at his splintered fingers, they began to grow back once more, claws of ice.

No sarcastic or bitter retort came from Hellboy. His eyes were wide beyond that shroud of ice, and his lungs, though large, burned with the need for air. He stared at Thrym through that blue-white, suffocating sheen, and a sadness deep as the marrow took root inside him, even as he struggled for air. Some unnameable power, perhaps that of the Norns—the Fates themselves—had drawn the spirit of the thunder-bearer back into the world to bring down the final curtain on an era, on a grand age of gods and monsters, and that knowledge filled him with a melancholy unlike any he had ever felt before.

Hellboy could not tell if that melancholy was his own,

or that of the spirit within him. Thrym did not belong here. None of these dead things did. Hellboy himself did not truly belong to this world, but he had made himself a home in it. The difference was, this was his time. This was his life, this age of man. Thrym might have preserved his essence and poured it from the Tankard back into the shell of his body, but it truly was nothing more than a husk.

Blackness edged in at the corners of Hellboy's eyes. What little breath remained in his lungs had run out. Bright lights flared behind his eyes and in his head. Thrym reached out, scratched a restored talon through the ice, and tore off the serpent pendant. The frost king held it up and gazed at it, grinning.

"This ought to have been cast in my image," Thrym said.

Hellboy set his teeth against one another, grinding. He stretched, muscles rippling. Mjollnir burned in his grasp again now, and he braced himself against the ice coffin in which he had been encased. In the encroaching blackness inside his mind, he met the thunder-bearer's essence. Together they reached out to the storm.

Lightning flickered in white veins across the sky and scorched the air as it reached tendrils down from the sky to touch Mjollnir, as it had done on the riverbank what seemed an age ago. The ice shattered and fell away from him, and the hammer glowed with an unearthly light.

"No!" Thrym roared.

Hellboy swung the hammer and splintered the giant's knee, snapping the leg nearly in two. Thrym's cry of rage and pain drowned out the thunder and fought back the wind. The frost king went down on his knees, one ruined and one still sturdy, but Thrym swayed forward, nearly falling. His eyes leaked that blue-white mist, like the frozen breath of a hundred men. The giant's horns were sharp and deadly, and Hellboy saw a cunning flicker in those eyes. Thrym's magic was given over to the resurrection of the other giants and to the mastery of the ice, but he might gore Hellboy with those horns.

Every instinct demanded he strike with Mjollnir again, but they were not his instincts, not really. Instead, Hellboy reached up with his left hand, the strength of the Aesir and the storm reverberating through his body, every nerve ending and every tendon rippling with that power, and he grabbed hold of the trunk of tree that jutted from Thrym's lower ribcage.

With a battle cry learned at the foot of the Allfather, he ripped the tree out of Thrym's body. Bones broke and flesh tore and ice cracked and when the roots of the tree

were pulled free, a hole five feet around gaped and puckered. It sucked at the air greedily, a cold deeper than any Arctic freeze blasting from it with each breath.

Thrym's mouth dropped open and he reached down to clutch at his belly. All around the courtyard, the bones of giants tumbled to the ground, still once more. The walls of Utgard shimmered and became translucent, the mountains visible through them all around; the ghost of that great fortress lost its solidity, little more than a specter again, an ancient phantom.

The frost king's eyes were wide, and he stared at Hellboy. "Bring the thunder, then," he croaked.

Hellboy did. He raised Mjollnir and lightning crashed down from the sky, shearing off Thrym's left arm at the shoulder. Then he brought the hammer crashing down and caved in the frost king's skull, snapping off his horns, flushing away that blue-white mist from his eyes in a blast of energy that might have been the giant's soul essence.

The bones of the king fell in upon themselves and clattered to the frozen ground.

Hellboy stood by those scattered bones, which now lay with the others, a graveyard of giants, and he staggered forward, weak from the loss of blood that no longer flowed, aching with wounds now closed, injuries already healing.

Above, the clouds began to clear and the last of the thunder rolled off across the sky. The ravens were gone.

As were the walls of Utgard, and the phantoms of Ragnarok.

Hellboy saw Eitri, bathed in blood that was not his own, picking his way amongst the bones. Only one other of the Nidavellim survived: his cousin Lit walked with him, arm dangling broken at his side. The blasted remains of the village that had once stood there in that mountain crag were grim testament to the truth of what had happened there, but somehow already the details seemed unclear to him.

"Abe?" Hellboy asked, glancing around as Eitri and Lit came closer. "Where the heck is Abe? Did you guys see him and Pernilla anywhere?"

"I know not where your comrade has gone," Eitri replied, voice quavering with exhaustion.

Hellboy turned to look at him. "I've got to find them."

"You fought well, thunder-bearer," Eitri replied, chin raised proudly. "We are all that remain now, but my cousins and my brothers were honored to die at your side. I will remember them, and you."

"I . . . look, Eitri, I'm not him. You know that, right?"

The dwarf hung his head, and suddenly he did not look like a warrior anymore. With his long, filthy hair and the iron rings in his beard, he looked only like some strange little homeless man. Lit seemed much the same.

"Yes, Hellboy," Eitri said. "We know."

But Lit did not look at

him. The ragged Nidavellim was gazing past Hellboy, eyes wide. Hellboy spun, fearing for an instant that Thrym had only feigned death. But it was not the frost king that approached across the ruined earth. The tall, long-legged being who strode swiftly toward them was familiar, however. It was Mist. The soul-gatherer carried her heavy spear in her right hand. On her shoulder sat Ratatosk the squirrel. Ratatosk chittered and squeaked as though he were some ordinary, earthly rodent.

Mist said nothing. She paused only inches away from Hellboy, her eyes in shadow, a slight smile at the corners of her mouth. She raised her left hand and with it reached out to tap Hellboy once between the stumps of his horns.

Mjollnir fell from his hand and thumped dully to the frozen ground. Astonished, Hellboy stared at the hammer for a long moment, relishing the emptiness in his head. He was alone again in his mind, the echo of that ancient age now gone.

When he looked up, Mist was gone.

"Eitri?"

The dwarf stared up at him, attentive and respectful.

"You'll keep the hammer?"

The two Nidavellim glanced at one another, and then Eitri nodded. "We shall. We will keep it in our care for all time. There are others of our kind in Stockholm and in Copenhagen and throughout the northlands. Mjollnir will be kept out of the hands of the unworthy and never will be wielded again unless the spirit of the thunder-bearer returns."

Hellboy nodded thoughtfully and glanced up at the sky to find only the night and bright, gleaming stars. "That's good. I don't think he's coming back, but I guess you never know. Wouldn't have exactly predicted all this stuff if you'd asked me beforehand." Again he looked to Eitri and Lit. "You guys'll make it back all right?"

Eitri bent and lifted Mjollnir. Hellboy was surprised at how effortless it seemed, but then he recalled that Eitri and his brother had forged the hammer to begin with.

"We will be just fine. And you?"

"I'll be all right," Hellboy replied. "Little fresh air'll clear my head."

There was an awkward moment where he felt he ought to have something more to say. Then he nodded once and turned away, toward the foothills on the other side of the crag, where he had last seen Abe.

The ground was broken and churned in many places. Homes had been reduced to rubble and frozen human corpses, some of them mutilated, their bones gnawed upon, were strewn amongst the debris. The giant bones were plentiful but easily navigated. Hellboy stepped around a small pile of stones that might once have been a chimney, and his hoof slipped. As he struggled to maintain his balance, a glimmer of starlight off metal caught his eye and he realized he was looking at the serpent pendant that Thrym had torn off him.

For a long moment he stared at it, tempted to leave it there.

"Hellboy!"

He looked up and saw Abe and Pernilla picking their way across the battlefield toward him. Hellboy let out a long breath he had no idea he'd been holding and started walking in their direction. Then he paused and bent down to retrieve the pendant. When he reached them, he handed it to Pernilla.

"This is pretty much all that's left. Except the bones. Figured you should have it. If you want to put it in a museum or something, or you want to keep it for yourself, either way is fine with me. Just . . . well, it might be a bad idea to wear it."

Pernilla took it from him gingerly and nodded. Then she slipped it into her pocket. She looked pretty bedraggled, but there was a kind of sheen to her skin and a brightness to her eyes that Hellboy figured came from having come so close to something so horrible and living through it.

"What happened to the hammer?" Abe asked.

Hellboy shrugged. "The dwarves took it. What was I gonna do with it? You didn't find any survivors, huh?"

"Three, actually," Abe said. He pointed back toward the foothills. "I've got them camped in a crevasse back there, out of the wind. We should all try to get some sleep at least until sunrise. Even if the walk to the nearest village isn't as long as the walk up here, I'd still rather do it under the sun."

Hellboy nodded tiredly, and the three of them fell into step side by side, walking back to where Abe and Pernilla had left the survivors. Abe had his arm slipped gently around her waist, but that might have been just to help her make her way through the rubble in the dark. Hellboy could not be sure, and he wasn't about to get nosy about it.

"All right," Hellboy said. "But just a few hours' sleep. At dawn, we hit the trail out of here. My stomach's already rumbling."

"There's still some food in our packs," Pernilla offered.

"Nah, none of that crap," Hellboy replied, chuckling softly. "I want to go home and get really bad Chinese take-out, maybe Kung Pao Shrimp and some Peking Ravioli. That's the ticket."

Abe turned to look at him. He paused a long moment and then grinned that weird, fishy grin of his.

"Good to have you back."

"Hell, it's good to *be* back."

"And the next time I say I don't want to go somewhere cold?"

"Bali, baby. We're going to Bali."